By J. K. Swift

The Forest Knights Series:

ALTDORF

MORGARTEN

The Hospitaller Saga:

ACRE

MAMLUK

HOSPITALLER

MORGARTEN

The Forest Knights Book 2

J. K. Swift

Printed in the United States of America

UE Publishing Co.
First Edition

10 9 8 7 6 5 4 3

ISBN-13: 978-1481179126
ISBN-10: 1481179128

For those who attempt the impossible.

MORGARTEN

The Forest Knights Book 2

THE BATTLE OF MORGARTEN

SCHWYZER ARMY

LEOPOLD'S ARMY

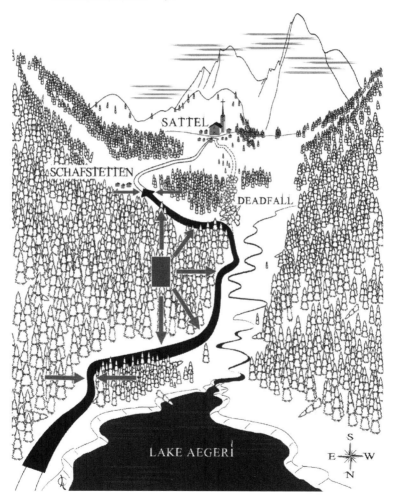

SATTEL

SCHAFSTETTEN

DEADFALL

LAKE AEGERI

Chapter 1

ERICH STOOD OVER Gissler's body and absently stroked the three stumps on his right hand that had once been fingers. A crossbow bolt protruded from Gissler's upper chest. Erich took a moment to admire the unknown archer's skill, for if the shot had struck a fraction of an inch lower, Gissler's chainmail vest may have spared his life. Or, perhaps it was merely luck. That was far more likely. Luck, or rather, its absence had killed far more people than skill ever would.

Erich's brows furrowed and he crossed his arms. There was something odd about the angle of the bolt. And the entire shaft was crusted in dried blood, all the way to the tips of its leather vanes....

A crash and the sound of splintering wood caught his attention. He turned away from the corpse and saw Reto climbing down from the top of the cage wagon. The bald, leathery-faced man cursed as he dropped to the ground.

"Nothing here. Found a strongbox but no coins,"

Reto said.

He pulled something flat and heavy that was tucked under his arm and tossed it into the trees.

"What was that?"

Reto shrugged. "Parchment. Maybe a book. That one got anything good on him?"

Erich nodded. "A fine sword. Take it and the mail vest, but leave the clothing." They were too stiff with old blood to salvage.

Reto scurried over and picked up Gissler's sword. He whistled in appreciation and tucked it into his belt. His small eyes darted over Gissler's corpse. "And what is wrong with those boots? Look broken in and comfortable to me. Might be my size, too."

Erich held up his hands. "Take them. But if you do, you offer up your own boots to one of the other men, if they want them. And you can carry that sword for now, but when we get back to camp it goes into the pool."

Reto flashed his teeth for only a second before bending to pilfer Gissler's corpse. Erich watched as his man tugged off the corpse's boots and ripped off his tunic to get at the chainmail vest.

Erich told himself he should be enjoying this moment more. This was, after all, one of the bastards who had killed most of his men those many months ago. The past half-year had been beyond difficult. But that was nothing new for him.

Erich's father had been a grain farmer until his wife died when Erich was ten. Life had been hard while she was alive, but with her passing, Erich's father and even the land itself seemed to give in. The crop shriveled and the next year blight finished it off. They starved for a season, earning what they could by begging, and, unknown to his father, some minor thefts. The next year the community hired Erich's father as an *alper*. He was to take everyone's animals up high into the Alps to forage for summer pasture and would not return for three months. He left in early spring, leaving Erich alone on their rocky land to fend for himself. When his father returned in late summer, Erich was gone.

He fell in with rough men, and realized that to survive, he would need to be rougher yet. After ten years, and many a hard lesson learned, he formed a brigand band of his own. They did well, flourished even, until he lost half his men when they made the mistake of ambushing Gissler's group.

Erich had built his band back up to twenty men, but he needed half again that number if he had any hope of seizing even the smallest merchant caravan. Especially considering the quality of his current followers.

He looked at the sword sticking out of Reto's belt and wondered if it was the same blade that had cut off his fingers. He could not remember the look of the sword, for it had happened too fast. The man behind the weapon, however, was another story. Erich could still hear the contempt in his words: *He will not be any good with a bow for the rest of his miserable life.*

He was right, of course. Erich also could no longer grasp a sword handle in his right hand, and had resorted to practicing with his sinister hand. It was still clumsy and awkward, but he knew with time he would adapt. What other choice did he have?

Erich wandered to the side of the road and peered into the trees at the leather-bound object Reto had discarded. Turning his head to protect his eyes, he squatted and retrieved the book from beneath a prickly bush. He turned it over in his hands, surprised by its weight.

So, this is a book.

It was the first time in his life he had ever held one. He unfastened the intricate buckle and fanned through the first few pages. He grunted with disappointment at the lack of pictures, then squinted at the flowing script and wondered at its meaning.

Reto was right. The book was worthless to men like them. He closed it and ran his hand once over the smooth cover. But there were others who valued these curiosities more than gold.

Erich tucked the book under his arm and walked over to a horse grazing at the side of the road. She cast him a sidelong glance as he approached and snorted, but did not consider him enough of a threat to give up the sweet tufts of grass overflowing into the road from the forest floor.

Someone had unhitched her from the wagon and left her to roam free. Her coat still bore harness marks, and unfortunately, a prominent Habsburg brand on her rump. Erich would have to leave her behind. No horse trader within a thousand leagues would buy a stolen Habsburg mount.

Four years ago Erich knew of another group of brigands that had been brazen enough to take three of Duke Leopold's horses from a stable in Andermatt. Habsburg soldiers hunted them for weeks, and when they found them, the horse thieves were hung and quartered. Their torsos were dragged through Andermatt until they fell apart. Their limbs received a similar treatment in various villages to the east, and the thieves' heads were sent to Altdorf to be placed atop poles in the town square. The Habsburgs placed a high value on their horses—much higher than the lives of men such as Erich.

He glanced around, wondering where the other half of the two-horse team was. If someone had been fool enough to steal one, why stop there? Why not take them both?

His eyes picked up two skid marks carved into the surface of the road. They were the width of a man's shoulders and led from the wagon to the forest edge. Puzzled, Erich followed the trail a few steps into the trees where the dense brush swallowed it up.

Reto came to Erich's side and scratched his stubbled head. "Looks like someone stole a horse and dragged something in there. What do you think it was? Another strong box maybe?"

Erich could see where something large had brushed aside branches to enter the woods, but then he could make out no further trail. He pointed to a single drop of blood on a rock at the road's edge.

"It was a person. Someone on a stretcher made of branches. Someone hurt."

"Should we follow them?"

"Follow what, exactly?" Erich said.

He stared into the trees. Their trunks swayed and creaked in the breeze. He swore he could feel them staring back.

He shook his head. Like the crumbled bits of a dried leaf on a windy day, the trail had simply vanished.

***

The whispers came for Seraina in sleep, as they often

did. Some time ago, or perhaps only moments before, she recalled sitting down against a giant spruce and closing her eyes. Seraina could still feel the ridges of rough bark pressed against her back. That sensation was a tie to the waking world and she latched onto it, resisting the pull of the voices.

Her visions were rare and, so she was told, a gift from the Great Weave. Something to be treasured. But these voices calling from afar, differed from the ones she had heard before. They grew, both in volume and quantity, and as they became louder, they seemed to insist that Seraina listen. No, they *demanded* to be heard. Finally, Seraina understood.

They were screams.

Wails of terror, pain, fear, and rage. The realization tore Seraina completely away from the waking world. The comforting reassurance of the tree's bark against her back was gone. She found herself hurtling through gray mist that clogged her nostrils and filled her mouth as she drew in deep breaths to ease the frantic pace set by her heart. The screams became louder, the anguish so unbearable, she clapped her hands over her ears knowing full well it would do little good.

She had to help them.

The mist cleared. Not gradually, but all at once, like the goddess Ardwynna herself had banished it from her forest realm with a clap of her hands.

Altdorf.

Seraina floated high above the ramparts of the Altdorf fortress. A great host encircled the keep, pouring through and over broken sections of the outer walls. In the distance, the sky glowed with the heat of a thousand fires as the town burned.

—

The winds carried Seraina lower, in an erratic swoop like a swallow chasing mosquitoes. But this bird had no control over her descent and Seraina soon gave up trying to direct her flight. She took a deep breath and surrendered herself to the Winds of the Weave, knowing full well where they meant to take her. She closed her eyes, but that only brought the gruesome images of war into focus. There was no way to shield one's eyes while trapped within a vision.

She watched as a man with a two-handed sword cut another in half from shoulder to hip-bone, and he in turn was skewered from behind by another man's blade. They fell, and other men ran over their bodies, howling, their faces red and twisted by the furies of battle.

Seraina winced as she felt their rage, their need to kill, and the great relief as a man slid his blade into the open mouth of another. His teeth dragged against the steel, ringing out a long, grating note. Tears filled her eyes and she tried to look away, but it was futile. The winds were merciless. They whisked her throughout the battle, from one gory scene to the next, like she was some wealthy patron of a macabre series of plays.

An old man sat astride a young soldier and pummelled his head with a bloody rock. A young girl, not yet in her teens, attempted to crawl through dirt muddied with blood, as two men tore the clothes from her back. Nearby, a group of soldiers laughed and passed around a wineskin. They watched a man grind against an unmoving naked woman, her arms and legs tied to stakes thrust into the ground. No sounds came from her broken lips, but Seraina could hear her screams. Shrieks that mingled with all the others, forming background music for the chaos.

Finally, relief, and no small measure of guilt, washed over Seraina as the winds took her away once more. They left her standing on top of a crumbled section of the outer wall.

In front of her, stood Thomas.

His tunic was drenched in blood, dripping with it, like it had been freshly pulled from a dying vat. He looked directly at her, and smiled. The scar, extending from the corner of his left eye all the way to his jawline, was so white it hurt Seraina's eyes.

He took a step toward Seraina but a man appeared between them. Thomas crushed his skull with a quick swing of his mace. More figures climbed onto the wall. Thomas stepped over the dead man at his feet and slashed with the sword in his other hand. Another man fell, only to be replaced by two more.

Seraina blinked. It occurred to her then, that of all the people she had seen thus far, Thomas was the only one she recognized. She had sensed the others' terror and pain, felt their need to kill or maim, but, thank the Goddess, she did not know their faces. And while she knew Thomas's face, when she quested out to him from within her own mind, she felt... nothing. No emotions whatsoever.

Thomas opened the throat of another and, when the dying man fell to his knees, Thomas brought his mace down upon his head. With every death, Thomas took one step toward Seraina. But he could never close the distance.

Seraina called out his name, and Thomas heard. He lowered his mace and sword and stared at her. He shook his head slowly.

Enemies flooded around him. A dozen swords

pierced his body and he stumbled. His dark, almost black, eyes never left hers until he tumbled backward over the wall.

Seraina gasped and leaned out between two crenellations. She watched his body fall, and though she was too far away to see his face, she knew he wore a contented smile. A moment before his body smashed against the rocks below, she felt the first hint of emotion emanate from Thomas's mind. It was only a simple pause, like a breath before sleep, and was gone in an instant. But she recognized it for what it was.

Relief.

Tears clouded her eyes as she stared at the blood-red form lying broken below. The Weave came for her then. Seraina shouted in protest and reached toward Thomas, but the winds plucked her from the walls and sent her spinning back into the mist.

Seraina woke with a start and she fought back a cough as breath poured into her lungs. She pushed her spine hard against the tree, and let it cradle her, as she allowed her senses time to recover from her vision.

The mist was gone, but now she was surrounded in darkness. Two sets of eyes stared at her, reflecting the glowing coals of a dying campfire. One set was blue and ancient, the other gold and wild.

"What have you seen, my child?" Gildas asked.

The violent images were still too fresh in her mind and they stole her voice. Suddenly cold, Seraina wrapped her arms around herself and shook her head. She stared into the hissing embers, jealous of their warmth. It took several minutes before she was able to answer the old druid, but Gildas waited patiently and did not press. He knew better. The wolf at his side, however, whined at her silence.

Eventually, Seraina forced words from her throat.

"Something is wrong," she said.

Chapter 2

DUKE LEOPOLD RODE at the front of a squad of fifty soldiers. Klaus, his ever-present man-at-arms, was at his side. The gray-haired veteran's hooded eyes swept back and forth on the road ahead, like a wary bird of prey waiting for a field mouse to break cover.

The only sign of movement came when a cold wind pushed its way through the trees and breathed life into a scattering of dead leaves, whipping them into a frenzy. They rose a foot into the air and hovered there for a moment. Then they began to turn in a circle, slowly at first. As the momentum built, they rose higher off the road and formed a column of spinning gold and tawny debris. The whirlwind floated back and forth across the road, in an erratic pattern that resembled a drunkard stumbling between taverns.

"Look!"

Leopold cringed as the sound of the Habsburg Fool's voice came from somewhere behind him. Much too close.

"The carpenter's fart!"

The little, purple-haired man sat sideways on a shaggy Norse pony. The Fool's face was split down the middle with white and black paint, a design his clothing also followed. Every now and then, when his pony stumbled, the Fool's pointed shoes tinkled with the sound of bells.

The Fool pointed at the twirling leaves. The soldiers nearest him laughed for everyone knew the story of the carpenter who had traded his soul to the Devil in exchange for two wishes. In a remarkable feat of balance and agility, the Fool stood on his saddle and acted out the entire story while standing on his moving pony's back.

"For the first, he asked for riches," he said in his best stage voice. It carried easily to the last soldier in line. "And the Devil made appear a kettle of gold coins! Far more than any man could spend in a lifetime. But the crafty carpenter paused before he made his second wish, knowing full well the Devil would own his soul once it was granted. 'Make your second wish,' the Devil demanded."

The Fool lifted his leg, screwed up his face, and farted; a necessary skill for any respectable court jester.

"My wish is for you to catch that and return it to me," he said, then he pointed at the spinning leaves. "And there goes the Devil now! Chasing the ever elusive carpenter's fart."

Most of the soldiers laughed, and more than a few crossed themselves when the Fool pointed out the Devil in their path. The Fool bowed in all directions, and then feigned to lose his balance. He fell split-legged onto his saddle, his eyes rolled up into his head, and he doubled over in mock pain.

That was enough for Leopold.

"I think the men at the end of the line have not had their fair share of you this trip. Go ride with them. If I see your painted face again, or hear your voice, I will have the men eat your pony and you can walk back to Habsburg."

The Fool clamped one hand over his mouth and covered his eyes with the crook of his other arm. Somehow, he managed to turn his pony around and plow his way through the soldiers all the way to the back of the formation.

Leopold did not balk when Klaus raised his fist and brought the column to a halt before the bridge spanning the Salzach river. Klaus had been responsible for Leopold's safety for all twenty-four years of the young duke's life, and his dedication to the task was genuine. He was one of only two people in this world that Leopold felt he could trust. The only other was his brother, Frederich.

Klaus stood in his stirrups and his head turned from side to side on his thick neck. He motioned for Leopold and his soldiers to remain where they were. He spurred his horse ahead and rode up to the narrow bridge. His horse hesitated, at first, but Klaus nudged it forward onto the wooden planks.

Leopold watched as Klaus examined the bridge and the far bank for any sign of treachery. A slow moving barge floated down the water. It was piled high with blocks of salt from the nearby mines. Klaus waited until it had passed beneath the bridge and faded into the distance, before he took his eyes from it and continued his inspection.

The old soldier had not yet forgiven himself for being absent when Leopold and Gissler had been ambushed on the forest road in Kussnacht. Ever since then he had been especially diligent when it came to his lord's security. Each of the twenty soldiers in Leopold's personal guard had been hand-picked by Klaus for their loyalty to the House of Habsburg. Although that thought did little to comfort Leopold, the fact that Klaus trusted each man did.

Leopold was confident Klaus would never betray him. He could never hope to gain a better position than the right hand of the Duke of Further Austria. Especially at his age. Leopold heard the whispers at court. Many thought Klaus was already too old to serve Leopold and they were lining up to suggest friends, sons, or cousins that would swear undying loyalty to the Duke.

But Leopold understood well the transient nature of loyalty. He pinched the top of his high-bridged nose and closed his eyes.

Damn that Schwyzer Hospitaller.

Gissler would have been the perfect replacement for Klaus. Unconnected at court and with not a trace of blue blood in his veins, his loyalty would have been easily bought. Owning a man with Gissler's skills would have been a great boon to the House of Habsburg.

And what would he have done with Klaus?

Leopold had not even thought about that. Of course he would have to keep him near, for the gruff veteran knew more Habsburg secrets than almost anyone. Perhaps even more than Leopold himself. But Klaus had served the Habsburg line well, and Leopold would ensure he lived out his last years in comfort. Still, he would need to be watched and kept near. For the man's own protection, Leopold told himself.

Leopold opened his eyes and stared at Klaus as he rode back toward them. For such a big man he rode well, and his body was as fit as any knight twenty years younger. Leopold realized it would be a few years yet before he would need to be replaced. That was a small measure of relief, for Leopold had no shortage of problems that required his immediate and full attention.

Chief among them, of course, was Arnold Melchthal and the ragtag army of peasants he had managed to raise.He had assumed it was Berenger von Landenberg's ineptness that had allowed the outlaw to remain at large for so long. But now that Melchthal was in full control of the new fortress in Altdorf, Leopold had to admit that he had underestimated the young man from Unterwalden.

He would not do so again.

The iron shoes of his own mount clattering against the wooden planks of the bridge pulled Leopold from his thoughts. He realized they were on the move again. Up ahead in the distance he saw the beginnings of Salzburg's Low-town, and perched five hundred paces above it, on a dramatic rock outcropping, stood Salzburg Castle; home to the Prince-Archbishop of Salzburg who, Leopold hoped, would be the solution to all his problems.

Farms and garden plots lined the road leading to Salzburg, and gradually gave way to the simple bungalows of the common classes. The grand Church of Saint Peter loomed high over these, and seemed to serve as a buffer between the cramped quarters of the simple townsfolk and the more elaborate two and three-story houses of the nobility. As Leopold and his escort came nearer to the base of the castle mountain, the houses became larger and more ornate; many with fenced off grounds of their own.

Leopold and Klaus dismounted in front of a stone gatehouse that seemed to grow out of the rock itself. Two soldiers snapped to attention in its arch and several crossbowmen leaned over the wall above to get a look at the new arrivals. The gate was the only access to the serpentine path that wound its way up the rocky slope to the main keep of the Castle.

Leopold ignored the guards and motioned for Klaus to follow him. Klaus grunted something to the captain of Leopold's men, then he followed Leopold through the great archway.

The Archbishop's steward stood waiting for them. He held the reins of two long-maned horses draped with silk blankets of red and white. On their heads they wore towering feathered headdresses to match.

The steward folded at the waist and held out the reins of the horses.

"Welcome to High-Salzburg, Duke Leopold. The Archbishop apologizes for being unable to greet your arrival in person, but commands we attend him immediately. He has supplied fresh horses to spare you the long climb to the castle."

Leopold did not even glance at the offered reins. Instead, he fixed the man with a withering glare and removed his gloves, one finger at a time.

"That command was intended only for you, I assume. For one prince does not command another," Leopold said. "Come, Klaus. We will take the rope-carriage. My arse has been beaten enough by horse flesh for one day."

The two men walked past the open-mouthed steward and approached the Archbishop's carriage. Decorated with ornate red and gold carvings, it had only two small wheels at its front, which made it list against the mountainside at an odd angle. The metal-rimmed wheels rested on iron rails and a series of ropes stretched from the carriage up the side of the mountain, disappearing far above.

Leopold made a show of opening the door for Klaus and gestured for him to climb in. Klaus hesitated and his usually emotionless face creased with the discomfort of having his lord open a door for him.

"Come now, Klaus. The good Archbishop would not have us thumping up these meandering paths on the backs of beasts when we could ride in comfort. Wipe your boots and climb in."

The steward managed to awaken from his stupor and scurried over. "My Duke, perhaps I could call another carriage from the keep if the horses are not to your liking."

"When there is a perfectly good one here? Nonsense. Why bother your stable hands?"

Klaus's huge boots had managed to collect enough dirt and manure to nurture a small garden, and when he scraped them off at the base of the door, more fell inside the carriage than without.

"It is just that… the rope-carriage… is reserved for the Archbishop's personal use. No one is permitted—"

Leopold held up his hand to silence the man.

"I understand completely. But, do not fret. I will be sure not to lend it out to any unsavory characters," Leopold said.

He resisted the urge to help the slow-moving Klaus squeeze through the narrow doorway with a shove. When the big man finally fell into a seat with his back to the mountain, Leopold stepped in and slammed the door shut behind him. He reached his arm through the half-door's opening and slapped his hand against the outside of the carriage like he would the rump of a horse.

"Do not stand there gaping, man. Get those oxen spinning their wheel. The bishop awaits!"

The steward puckered up his face and replied in a small voice. "The *Arch*bishop, Duke Leopold."

Leopold narrowed his eyes at the man. "The *aged* Archbishop. In fact he is getting so old he may no longer be with us by the time I get to the top of this mountain. You, on the other hand are much younger, and if fortunate, will be on this earth much longer than your bishop. I wonder who your next lord will be?"

The steward took a step back and bowed his head. He turned and shouted at the wheel house. "Hitch up the oxen! Send runners to the top. The Archbishop's cart is coming up!"

Leopold leaned into his upholstered seatback, out of the sun's heat, and tried to ignore the stench of disturbed manure wafting up from Klaus's boots.

Chapter 3

NOLL MELCHTHAL FOUND himself alone in the Altdorf keep, and he did not like it. He sat on the lowest step leading up to the throne platform and kept his eyes locked on the stone floor, for every time he looked around the cavernous room he could not help but be overwhelmed by its man-made grandeur. Four tall men could stand atop one another's shoulders and still be unable to touch the timber supports of the floor above. The cold, flagstone floor, white with the recent dust created by mason chisels, stretched far into the distance.

He stared across that gray sea with an unfocused gaze. The cracks between the blocks of stone faded away the nearer they came to the dark alcove of the main doors, and once again, Noll could not keep his thoughts from settling on Seraina.

He had sent messengers to Habsburg Castle proposing a trade. Landenberg, Vogt of Unterwalden, for Seraina and the ferryman, if he yet lived. His messenger had returned two days ago with the news that Duke

Leopold had refused to see him, and rumor had it that the Duke had departed for Salzburg.

Noll was crestfallen. If Leopold had taken his prisoners to Salzburg, they could at this very moment be in the hands of the Archbishop's confessors. A vision of Seraina defiantly holding back her screams as Leopold's torturers worked their dark trade forced Noll's stomach into the back of his throat. He clenched his eyes in vain and ground the heels of his hands hard against his temples.

Crippled by the strength of his own imagination, he could not bring himself to look up when the great doors grated on their hinges. He waited for the sound of boots on stone, the inevitable approach of someone who needed him to make yet another decision. But the footsteps never came. Whoever it was, must have recognized this was not a good time to seek Noll's counsel, and had left him alone with his grief.

Noll let out a breath, thankful. But as he breathed in, he sensed a presence. There was a life besides his own in the cold stone room. And it smelled of pine.

The realization that he was not alone saved him from jumping when a warm hand touched his shoulder.

"Noll," Seraina said.

He raised his head, and although he did not jump, his heart almost burst in his chest when he saw Seraina standing before him. Her green eyes flashed, filling the keep with more life than if it had been packed shoulder-to-shoulder with people. For the briefest moment, he thought it was the cruelty of his imagination at work once again, but when she smiled and pulled him to his feet, he knew it was no trick.

"Seraina!" He pulled her into his arms and laughter

20

flowed from her lips. The sound settled over him like a hot bath. He closed his eyes, and breathed in great mouthfuls of the pine and sunshine from her auburn hair, hardly daring to believe she was there.

"I thought you lost," he said, and pulled her in even tighter. He would have been content to stay that way, but Seraina gently eased out of the embrace.

"Gissler is dead," she said. "Thomas found me."

Noll nodded, and let her escape from his grip.

Then he remembered Leopold had been together with Gissler when they had taken Seraina. Perhaps that was why his messenger could not make contact with the Duke. Perhaps he too was dead.

He could not keep the excitement out of his words. "And Leopold? What of the boy tyrant?"

Seraina shook her head. "He escaped. The Red Lion lives. The Habsburg threat is still very real."

He should not have let his hope go unchecked. Leopold would not give up his place in the world so easily. "But the ferryman is still alive as well. Your face tells me as much."

"I would have come sooner, but Thomas was badly injured. I have been by his side these many days past," Seraina said.

"He is here then?"

"No. Thomas is still too weak to move. I left him in good company, but I cannot stay long."

"Why come at all then?"

He could not keep the hard edge from creeping into his words, as it always did when he spoke of the ferryman. Was it the man himself who he disliked so much? Or was it the way Seraina spoke his name? Noll closed his eyes and shook his head. This was madness.

21

His people were now at war with the Holy Roman Empire. A war he had started. And he was fawning over a girl like some fresh-faced boy yearning for manhood.

"I had to see you Noll." Seraina paused before continuing. "I had another vision."

Noll studied her face. She tried to smile, but it was an awkward attempt. "I would wager the omens were not good," he said.

Seraina turned away. Her nose crinkled as her eyes swept the room from the flagstone floor to the heavy timbers supporting the next level of rooms high overhead.

"There is something wrong," she said. "Something I do not understand."

"There is plenty wrong," Noll said. "For starters, I have an army of only five hundred men. Farmers and woodcutters, with only one sword for every ten men. The defenses of this fortress are only half complete and all my master builders have gone back home to their families. The Austrians could march in here with a thousand real soldiers and take this pile of stones before nightfall. And now, I have word that he has gone to Salzburg, where he will surely demand that the other princes rally to his cause. What about this situation is *not* wrong?"

The lines of worry that had creased Seraina's face only a moment before, faded. She stepped in closer to Noll and pulled one of his waving hands out of the air and covered it with her own. As always, all concern for her own troubles vanished when confronted with someone else in need.

"There is still so much to be thankful for," she said. She let go of him and spun away, her dress swirling with the sudden motion, and began pacing. Her steps were light and silent. "We have all this," she said sweeping one arm around the room. "Whereas, only a short time ago, we had nothing. You have awoken our people, but even more than that, you have shown them what is possible. Surely, that is worth more than a few soldiers?"

"But have I woken enough of our people? There is still no word from Berne or the guilds of Zurich. Nor has Lucerne offered any support for the Eidgenossen."

"Do not worry about them. More will come. I have seen it, remember? There are many yet who wish to awaken and climb out from under Habsburg rule."

Noll shook his head. "I hope you are right, Seraina. I truly do. But I also know it is impossible to awaken a man who only pretends to sleep."

Seraina laughed. "This is a fine turn," she said. "It is usually you accusing me of talking in riddles. We become more alike everyday." She took Noll's arm. "It is damp and lifeless in here. Come, my mushroom-man, let us put some sun on that frowning face."

She led him to the balcony overlooking the courtyard and they stepped out into the fresh air. Noll squinted into the afternoon light, and a soft breeze tousled his hair. He immediately felt better. Seraina was right, Noll thought. Shutting himself away in that cave, trapped alone with only his self-doubts for company, had dampened his spirits.

"Now tell me. What preparations have you made and what can I do to help?" Seraina asked.

Noll pointed to the gatehouse. "I have directed most of the work, so far, on finishing the gatehouse and the outer walls. But as it stands now, there are still a dozen breaches."

"How long before Leopold comes?"

"That is the only good news in all of this. The first snows will be here in another six weeks, so he has missed his opportunity for this year. He could possibly attack in spring, but the passes will still be too soft for an army. And besides, Leopold is too practical. He will wait for us to bring in the first crops so he has food for his men."

"Midsummer then?"

Noll nodded. "Those are my thoughts."

Seraina's face brightened. "So we have time. Time to find more allies and prepare. You see, things are not as bad as you feared."

Noll rolled his eyes. "Perhaps. But I will feel much better when I have Pomponio."

Seraina frowned. "What is a *pom-pony-o*?"

"Not what, who. Giovanni Pomponio. He is a Venetian, and a master swordsman. I have contracted him to come and train the men."

The way Seraina's eyes narrowed told Noll she was not keen to the idea.

"How much is this mercenary charging you for his services?"

"Not just him. He says he will bring a dozen of his best men as well. And it is Habsburg gold anyway, for we found a small chest in Leopold's room."

"How much?"

Noll hesitated. "All of it," he said.

Seraina shook her head and stepped away from the balcony railing. "Noll, you could have bought swords for your men with that money. And really, do you think it wise to bring in outsiders?" she asked.

Noll felt his jaw tighten. He grabbed Seraina by the arm.

"What good is a sword in the first place if a man does not know how to use it? Ten months from now, an army of battle-hardened killers will be at our doorstep. We need to surround ourselves with men like these, learn from them, if we are to survive. And the sooner the better."

He let go of her arm. "I am sorry," he said. "I forget myself at times."

"It is all right, Noll," Seraina said. "I understand. Outsiders make me nervous, that is all. But, you may be right."

Seraina had once told Noll that it was his fire that made him who he was. She could no more blame a cat for eating a wounded bird. And that so long as his laughter came just as often as his bursts of anger, he was living the life the Weave had intended for him.

But it had been some time since Noll had last laughed.

Right or not, it was done. The Venetians would be here tomorrow, or the day after. It did not matter how much gold it cost, Noll was not going to ask any man to fight beside him if he was not prepared.

"Will you stay here for the night?" Noll asked.

Seraina stared out over the courtyard. Her green eyes were fixed on a section of the outer wall. She seemed to not have heard him.

"Seraina?"

She blinked, and turned toward Noll. "Yes? No, I cannot stay here. I must head back to Thomas tonight."

Noll nodded. "Of course," he said. "How far do you go? I can get you a horse…"

"An hour north of White Elk Glade. It is easier to go on foot."

Noll felt the previous worries over Seraina's safety begin anew. "Stay off the roads, then. Habsburg patrols have begun to blockade the northern ways. It will not be long before they close them down completely."

"I have little use for roads," Seraina said. "You should know that by now."

Chapter 4

THE BLACKNESS CLEARED, one dark layer at a time, and Thomas forced his eyes open. His chest heaved and air rushed into his lungs, which sent his heart thrumming like the wings of a hummingbird.

"Easy now. The Weave welcomes you back, but no need to rush into her embrace."

The voice's owner, an old man, appeared above him and, for a moment, Thomas thought he dreamed again of the trapper that had taken him in after the death of his parents. But this man's long, powder-white beard and wizened eyes did not belong to the trapper of his memories. The man placed the palm of one leathery hand against Thomas's chest and within seconds the palpitations slowed.

Glancing around him, Thomas saw he lay on a bed of spruce boughs covered with a plush lambskin blanket. Another heavy skin was on top of his naked body and pulled right up under his chin. Though he could not see them, he felt the snugness of bandages wrapped around his middle and one leg.

At first he thought he was in a large tent, but then realized his head was inches from the base of a giant spruce, and the walls of the tent were, in fact, the tree's overgrown limbs stretched down to the ground. A tiny, smokeless fire burned on the far side of the natural room, and beyond that was an opening in the evergreen wall just large enough for a person to squeeze through.

The old man held a wooden bowl to Thomas's mouth. The lukewarm broth, thin but pungent, flowed past his cracked lips and traced a route clear down to his stomach. The man pulled the bowl away before Thomas could drink his fill.

"Enough. For now. It would not do to sodden your roots just yet."

After working the saliva around in his mouth and swallowing, Thomas found his voice.

"Seraina?"

The old man smiled. "She is fine. Do not fret over her whereabouts, as I suspect she will be along shortly."

"Who are you?" The strength and clarity of his own voice surprised Thomas. Starting at his toes he began flexing his muscles one by one, in an attempt to gauge the severity of his injuries.

"Some names are worth knowing, Thomas Schwyzer. Mine is not one of those. I did not kill you in your sleep, so I suspect you can tell that I am a friend, and that should be enough."

A rustle to Thomas's right made him risk turning his neck, and what he saw sent his heart hammering off the walls of his chest once again. An enormous wolf, its fur the same downy white as the old man's hair and beard, sat on its haunches less than two strides away. It caught

Thomas's sudden movement and turned its great head toward him. Its lips curled up to bare pink gums and jagged teeth longer than a man's finger. A guttural warning echoed up from somewhere deep in the back of the beast's throat.

Thomas found himself scrambling back to lean on his elbows and his head banged against the trunk of the giant spruce. Pain lanced down his side and his leg throbbed as blood coursed through the limb.

"Oppid! Get back. Our patient does not need to see the likes of you just yet."

He reached out and pressed his hand against Thomas's chest. Thomas risked a glance at the old man and wondered if he had been saved by a hermit touched by madness. But there was something about the way the man spoke and the rhythm of his words, and before he knew it, Thomas was once again lying under the warm lambskin. His eyes, however, remained fixed on the snarling wolf.

The old man began talking to the beast as though Thomas was no longer present. "Even if he meant us ill, a man in his condition is no threat to either one of us. Surely you can see that? Settle down now."

The beast kept its amber eyes fixed on Thomas and slowly lowered itself onto its belly. After a moment it rested its massive head on top of paws the size of full-grown rabbits.

"Is that your animal?" Thomas asked once he could speak.

"Oppid is my companion," the old man said. "You have to forgive him. He is not the trusting sort."

"But he is tamed?"

"Tame?" The old man looked at Thomas and

laughed, revealing straight teeth even whiter than his beard. "By Ardwynna's Grace, of course he is not tame. He is a wolf."

That did little to set Thomas at ease. He could not keep his eyes from the wolf, and finally the old man sensed his discomfort. He said a few words in a tongue unfamiliar to Thomas and the wolf padded to the doorway. But before he exited the tree shelter, he turned his golden eyes on Thomas and gave him one last blood-curdling snarl, as if to say, *I will not be far.*

With the wolf gone, Thomas relaxed. He continued the self-assessment of his injuries. He felt the stiffness of stitches on his thigh, as well as his torso and chest, but there were no severed muscles or ligaments from what he could tell. Even though he was concealed beneath the blanket, his nakedness was uncomfortable. The Knights of Saint John were forbidden to sleep naked, and it was a rule that was strictly enforced.

"I owe you my life," he said.

"Not me. Seraina is the one that tended your wounds. And she did a fine job, I should say. You were already on the mend when I first saw you."

Thomas glanced down at the line of stitches stretching down his side. "It would seem her skill rivals that of Hildegard of Bingen," Thomas said.

One side of the old man's mouth turned up in a smirk. "Ah, you mean Sibyl of the Rhine? Your church did well to claim her as one of its own, I will give you that. But tell me, why has she not been ushered into Sainthood when so many undeserving ones have?"

The hostility in his words caught Thomas off guard. "It was meant as a compliment. I know very little of Hildegard. If not for her texts on healing, I doubt I would even know her name."

"You know only what the church would have you know. Nothing more."

"I know God saw fit to imbue her with great healing skills. Is that not enough?"

"Why is it that you Christians are so eager to attribute all the good in this world to God and all things evil to the Devil?"

"God sets us all on the path He sees fit," Thomas said.

"Well, your god had nothing to do with Seraina's skills. Seraina worked hard for her knowledge. I have never seen a disciple so devoted."

"You were her teacher?"

"One of many."

There was a slight rustle at one of the makeshift branch-walls and Seraina slipped through. Her eyes went wide when she saw Thomas sitting up.

"You are awake!"

She dropped the sack in her hand and was at Thomas's side before he could speak. She took his hand in hers and placed the other on his forehead.

"How do you feel?" her eyes glowed in the half-darkness of the shelter and Thomas found himself unable to look away.

"Good," he said. "Better than good, all things considered."

Seraina took his hand in both of hers and lowered herself onto the edge of the bed. "And you will feel even better soon. The worst is over." She turned to the old man. "Gildas, give him some broth."

Gildas cleared his throat. "I already did."

"He needs more," Seraina said. "I can feel it in his

heart rhythms."

The old man grunted. "Very well. He is your patient, after all." He held out the bowl for Thomas to take. "But if he needs more he should be strong enough to feed himself."

Thomas began sipping at it slowly, and his hands shook at first, but once the liquid reached his stomach he drank in greedy gulps. Before he could empty the bowl, Seraina laughed and reached out her hand to cover his own. She took the broth from him and he fell back into the bed.

"That is enough," she said. "For now. I can see Gildas is about to throw a fit."

"How long have I been here? And, for that matter, where is here?" Thomas asked, glancing around at their cave-like shelter of tree branches.

"Six days," Seraina said. "We are only a few miles from the hollow in Kussnacht where you found me. You were too injured to move any further. But no need to worry. We are well-hidden. Leopold's men could never find us here." The words bubbled out of her and she seemed to take great delight in wiping the remains of broth from Thomas's chin with the sleeve of her dress.

Six days? Thomas clenched his fingers and flexed his leg muscles. They responded well and did not feel like they had been inactive for six days.

Gildas seemed to sense what was going through Thomas's mind. "Seraina exercised your limbs for you, when you could not. Your recovery may seem *miraculous* to you, but it is nothing of the sort. It is thanks to Seraina's hands keeping your blood flowing from your heart to your extremities and back again."

Thomas stopped flexing his thigh muscles and was

suddenly very aware of how naked he was under the lambskin blanket. He looked at Seraina.

"You have my gratitude," he said. "I hope it was not too… much trouble."

She shrugged. "You would have done the same for me, I am sure."

Thomas caught the trace of a smile on her lips before his eyes dropped to his hands. A breeze rustled the walls of their shelter, and a few green needles drifted down onto his bed. He was grateful to have something to focus upon.

"And my clothes…?" he said, to no one in particular.

"I burned them," Seraina said. "They were ruined and bore the stink of memories best forgotten." Her eyes dimmed for just a moment, and then flared to life again like a candle burning too hot for a thumb and finger to extinguish. She pointed to the sack on the ground. "I have brought you all new clothing. It is time to make some new memories."

Her words came too late for Thomas. His mind had latched onto the colossal form of his boyhood friend lying still and filthy in a dark prison cell. Thomas closed his eyes to shut it out, but that was a mistake, for the image only grew more real. He could see Pirmin's swollen face, beaten beyond recognition. Bruises and great purple welts in the shape of hobnailed boots lined his chest and ribcage, and his once muscular arm lay blackened at his side, seeping puss and a foul, cloudy liquid. He snapped his eyes open before his mind could force him to relive the rotting stench that went along with the death of his best friend.

Thomas looked at Seraina and worked the dryness from his mouth. "And Pirmin? Do you know what became of his body?"

Seraina nodded. "Noll saw to him, but do not worry about that now. You should focus on your own recovery."

Thomas pushed himself up on one elbow. "Was he buried on holy ground? I saw to his shrivening, but it would all be for naught if he is put to rest anywhere but church land."

"I have not yet visited his grave," Seraina said softly. "But I am sure Noll would have seen to it."

Thomas grimaced as he raised himself higher. "I must go and see for myself. Will you take me there?"

He attempted to swing a leg out from under his blanket but the movement pulled at his stitches. Pain swept up his side and his head pounded.

Seraina placed her hands on his shoulders. When she spoke her words were soft but firm. "I will take you, in time. But not until you are strong enough."

Thomas resisted for only a moment before he felt his strength drained away by the effort. He collapsed back into the blankets and closed his eyes until the throbbing in his skull subsided. He had to see Pirmin's resting place. He would not risk his friend being turned away at Saint Peter's Gate because Thomas had neglected his duties. But, he also knew his limits.

He opened his eyes and stared at the green canopy above. "Tomorrow, then," he said.

Seraina leaned back and lifted her hands from his shoulders. "That is not for us to decide. You have been through a great deal and we must allow the Weave time to welcome you back into her fold."

"I will be capable of travel tomorrow," Thomas said.

They stared at each other, locked in a battle of wills,

until Gildas spoke up. "Ready or not, he means to set out tomorrow, Seraina. I suggest we be prepared to accompany him."

Later that afternoon, with a little prodding from Gildas, Seraina agreed to let Thomas stand. After pulling on his new breeches, Thomas stood with Seraina's help. With his arm around her shoulders, the two of them shuffled between the bed and fire until a light sheen covered Thomas's brow and the breath rattled in his chest.

Gildas and Oppid sat together on the ground and watched. The old man, with his back pressed up against the trunk of the tree, chewed thoughtfully on a blade of grass. The intense way the pair eyed Thomas made him nervous, but he tried to dismiss the feeling and concentrate on taking one painful step after another. After all, who *would not be* uncomfortable limping about in front of a giant wolf?

When Seraina finally eased Thomas back into his bed, he grunted with relief. As darkness settled in, Gildas stoked the fire and they ate a simple meal of cheese, blackberries, and crunchy white tubers Thomas had never before seen. Although suspicious at first, he found them to be delicious and, because of their high water content, thirst quenching.

"He eats well. That, at least, is a good sign," Gildas said.

Seraina smiled at Thomas and nodded. "His body has begun to take over the healing process. I suppose I am no longer needed. Of course, I suspect someone will have to help him into his boots in the morning."

Thomas smiled weakly. The exercise had exhausted him, and his body demanded sleep as it attempted to digest the simple meal. He fought off the closing of his eyes once, but could not find the strength to resist when they shut a second time.

Later, he was woken by a hair-raising howl that belonged in the coldest hours of a full-moon night. Confused and disoriented, Thomas tried to sit up. He clutched at weapons that were not there.

But Seraina was. She stood over him and placed a hand on his bare shoulder.

"Shh… it is only Oppid," she said.

There was still enough light from the fire for Thomas to make out the fine features of her face, and of course, her eyes. "Lay back now…"

Somewhere outside their forest shelter, Oppid cried out to his kin once more. This time it was longer and, it seemed to Thomas, filled with anguish. Despite the comforting sound of Seraina's voice, and the warmth of her hand on his skin, Thomas felt a chill roll up his spine.

Sleep finally overtook Thomas, for Oppid did not howl again. Nor did any wolf answer his calls.

Chapter 5

THE MEETING CHAMBER was on the uppermost floor of Salzburg Castle. It was a long, rectangular room with high ceilings and smooth leather over the lower half of the walls. Wooden panels with intricately carved golden rosettes covered the wall's upper reaches. At one end of the room, upholstered benches lined the three walls. At the moment, a half-dozen men sat on them, doing their best to appear comfortable and relaxed.

The architect had had a good sense of court politics, and Leopold appreciated the irony of the room. The horseshoe seating arrangement allowed no obvious head of the table position and every person in the room was able to press his back up against a wall. The design was meant to put members at ease, but Leopold thought everyone looked small and feral the way their eyes darted around at one another when he entered the room. One by one they slid themselves up their respective walls and stood to greet the Duke.

There was not a prince among them, Leopold noted.

They had all sent stewards or marshals on their behalf, as was the minimum requirement when summoned to a war council by another prince. Leopold had expected as much. The other princes had no love for Leopold, or loyalty for that matter. But they would obey the King's Law. However, there was one man present Leopold had not expected to see: Sir Henri of Hunenberg.

Only one person remained seated: a portly man of late middle years, but with the powder-gray hair of someone much older. His deep red robes splayed onto the bench on either side and contrasted with the dark leather of the walls. He made no effort to leave his seat in the center of the horseshoe.

Leopold briefly acknowledged the greetings of the other men then strode directly to the Archbishop.

"Duke Leopold," he said holding out a hand bearing only one single ring of gold, but mounted with an almond-sized gem.

Leopold dropped to one knee and kissed the ring. "My dear Archbishop," Leopold said, raising his head. He seemed to notice the red robes for the first time. "What is this, your lordship? Has the Pope finally welcomed you into his house and promoted you to a cardinal?"

The Archbishop eventually smiled at Leopold, but it took some time to appear on his lips, and there it died without ever reaching his eyes. The Arse-bishop of Salzburg, as Leopold liked to call him, held the position of *Legatus Natus*. It permitted him to wear red, although a different shade than that of a cardinal, even in the presence of the Pope.

"Your eyes deceive you," the Archbishop said. He held one arm out to the side. "This is not the scarlet of a cardinal. Merely the red vesture of my station."

Leopold squinted. "Ah, so it is. Now that I look more closely I see that it is a much deeper shade. My mistake. Still, I am sure your time must be near. Frankly, I do not know how you do it."

"Do what, exactly?" the Archbishop asked.

"Labor in the shadows of the church, of course. I should think it would drive most men to the brink of insanity to devote one's life to a cause and never be justly recognized for it."

"On the contrary. I am the First Bishop of all German lands. His Eminence has entrusted me to preside over the Princes of the Holy Roman Empire. I imagine you, better than most, can appreciate the significance of this."

"It seems you have lost half your flock, then. For half of the princes side with Louis the Bavarian," Leopold said.

"For the time being, perhaps. But they will come to reason, for Frederich is the rightful King. I have the utmost confidence that, with our help," the Archbishop made a grand sweeping gesture around the room, "your brother will prevail."

"I am sure he will," Leopold said. "But that could be years in the making. In the meantime, we have a responsibility to our future King to ensure he has a kingdom left to rule once Louis is defeated."

"Of course, Duke Leopold. Is that not why all of us are here today? Come, take your seats councilors."

There was a commotion on the other side of the heavy chamber door. Words in raised voices were exchanged, followed by a short period of silence. Then someone eased the door open. The Archbishop's Chief

Steward, the man who had met Leopold and Klaus at the entrance to High-town, stepped into the room.

Every man in the room stared at him. To his credit, he stood at attention, unflinching, looking straight ahead, and waited to be acknowledged.

"Well," the Archbishop said. "What is it?"

"A messenger, my lord, he—"

The Archbishop waved him away. "I will see him after we are done here."

"He is a King's Eagle, my lord."

The room went from quiet to complete silence.

"Show him in, of course," the Archbishop said.

The steward had just enough time to open the door, before a bearded man garbed all in black, with a huge yellow eagle emblazoned on his chest strode through. His hair and face were coated in dust from the road, and streaked darker in places wet from sweat. He took two steps into the room; large clumps of mud fell from his boots. He dropped to one knee, and locked his eyes on the floor. The only thing about him that moved, were the saddlebags that swayed off one shoulder. As was the custom of all King's Eagles, he kept his messages, and anything else of value, in two small bags joined together with a flat piece of leather. That way, when he changed horses at an outpost, no time was wasted in transferring his supplies to a fresh mount. If his horse died from exhaustion, the Eagle was expected to take his saddlebags and continue on foot until he could expropriate a horse from someone. And if he should ever lose his bags, well, there was a reason for the saying 'a bagless King's Eagle, shall fly no more.'

"You bring the King's word?" the Archbishop asked.

The man reached into one of his saddlebags and

produced a small scroll. He stood, asking permission of no one, and stretched out the roll between his hands. In a strong, clear voice, he began to read.

Princes and Loyalists of the Holy Roman Empire:

We are beset by dark times, for treachery approaches from all sides. Pretenders threaten to usurp our Divine Right to Rule.

I am forced to take up arms against my own cousin, who I am convinced, acts upon misinformation supplied by unscrupulous advisers. Meanwhile, on the other side of the Empire, in Further Austria, you are faced with your own challenge; an open rebellion by the peasants of the Forest Regions.

You may be tempted to consider your situation less grand, or not as worthy, as my own. However, if this were truly so, I would not have taken the time to send this decree.

On the surface, this rebellion appears to be nothing more than mountain peasants laying claim to Habsburg lands and defiling property of the monks at Einsiedeln. But this is no benign threat and I urge you, do not take it lightly. Much is at risk.

From Paris, comes word of a diseased class who call themselves "bourgeois". Their guilds grow in power and greed everyday, threatening to topple the Divine Order, the very pillars upon which society is built. These mercers would raise themselves up and be your equals. Mark my words. This movement is a plague waiting to spread.

If we stand by and allow the peasants of Schwyz, Uri, and Unterwalden to take even one farmer's field, we are remiss in our duties as Lords of this Land. For, in the end, they will only succeed in abusing God's gardens and destroying themselves while doing so. But even worse, by not acting, we are in direct defiance of God's wishes. For, by His Word, "Kings are to rule the hands of men, and the Church, their hearts".

———

41

I deeply regret my absence at your council, but as you know I fight another battle. The Empire faces war on two fronts, and neither poses a more dangerous threat than the other.

As these are my thoughts, I exert my right as your vassal lord, and call upon each and every one of you to fulfill your oaths of fealty. It is my wish that you raise from your lands the prescribed number of infantry and mounted knights as set out in your Oath to the Throne, and make them available to my brother Leopold, the Sword of Habsburg, at a place and time of his choosing.

It may be Habsburg lands today, but mark the words of your King, if this threat is not properly addressed, tomorrow it will be yours.

The messenger cleared his throat and looked up. He threw his shoulders back and drew himself to full height.

"Signed and dated by his Grace, Frederich of Habsburg, King of the Germans, and Rightful Emperor of the Holy Roman Empire," he said.

The room was silent. The Archbishop beckoned the Eagle to him and accepted the scroll. He studied it with narrowed eyes. Eventually, he nodded.

"It is indeed the King's seal. I did not know your brother was capable of such eloquence, Duke Leopold."

Of course he is not. They are my words, and my scribe Bernard's script. You and I both know it.

"Unlike myself, Frederich was gifted with a golden tongue. I have always envied him that," Leopold said.

Even you, my Arse-bishop, cannot refute the Royal Seal. I am sure it will drive you mad wondering how I got my hands on that.

The old cleric handed the scroll back to the Eagle. "You discredit yourself. I am sure you have your own set of talents that we have yet come to appreciate, Duke Leopold. Or, would you prefer I call you *Sword of the*

Habsburgs?"

One of the stewards chuckled until he saw the young Duke looking at him. It was the Count of Kyburg's man. Leopold fixed his face in his memory.

A deep voice broke in on the conversation. "My lords, may I have leave to speak?" Count Henri of Hunenberg asked.

Leopold was glad the man had spoke up. A veteran of the wars in the Holy Lands, Henri was the only lord in the room, except for the Arse-bishop, who was there in person to represent his own title and lands. But, he looked uncomfortable in the council chambers. He had spent too much time in the Levant and seemed out of sorts with court politics.

Why was he here, anyway? None of the other counts or princes had come themselves. Why should he?

Leopold suddenly recalled that he still owed Henri partial payment for one of his estates near the Gotthard Pass. Surely the man had better sense than to come looking for a handout here. Leopold would pay him when he had the funds, and not a moment before.

"Of course, Count. You require no man's permission to speak in this council. We are grateful for your presence," Leopold said. He gestured for the man to retake his seat.

Count Henri bowed his head but remained standing. "We all understand the King's message. But we have not yet heard from the man who is to command this army we raise. Perhaps you could tell us what you plan, Duke Leopold."

"Plan? I think it should be obvious. I will march into Schwyz, punish those responsible for the attack on the Einsiedeln monastery, and rest up my men. From there, I march to Altdorf, retake the fortress, kill all who resist, and put the mountain peasants to work repairing the damage they have caused."

"Enslave them, you mean."

"Ah, Henri. I believe I know where this is headed. You knew some of the rebels in Outremer, did you not? You fought alongside them and counted them friends, I imagine."

"Aye. I knew both Pirmin and Thomas. But friend is not the exact word I would use to describe Thomas. Pirmin maybe, but not Thomas."

"And what of Hermann Gissler? The man this Thomas Schwyzer cut down before my very eyes. Would you count him as a friend, if he yet lived?"

Count Henri shifted his weight and stared at the Duke. "I just think there may be a better solution to this mess than marching through those villages with a full blown army. I have seen what an army can do to a land and its people. It will take years for them to recover."

"I appreciate your forthrightness and will take your concerns under advisement. Now, I trust you will heed the commands of your King?"

Henri cast his eyes downward at his hands. They were heavy, with thick digits and a crescent shape to them that looked permanent. He let them drop to his side and one slowly curled into a fist.

"I am bound to the Crown for fifty knights and fifty infantry, and I will honor it. However, I will be commanding the men myself. As is my right," Henri said.

"Of course. Having a man with your experience in my army will be most welcome," Leopold said, and he meant it. Henri may have a sentimental streak but when it came time to fight for his King, he would do what was required. His sense of honor would permit nothing less.

He did a quick mental calculation. Adding Henri's soldiers to those the other lords would be required to furnish, came to just shy of two thousand men. Leopold's own force consisted of three thousand, and how many would the Archbishop be required to contribute? Another two thousand? Perhaps three? The Salzburg Barracks was home to full-time, battle-hardened soldiers, who had seen active duty all over the Empire. They would be the best trained of them all. It was shaping up to be the ultimate punitive force.

"Archbishop. Do you recall what the size of your contributory force shall be?" Leopold asked. He kept his eyes wide and innocent, and was proud of himself for not allowing a trace of smugness to creep into his voice.

The older man steepled his fingers in front of his face.

Was the old goat actually hiding a smirk?

The Archbishop opened his mouth to speak, and then stopped himself for a moment before finally continuing on. He looked like a man about to eat a roast pheasant, but could not quite decide which wing to tear off first.

"Regrettably, all of Salzburg's military forces are already committed to the King's cause. I have my own writ from the King that I must follow. You see, Salzburg is to be kept as a place of strength should Frederich need to withdraw from the war with the Bavarian for a time. The King has commanded me to ensure all of Salzburg's soldiers are available to him at a moment's notice. All of them. God forbid that should ever happen, of course."

You dung-eating buggerer of….

"So the answer to your question, Duke Leopold, is

regrettably, not a one."

The Archbishop leaned back into the leather of his bench and crossed his arms. He shook his head in a display of regret, but the thin smile on his lips told another story entirely.

***

"In all your years, have you ever known a more repugnant, holier than thou, greedy, arse licker? Have you?" Duke Leopold asked.

"Yes, my lord. Several," Klaus said.

Dressed in only his nightshirt, Leopold paced laps around his assigned room. Klaus was sure it must be the smallest guest quarters in Salzburg Castle. He thought of mentioning that to the Duke, but quickly changed his mind. Klaus did not know of another man Duke Leopold hated more than the Archbishop of Salzburg, and fanning those flames would not be wise.

Leopold puffed up his face and squinted his eyes. "*So the answer, Duke Leopold, is not a one.* How long did he practice to get that pompous tone just right? And what cruel bastard ever decided someone could be both a prince and a bishop?"

"Your grandfather, I believe," Klaus said. *God rest his soul.*

"Well, that explains it. Yet another failing of dear old grand pappy that I have to live with. If I did not need the Arsebishop's cavalry I would have spit in his face right then and there. And watched it drip down his double chin onto his precious red robes. Really, why should a cleric be in charge of some of the best soldiers in the Empire? Who decided that?"

46

"Your grandfather as well," Klaus said.

"The man was truly an idiot."

Klaus said nothing. He stood ramrod straight, with his hands behind his back, and eyes in front.

"Well, what do we do now Klaus? Go back to his holiness tomorrow and beg for his cavalry?"

Klaus shook his head. "We do not need his soldiers, my lord."

"No, we do not *need* them, Klaus. I *want* them. When we march into Schwyz and Altdorf, we must do so with a full display of Habsburg might. I want drummers, trumpet men, infantry, and if I can't have the Sturmritter, I want the next best thing. And that, sadly, is the Arsebishop's cavalry. And now that he has told me I cannot have them I want them even more!"

Leopold grabbed a pitcher of wine from the bedside table and filled a mug. He lifted it to his nose and sniffed it. He was about to take a drink and then groaned and threw it against the wall.

"Probably poisoned," he said. "Would that not be the perfect end to a perfect day? Or the perfect week for that matter? What do you think, Klaus?"

Klaus paused before answering. "I think the Ars… Archbishop did not believe the messenger was a true Eagle."

"I could care less what he thinks, as he obviously does not spend much time catering to my wants. He does not care if Louis trounces my brother in this war. He will still be the High Bishop for the German Empire. The only person's favor he really needs, is that of the Pope."

Leopold paused. He stared at Klaus and cocked his head. Klaus had seen that look many a time. He let out a deep breath, and waited.

"The Pope…" Leopold repeated. "Klaus, why is it that I get some of my best ideas while yelling at you?"

Klaus gave no indication that he had heard the question. But he had, in fact, heard everything. Not many men could say they had served two kings and outlived them both. Klaus suspected he knew which plan Leopold was about to hatch.

It was going to be a long night.

Chapter 6

THEY SET OUT mid-morning with Thomas riding bareback on their one horse and Seraina and Gildas walking alongside. Thomas was grateful that Gildas had sent the wolf away earlier when he saw how much Oppid upset the horse, for Thomas doubted he had the strength to control a fidgety animal. And Gildas too, mumbling something about towns filled with small-minded people, seemed to relax when Oppid bolted off into the woods.

They emerged from the trees onto a road some time later. Thomas knew it was for his sake that they avoided the forest trails but he wished Seraina would stop looking at him every time he winced or shifted to a more bearable position on his mount. He kept one arm pressed tight to his side, as it lessened the jostling of his stitches. He was weak, he knew that. But the pounding in his skull had subsided to a tolerable level and he was actually beginning to feel the first pangs of hunger.

"Do you need to stop for a rest?" Seraina asked.

"No."

"We have time. I know of a place we can spend the night and push on to Schwyz at first light."

"I said no. I would see us at Sutter's inn before dusk."

"Very well. But we will stop here for a few moments. You may not be tired but your horse is. You ride with all the life of an iron anvil."

Thomas began to grunt back a reply but the vibration of speech sent a shiver of pain rippling up his side. He settled for a dark look.

Gildas stopped and leaned on his staff. "A rest sounds good. You set a swifter pace than I am accustomed. Whatever happened to the little short-legged girl of yesteryear that used to have to run to keep up with me?"

Seraina laughed. "Why I willed my legs to grow, of course, because I was sure there must be more to see in the world than thinning white hair and a crooked back."

"It seems that a great deal of that will was directed at your tongue as well," Gildas said.

Seraina was still smiling as she looked at the road before them. It rose up a steep hill and turned to the right.

"I think there are heidelberries nearby. Gildas, help Thomas off his horse and I will be back in a few minutes."

She was already several strides up the road before either man had a chance to voice their thoughts. Thomas watched as her lithe legs carried her away from them. Her strides were long and graceful, and although she was no taller than an average woman, the way she moved was more feline than human. She crested the hill and, with one last glint of sunshine off her auburn hair, Seraina disappeared around the bend.

Thomas realized he had been holding his breath. He looked down and saw Gildas staring at him. The old man shook his head.

"She is not for you, Thomas Schwyzer."

"What are you talking about?" Thomas met the old man's stare with one of his own.

"Deny it if you will. But your eyes are the scouts of your heart, not its spies. They cannot conceal what you feel."

Thomas looked down at his horse's mane. "You are full of crazy talk, old man." He swung his right leg over and eased himself to the ground. His pulse beat at a furious pace.

Gildas looked up the road.

"I tell you this to spare you. Not because of some fatherly need to protect a daughter." He turned back and Thomas tried to avoid the man's fierce blue eyes, but they were a current that he could not fight against.

"Seraina is much more than a daughter to this world," Gildas said. His eyes softened to reveal a sadness that had perhaps always been present, but hidden. "Your priests tell us women are sin. My own people view them differently. We say *woman is life*."

"Then what do you say of men?" Thomas asked.

Gildas smiled. "*Man is the servant of life*. Fitting is it not?"

Thomas shook his head. "I do not understand what you are trying to…,"

Thomas blinked, and caught a sense of motion from the top of the hill. At the same time, Gildas too seemed to register a change of some sort, for he turned and looked up the road.

Seraina rounded the corner in the road and was coming toward them at an all-out sprint. She slipped as she started down the hill, but without slowing down, she reached out one hand, pushed off the ground to regain her balance, and continued running. The sight of her reddish-brown hair, streaming behind her as she ran, had a much different effect on Thomas now than it did earlier. It filled him with dread.

He reached to his belt for his knife, but it came away empty. He looked to his horse, but realized its back was bare, save for Ruedi's crossbow wrapped in a sheepskin blanket. The quality weapon was worth a small fortune, but now, with no bolts, it was worse than worthless. But even if he had a quarrel, Thomas knew he would be unable to cock the weapon without the assistance of a belt hook. The heavy draw weight of the string would sever his fingers before he could pull it even half way.

"A sword," he said, looking at Gildas. "I need a weapon." Gildas stepped away from him and shook his head. Thomas's eyes locked onto the walking stick Gildas held. It was crooked and worn smooth from a lifetime of use, but being made from hard, solid oak, it was heavy enough. He reached out and tore it from the old man's grasp before he could protest.

Seraina was there much sooner than Thomas thought possible. She walked the last few paces with her hands on her hips to catch her breath. Her cheeks were flushed and the sides of her hair wet with sweat. One unruly strand curled over a cheek and fluttered with every exhalation.

"Habsburg soldiers," she said. "And I think they saw me. Quickly! We must take to the trees."

Gildas put his arm on her shoulder. "It is too late for

that now." He nodded toward the road. Two riders, the sun glinting off their helmets, trotted toward them. They seemed to be in no rush, but they were obviously focused on the three travelers standing directly in their path.

"We must run," Seraina said.

"We cannot." Gildas nodded toward Thomas. "He is in no shape to flee. I doubt he could even get back onto his horse in time."

"He is right," Thomas said. "You and Gildas go. I will be fine. They will not know who I am."

Seraina's voice rose to a frantic pitch. "Are you mad? Of course they will know who you are. You killed the Duke's soldiers and stole one of his horses!"

Thomas looked at his mount. The Habsburg brand jumped out at him. Cringing, he pulled the bundle holding Ruedi's crossbow forward so it covered the mark. By the time he turned around, he was greeted by the pattering of hooves on hard earth. He tightened his grip on the walking stick.

"You there. What cause do you have to run from your Duke's patrol?"

Gildas stepped forward. "Please forgive my daughter, my lords. She is mute and scares easily. She mistook you for highwaymen and rushed back to warn us."

The riders pulled up before them. The one that spoke was much younger than the other, and the way he barked out his words, made Thomas think he was eager to impress the veteran he rode with.

"Show me your trade pass," the younger man said.

"Trade papers, my lord?" Gildas said.

"This road is closed to all but those certified by the Trade Commissioner."

"Since when?" Thomas asked. "I have not heard of these roads being off limits to locals." He regretted speaking almost immediately. Not because the younger man turned on him instantly, but more so because he felt the older soldier also take an interest in him.

"Do you expect to know all that transpires in the Commissioner's office?" the young soldier said. "Are we to knock on every hovel's door and deliver each command of his lordship personally? Who are you, man, to speak so out of place?"

"He is my daughter's husband, my lord," Gildas said, shooting a scowl at Thomas. "He is a miserable man at the best of times, and often speaks out of turn to make up for his wife's eternal silence."

To emphasize the old druid's story, Seraina punched Thomas in the shoulder and flashed her teeth at him.

"Well, if he speaks again without my leave, I will have his tongue at my belt. That should make the conversations at their dinner table more balanced."

He chuckled at his own threat, and Thomas forced his eyes to look at the ground. The older soldier nudged his horse forward and slowly began circling around to the rear of Thomas's own mount.

The young man continued questioning Gildas. "If you have no trade papers, then you did not pass the checkpoint. How did you get on this road?"

"Not far from here, there is a trail in the woods that leads to our farm," Gildas said, his words especially slow to Thomas, and as he spoke he stepped toward the young man, holding his hands low and out to the side. "This path meanders between lichen-coated rocks, and under trees draped in giant-beard. The sun appears, now and then, and when it does, its rays warm your skin, and if you listen carefully, very carefully, the sound of running water hums in the background..."

Gildas continued speaking and if Thomas had been standing closer to the old man he doubted he would have been able to focus on anything but his words. But, with effort, he shook off the sound of Gildas's voice. He took hold of his horse's halter, then angled himself toward the other soldier walking his horse behind them.

"A word of caution, my lord," Thomas said. "This horse likes to kick out at others that come too close from the rear."

The soldier drew his sword. "I shall have to be careful, then," he said. "What do you carry under this blanket?"

Seraina stiffened beside Thomas. He could tell it was all she could do to hold back her words.

"Firewood," Thomas said.

"Firewood," the soldier repeated, like it was some exotic foreign word.

"And a few onions," Thomas said.

The soldier nodded. And then thrust his sword point between the blanket and the rope securing the bundle in place. The rope sprang away, the horse skittered sideways a step, and the load slid off and crashed to the ground.

Ruedi's Genoese-made war bow flipped out from its concealment and skidded to a stop at Thomas's feet. The veteran's eyes picked up on the horse's Habsburg brand in the same instant.

He raised his sword, and then screamed in pain.

Seraina was on his other side. She had thrust her hand behind his knee and had a hold of something, a ligament or tendon, or God only knew what, but whatever it was, the soldier's face was pale with agony.

He dropped his sword and leaned in his saddle to get away from her. Thomas shuffled over and obliged him. He grabbed his arm and yanked him from his horse. Thomas grimaced as his stitches stretched to their limit, but held.

Thomas heard the ring of a sword being drawn from its scabbard. He looked over his shoulder as the young soldier, seemingly no longer under Gildas's trance, kicked the old man to the ground.

Seraina screamed the druid's name and rushed to help him. Thomas gripped the walking stick in his hands and brought it down on the head of the soldier lying at his feet. He hit him again for good measure, then turned to help Gildas and Seraina.

But he knew he was too far away.

As Seraina ran at the two of them, the young soldier, with a wild look in his eyes, hefted his sword high above his head. Gildas, having pushed himself up to his hands and knees, looked up as the sword began its downward arc toward his neck.

Then Thomas saw fear twist the ears of the soldier's horse. Its eyes went wide, and before it could bolt, its master was carried clean out its saddle by a blowing cloud of white fur.

Oppid's momentum carried him and the soldier twenty feet away from the terror-stricken horse. The white wolf had his massive jaws wrapped over top the soldier's helmet, so he lived long enough to know he was in a nightmare. The man screamed as Oppid stood over him, snarling, his yellow teeth dripping streams of thick saliva. Then the wolf snapped him up by the throat, lifted him off the ground, and shook the soldier back and forth like he was nothing more than an old dusty blanket. The cracks of his neck and spine splintering made Thomas look away.

The older soldier let out a groan, so Thomas hit him again with the walking stick. Then he retrieved the soldier's sword and turned back to finish the man, but Seraina stepped in front and put her hand on Thomas's chest.

"Thomas, no," she said.

"He will bring others," Thomas said. "They said there was a checkpoint near here."

"We have two more horses, now. We will be in Schwyz before they can send others," Gildas said.

Thomas watched Oppid drag the broken corpse of the other soldier into the woods. "God have mercy. Is he going to do what I think he is?"

"At times, nature may appear cruel," Gildas said. "But look at it through Oppid's eyes. True cruelty lay in letting a perfectly good set of entrails rot in the sun." The old man's eyes sparkled. "Come, Thomas Schwyzer. Let us be on our way, and leave an old wolf his privacy. For, as those of your faith are fond of saying, it is God's Will."

As they came over the last series of low, velvety green slopes, and Schwyz lay at the head of the valley below, Gildas slowed his horse and began to stammer excuses for not going any further.

"Why not come in with us?" Seraina asked. "Sutter has a warm, comfortable inn with even a few private rooms, and the best chamois stew—".

Gildas shook his head and the downy white hair of his beard and head floated in the breeze. "No. It is time for me and Oppid to be on our way."

He slid off his horse, stroked her neck once, and whispered something in her ear that sent her trotting off back the way they had come. Thomas and Seraina also dismounted and, after Thomas removed Ruedi's war bow, they too sent their mounts away. They would not risk any harm coming to Sutter by bringing the Duke's horses into his stable.

Gildas whistled and Oppid loped out of the woods, turning his massive head warily from side to side as he crossed the open grassland between them.

"Luck is not one of my beliefs. But, I will wish it to you all the same, Thomas Schwyzer." The old man held out his arm and Thomas took it.

"How long will you be gone?" Seraina asked. Her voice was small and Thomas could hear the fear of abandonment in her words.

Gildas shrugged. Oppid was at his side now, and the old man absently grabbed and released great handfuls of the wolf's white coat. "As long as it takes. The others are scattered and will be difficult to find. But I will. And when the time is right, you must meet us on the Mythen."

Seraina nodded once, and then dropped her chin. The old man looked at her and his face softened.

"I will be back, my child. Remember, I too have no small touch of the sight, and that much I have seen."

He reached out and lifted her head. She looked up and her eyes shimmered. A tear broke free and crawled down one cheek. The sight of her in pain made Thomas avert his gaze.

"Ah, Seraina. Your eyes remind me so much of the waters we lived on when you were a child. Do you remember our lake?"

"Yes… I think so," she said, dabbing at her eyes with her sleeve. "But only bits and pieces. I was so young."

"And so full of questions for one just learning to speak. Why, why, why! How, how, how! It could have been the most peaceful place in the world, if not for your endless nattering."

Seraina smiled. "I do remember. I was happy there," she said.

"You were, and so was I. Happier than at any other moment in my long years. And when I look at you now, it gladdens me to see that green lake reflected so clearly in your eyes. Somehow, you have preserved the same wonder and innocence as back then, but like those waters, I see the strength of steel as well. There has never been a prouder man, than the one that stands across from you now."

Seraina hugged him and buried her face against his white robe. Her shoulders shuddered and he kissed the top of her head. After some time, he eased her to arm's length.

"Come, now. You will upset the wolf. It is best you say your goodbyes."

Seraina wiped once more at her eyes and nodded. She called the wolf by name, then dropped to her knees and threw her arms around his neck, her fingers not even close to touching. She forced a laugh and whispered strange words into his ear.

Thomas became aware that the old man had locked his eyes on him. All traces of the kindness that had been in them only moments before was gone.

"Look after her," Gildas said. "As she has done for you. And remember what we discussed."

"It was not much of a discussion, as I recall,"

Thomas said.

Seraina stared after Gildas and Oppid for a long while after they disappeared into the forest. Finally, she and Thomas began walking down the slope toward the village.

"I do not understand why Gildas refused to stay at Sutter's for even one night," Thomas said. "Surely a comfortable bed and a hot meal would do the old man some good. Is he in that much of a hurry?"

Seraina held out one hand and dragged it through the waist-high grass. It was late afternoon and Thomas was beginning to feel the autumn chill through his cloak, but Seraina did not seem to notice.

"Gildas does not like to be around people much. Even the smallest village unnerves him," Seraina said.

"He cares about you, though. How did you come to be raised by him?"

"He bought me," Seraina said.

"Bought you? Such as at a slave market?"

"You are one to talk," she said. "It was not like that. I was only a baby when Gildas found me. My parents were very poor and already had five children, so Gildas convinced them to give me up."

"Why did he choose you over one of the others?"

Seraina smiled. "Because I was special. Can you not see that?" Her spirits seemed to be improving.

Thomas shrugged. "He may have been able to get two, or even three, of the other children for the same price as one *special* one."

Seraina slapped him on the arm. Thankfully, it was his uninjured one.

"We are a pair, you and me," Seraina said. "Each sold

to the highest bidder. I wonder what our lives would be like if that had not happened..."

That was a question Thomas had never once asked himself. He remembered almost nothing about his life before the *Long March* to the port of Genoa, where he and the other Schwyzer children were loaded onto a ship bound for the Holy Lands.

Sometimes, late at night, he would catch a glimpse of a tall man cutting wood, or a woman with sandy hair, standing in a black earth garden and wiping her brow with the back of her arm. But they were fleeting images, just as likely to be based on dreams as reality.

Perhaps the only true memory he could claim of those early years, was that of a shivering boy trying to spread a small blanket over the half-frozen bodies of his dead parents. Since that was what he usually saw whenever he attempted to remember his parents, he eventually stopped trying altogether.

"My parents died when I was very young," Thomas said. He was not sure why he had said that.

"I know," Seraina said.

When he looked at her with confusion on his face, she added, "You talked out loud, and often, when you were stricken with the blood fever."

"Ah," he said.

"In fact, I think you talked more when you were at death's feet than you do now."

"Perhaps my silent nature is the reason the Hospitallers paid more for me than Gildas did for you," Thomas said. He found himself smiling, and if the scar on the left side of his face tightened, he did not notice.

"Oh, ho! The fox bares his teeth," Seraina said. "Speaking of Gildas, what was it that you and he *discussed* when I was gone?" If anyone looked like a fox at that moment, it was Seraina.

Thomas shook his head and tried to keep his eyes locked on the thatched roof of Sutter's house in the distance.

"Was it about me?" Seraina asked, innocently. But her grin and the tilt of her head told Thomas she knew that it was.

***

Seraina saw Sutter cutting wood behind the inn as she and Thomas approached across a field. He straightened up when he saw them coming and, after shielding his eyes from the sun to get a better look, shouted something toward the kitchen window. Within seconds, both Vreni and her daughter Mera ran out the back door.

Seraina left Thomas behind and ran to meet the two women with tearful embraces all the way around. By then Sutter was there, and even the gruff innkeeper wrapped his long arms around Seraina.

Mera had her crying under control by the time Thomas limped up, but one look at him and her pretty features began to waver. She ran at Thomas, as though it were a race to get to him before her tears exploded, and threw her arms around his neck. She got her head on his chest just in time.

Seraina looked on as Thomas held his arms out to the side for an uncomfortable moment, but then in small jerky movements, managed to put them around the girl and comfort her as best he could.

"I am so sorry Thomas," Mera said. "None of us deserved to have Pirmin taken from us, but you least of all."

Thomas said nothing, but Seraina was sure she saw his arms squeeze the girl a little tighter.

While Vreni and Mera disappeared upstairs to make up two rooms, Seraina and Thomas sat with Sutter at the small kitchen table, since it was the dinner hour and there were a few guests in the main room.

"You have been to Altdorf, then?" Sutter said to Seraina.

She nodded. "More men flock to Noll's fortress every day, from all corners of the Forest Regions," Seraina said. "If Leopold comes next year, he will be in for a surprise."

Sutter's mouth became hard. "That is good to hear. And what of Landenberg?"

Seraina feared he would ask about the Vogt of Unterwalden. "The Council will meet and decide his fate," she said.

He looked up at the ceiling for a moment and then lowered his voice to a whisper. "He should be hung."

Seraina could feel Sutter staring at her, but she could not be sure because her own eyes refused to leave her fingers. "I know how you feel, and if it is any consolation, Noll punished the man. I saw his injuries."

"That will not stop him from coming right back here and terrorizing us all over again." He paused. "I have given this some thought. I am going to join the Confederate Army."

Seraina could not believe what she was hearing, but it was Thomas who responded first.

"No, that is a very poor decision. Look around you, Sutter. You have a business, a family, and both need you more than any band of Melchthal's. If you go to Altdorf, you throw all of this away."

"I believe in what Noll is doing," Sutter said.

"War is for young men," Thomas said.

"You serve this cause better by staying alive," Seraina said. "Your family needs you."

Sutter closed his eyes and massaged his temples with one hand. "You are both right. I am not thinking straight these days." A dry laugh forced itself from his chest. "I am just a tired, old innkeeper."

Seraina could tell Sutter was lying by the way he laughed. He was telling them what they wanted to hear. Thomas seemed to sense it as well, for in a rare show of affection, he reached over the table and put his hand on Sutter's shoulder.

"Do what is best for your family. You will never regret that," Thomas said.

"What will you do?" Sutter asked.

As Seraina waited for Thomas's response, bits of her recent vision flashed through her mind.

"I have not given it much thought," Thomas said, leaning back slowly in his chair.

"You could come stay with us. We need an extra set of hands around the inn."

Thomas smiled, but there was more sadness about it than joy. He looked around the kitchen.

"Thank you, Sutter. I would like that," he said. "But I think I had better ask Pirmin first. He was always rather protective over this place."

While Sutter chuckled at the joke, Seraina looked into Thomas's dark, almost black, eyes and trembled at what she saw.

Chapter 7

THE ARCHBISHOP'S MESSENGER walked his horse through the gates of High-town just after midnight. A bank of clouds had moved in an hour before, and the evening air was muggy. When the rain finally broke loose, it came in the form of a mist so fine and light he did not bother putting up the hood of his cloak.

He kept his horse to a walk as he passed through Low-town. The sound of a cantering horse in the dead of night made people nervous and was sure to draw attention. But once he had navigated the maze of cobbled alleys and streets, and the last group of houses lay behind him, the messenger dug his heels into his horse's side and urged her into a gallop.

The horse's shod hooves hit the bridge over the Salzach a minute later, and the sound echoed off the trees and drowned out the noise of water rushing below. The rider did not let up on the reins. Time was more important than stealth now. He knew he was far enough out of the city that no one would hear.

But he was wrong.

After the end of the bridge the road banked to the left and narrowed. With the cloud cover, and the drizzling rain, he had no hope of seeing the black-dyed rope stretched taut in his path. It caught him high in the chest and snapped his head back to bounce off his horse's flank. He rolled backward off his mount and landed hard in the middle of the road. It took several moments before he could breathe, never mind push himself up to his hands and knees. His head cleared enough to realize what had happened and he drew his sword at the same time as he staggered to his feet.

"Take your time," a rough voice said. "Neither one of us is in a hurry now."

A man, huge as the night was dark, stood on the road a few feet away. His sword was drawn, but rested point down in the road. His hands were folded over one another on the hilt of, what would be for most men, a two-handed sword.

The messenger pointed his blade at the figure. He glanced around warily. Emboldened when he saw no others, he at last found his voice.

"Who are you to waylay a messenger of the Prince-Archbishop?"

"At this point, it no longer matters."

The Archbishop's man squinted his eyes and took a step sideways. "I know you", he said. "You are Leopold's man. What is the meaning of this?"

Klaus grunted, and lifted his sword. "You sound plenty rested enough now," he said.

The messenger's eyes widened. "You would raise swords against an official representative of a Prince of the Empire?"

"No. I just mean to kill one."

Klaus shuffled forward and aimed a slow thrust at the man's midsection. The messenger was surprised by the attack, but he was light on his feet and managed to step back and block. Klaus thrust again, another cumbersome stroke, and this time, encouraged by his opponent's lack of speed, the messenger countered with a slash at Klaus's throat.

Klaus's sword came alive. It deflected the blow downward and then Klaus whipped the flat of his blade against the man's leg and head so fast the pain registered in both places simultaneously. He cried out and fell to one knee. Klaus grabbed the wrist of the man's sword-arm in one of his own massive hands, and squeezed until the messenger's fingers went numb and the blade fell to the road. Klaus elbowed him in the face, and he fell over with the criss-cross pattern of chainmail covering both eyes and a freshly broken nose.

Klaus leaned over, took up the man's sword and threw it as far into the bush as he could. He sheathed his own weapon, grabbed the messenger by his long hair, and dragged the half-unconscious body into the woods. He slowed to pick up a shovel leaning against a tree, and then continued with his prize deeper into the black forest.

When he felt they were far enough from the road, Klaus let go of the man. His head bounced off a root and he groaned. He kicked the messenger's feet.

"Wake up," he said.

Only a fool would throw a body into a river. They have a tendency to bloat, rise up to the surface, bounce along on currents, and eventually show up in a fisherman's net, or get mangled in some miller's wheel.

Careful men preferred holes. So long as they were deep enough to keep the meat from prying wolves, holes were always a better alternative than water.

Looking after Duke Leopold had made Klaus a careful man. And sometimes, a lazy man. Digging holes was hard work, and Klaus was no longer a young man.

Klaus kicked the messenger's feet until his eyelids flickered open. He threw the shovel on the ground and its sharp tip broke the earth, spilling soil over his face. The man turned his head and spit dirt from his mouth. His eyes were white with fear as he looked up at the giant above him.

"Dig," Klaus said.

***

The sound began as a *pitter*, like the first few drops of rain hitting an oiled cloak. Rhythmic, almost comforting, it did not penetrate far enough into Leopold's sleep to wake him. But the pitter grew into a thump, followed by two more, and then a series of bangs. Finally, a frantic whisper cut through the heavy door and reached Leopold's ears.

"Dawn approaches, my lord. You said to wake you well before. Do you hear me?"

The voice was coarse and gruff. Completely unsuited to whispering.

Klaus! What time was it?

Leopold's eyes snapped open. He threw back the heavy down quilt and tried to stand, but his foot caught in the blanket. He crashed onto the floor. His head ached and his tongue felt like the wings of a giant moth. He cursed as he scrambled about on the cold flagstones, thankful that he had had the foresight to sleep fully clothed. He pushed himself up and swayed unsteadily until his head cleared.

By the blood of Mary, I hate mornings.

The banging started anew.

"Stop it!" Leopold pulled open the door and Klaus took a step back. "I am up. No need to wake the entire castle."

"You said to wake you before first light. No matter what," Klaus said.

"Do I look like I am sleeping?"

"I have seen dead men look more awake," Klaus said, as Leopold scrubbed his face with the palm of one hand.

"You have somewhere to be," Leopold said and slammed the door shut.

Leopold watched the Archbishop from an alcove in the keep's outer wall. He was right on time for his morning ritual of walking the entire length of his fortress wall. As the autumn sun crested the surrounding peaks, it began to bathe parts of the city in a warm glow. From this vantage point, the Archbishop could see almost every single household in his city state.

Leopold rolled his eyes as the Archbishop stopped and stared out over the wall. Seeing his lands and subjects spread out before his feet like that must feed the man's already bulging sense of self-worth, he thought. He took a breath and stepped out from his hiding spot.

"Salzburg has indeed flourished under your rule," Leopold said, strolling forward casually to join the Archbishop.

He twisted his head at the sound of Leopold's voice and the bulk of his body followed later, as though they belonged to different people. His eyes narrowed and his tongue flicked his lips. Extreme annoyance twisted his features for only the briefest of moments before it disappeared, but not before Leopold could notice.

What is the matter, my Archbishop? Did I interrupt your daily moment of solitude?

"I hope I am not intruding, Archbishop."

"Of course not. You surprised me is all. I did not take you for an early riser, Duke Leopold."

Leopold put his elbows on the wall and gazed out over the landscape. He let out a breath and the cool morning air turned it to vapor.

"Oh, I do so enjoy a morning walk. It clears one's mind and presents previously unimagined possibilities." Leopold's puffy eyes squinted against the brightness of dawn. "Salzburg truly is a beautiful city. I must make the time to visit more often."

"You are welcome here whenever you wish, Lord Leopold. Your father was a great friend to me and it is my hope that our friendship will live on in our own relations."

You hated my father. Perhaps even as much as I did.

"Why thank you. I do always enjoy the time we spend together. And I apologize for not calling upon you the last time I was in Salzburg."

The archbishop blinked. "You were in the city recently? I wish I had known."

I am sure you do.

"I meant to come up to the castle, but my business confined me to Low-town, and before I knew it, I had to leave again for Habsburg. I am sure you understand. Men in positions such as ours have so many demands placed upon our short time here on this earth."

"And some men's lives are cut shorter than they would like," the Archbishop said.

Some live far too long.

Leopold laughed. "All men's lives are shorter than they would like. Young, or old, it does not matter."

"I trust your business went well?"

Leopold stopped smiling and put on his best disinterested look. "Business, archbishop?"

"In Low-town. You claimed you were there on some sort of *mercantile* endeavor." When he mentioned the merchant class, the bishop's face soured like he had drunk week-old milk.

Leopold chuckled. "A slip of the tongue. I was unclear. When I said business, I really meant nothing of the sort. It was mercy that brought me to Salzburg that day. A weakness of mine, some say. You see, I have a soft spot for widows. Especially ones with children to care for."

The archbishop said nothing. The skin at his neck turned a mottled shade of red and gray.

Leopold patted his chest while he gazed out over the wall at the city below.

"Ah, here it is." He removed a cylindrical object from a pocket beneath his vest. He carefully unwrapped it from a short length of yellow silk and held it up for the Archbishop to inspect.

"Have you seen one of these looking glasses?"

The Archbishop nodded. "I have. The church still debates the godliness of these instruments. I must say, it saddens me to see one in your hand."

Leopold slid the looking glass open to its full length. "It is only a matter of time before the Pope himself has his very own."

Leopold stepped near the wall and held the scope up to one eye. He looked toward the snow-capped peaks in the distance and then slowly lowered it until it passed over the Salzach River. He scanned the three-story noble houses of Low-town until he found what he was looking for.

"Very useful tool," he said. "Oh, look. Is that… why, yes it is! The red lion of Habsburg held by my very own flag bearer. Incredible."

He pulled the looking glass away from his eye and held it out to the Archbishop.

"You really must see this."

When the Archbishop made no move to take the scope Leopold said, "Do not worry. This one was made in Strassburg, by German craftsmen. It is not an original from the Mohammedans' land. No infidel hands have touched it, I assure you."

The Archbishop took a half step back. "I would rather—"

Leopold thrust out the looking glass and pressed it against the Archbishop's chest.

"I insist," he said.

The Archbishop's hands shook as he held the glass up to his eye. For all his resistance to the idea of the instrument, he seemed quite familiar with its use.

"Did you really think you could keep your whore and her five children a secret?"

The Archbishop said nothing. He kept the glass pressed against his eye.

What part of the scene below holds your attention so? Is it the sight of my soldiers standing in your secret mistress's courtyard? The woman herself, kneeling, in tears? Or is it her children being loaded into a carriage by armed Habsburg men? These clerics can be so hard to read at times.

"How old was the whore when she bore your first bastard? Eleven? Twelve, perhaps? Surely not thirteen. What a hag she must have been."

The Archbishop whirled on Leopold. He threw the looking glass to the ground and the lenses shattered.

"She is no whore," he said. A vein throbbed at his temple and his skin flushed with rage.

Leopold took a step back and held up his hands. "No? Well, perhaps I am wrong. Maybe we should ask the Pope to be the judge of what she is or is not."

The Archbishop's face paled instantly. But to his credit, his voice was steady and in control when he spoke.

"What is it that you want, Leopold?"

"Two thousand infantry, a thousand knights, and five hundred gold. To provide for the upkeep of your men while in my care."

"Their upkeep would not cost half that," the Archbishop said.

Leopold shrugged. "I treat my men better than you, I suppose. And one more thing. I should think a public holy blessing would not be too much to ask."

"What of the woman?"

"She may remain in Salzburg, in that lovely house you had built for her. But the children will come to live in Habsburg for a time, as my wards. Their mother being a poor widow and all."

The Archbishop turned away and stared down once more at the city. In a few short moments his body had experienced a full gamut of emotions. They had taken their toll, and now he just looked like a tired old man. Even his flowing red robes could not hide that fact.

Leopold put his hands on the wall and, like the Archbishop, gazed out over the city.

The sun was at full light. Soon the city would come alive.

"What a beautiful day. I do so love mornings," Leopold said.

Chapter 8

ALTDORF'S SMALL, stone church, situated on top of a hillock at the eastern edge of town, was a squat, gray structure seemingly as old as the hills themselves. Thomas stepped into the shadow of the cross erected on its roof and walked around to the back of the building.

Most people hated cemeteries, but Thomas had always found them comforting. As a child, whenever he felt the need to be alone, he would leave the stench of the city behind and run to the cemetery outside Acre's gates. Later, as a young man in Cypress, he would spend hours walking amongst the graves, trying to read their inscriptions. Of course he felt closer to God when he set foot on holy ground, but, he doubted that was the only reason for the attraction. He suspected it had more to do with escaping the world of men, even if it was for only a short time.

Today, however, his steps were heavy, and not just because of his injuries. He avoided looking too closely at the crosses until he was surrounded by them. When he did finally look up, wondering where he would find Pirmin's grave, he saw a young boy and a dog. The boy sat on the ground next to a mound of dirt, blacker than the other ones nearby, and much larger. He looked up at the same time Thomas saw him. He jumped to his feet, gave his backside a quick brush with his hand, and ran away toward the far gate.

Thomas paid the boy no mind, for his full attention was captured by the dog. It was Pirmin's young pup. He tried to remember the dog's name, but the boy was quicker.

"Vex! C'mon boy!"

The dog stopped sniffing the ground and bounded after the boy without any hesitation. The boy gave Thomas a scowl and then both he and the dog disappeared through a gap in the fence.

Thomas limped to the fresh grave. *If that is indeed Pirmin's grave and the street rat has defiled it in any way, I will make him sorry....*

Sure enough, as he got nearer, Thomas saw that the boy had left something behind near the head of the grave. An old, chipped, clay pitcher stood on the ground. Thomas picked it up and liquid sloshed inside. He smelled it.

Wine. Cheap wine.

A wet bit of dirt in the middle of Pirmin's grave told Thomas the full story. The boy had brought Pirmin wine, and then shared a drink with him. Thomas shook his head in amazement. Even in death, Pirmin had more friends than most. Thomas suddenly regretted thinking the worst of the ragged child.

The cross marking Pirmin's grave was thin, frail, and unassuming. It was so unlike the man and his life that it brought a sad smile to Thomas's face. He could almost feel Pirmin's giant hand patting him on the head like when they were children.

"Thomi, Thomi. So this is where you will dump me. Marked with nothing more than a couple of twigs, for the rest of eternity. When did I ever piss in your oats?"

Thomas gazed out over the rolling hills. With the small church at his back, the elevated grounds provided an idyllic view that stretched for miles down the mountain-lined valley.

"Easy now," Thomas said out loud. "This is a fine spot. You have your own cherry tree for shade. And you will have many visitors, for this rise will give them far more interesting things to look at than just your horse-sized pile of dirt."

"Only you could make being dead sound not so bad. But you better do something about that cross. I want a proper headstone. One with letters saying my name and all the great deeds I did over my life."

Thomas looked at the two uneven sticks lashed together. The crosspiece drooped so much the cross looked more like an 'X'.

Thomas nodded slowly. "I will write the words myself," he said.

He stood for a long time, staring at the grave.

When he started to imagine he could see Pirmin's outline beneath the mound of dark earth he closed his eyes and admitted it was time. He scooped up a handful of soil and bowed his head to pray for the soul of his friend. When he was done, Thomas released the soil from his stiffened fist and watched as the wind carried it the length of Pirmin's final resting spot.

When Thomas turned back to the church, he saw

Noll standing in the shade of one of its walls. He leaned against the stone, unmoving, as though he had been there a long time. When he pushed away and started walking, Thomas could see he held a long staff in one hand. As he closed the distance, Thomas realized it was not a staff after all, but rather, Pirmin's great ax.

Noll held out the ax to Thomas and he took it in both hands. At over eight feet in length, it appeared cumbersome and unwieldy. But Urs had designed the handle and weighted it perfectly to serve as a counter-balance to the heavy, flanged ax head. He had also cut a small cross from the head's center to make it lighter. Urs had created a number of shafts for Pirmin over the years, with each new version an improvement over its predecessor, but he had never managed to come up with a design superior to the current steel tube version.

Thomas gripped it with both hands, squinting his eyes against the sun's glare as it danced from the finely honed cutting edge to the pick-like hook extending from its opposite side like a giant finger. A digit Thomas had seen Pirmin use to flick many a man from the back of a horse or off a battlement's wall.

"I found it in the jail's armory," Noll said. "Thought you might want it."

Thomas shifted his grip and powerful emotions swept forward as an old memory of Pirmin overtook him. Dressed in his full red battle kit, Pirmin stood amongst several other Hospitallers as a few Genoese crossbowmen, their bolts spent, retreated behind the line of the Knights of Saint John. The Hospitallers braced themselves for the enemy's charge. Pirmin held his ax horizontal to the ground with both hands. He gave the shaft a quick roll, making the ax head flip toward heaven, for the briefest moment, before it descended back down to point at Hell. It was Pirmin's ritual salute to the Two Powers That Be, and he always followed it with an unabashed grin in Thomas's direction. Like it was a jest only Thomas could appreciate.

The image of Pirmin's face faded and Thomas found himself staring at his hands as they clutched the cold steel shaft.

"We are glad to see you alive, ferryman. For some time we feared the worst," Noll said. He cleared his throat before continuing. "Seraina told me what you did for her. I am in your debt for that."

With effort, Thomas pulled his eyes from Pirmin's ax and looked at Noll. "No one owes me anything," he said.

Noll stepped around Thomas to stand in front of Pirmin's grave. "I know I only met him a short time ago, but Pirmin was one of the best men I have ever known." He turned and looked down the valley. "I chose this spot for him, but I will understand if you want him moved."

Thomas studied Noll's face. The young man had aged ten years since he had seen him last. His chiseled features were overgrown with stubble and haunted by the shadows and creases of responsibility. He had finally gotten his war, and if he was anything like most people, it was not what he had envisioned.

"It is a fine spot," Thomas said. "Pirmin would complain, of course, but I believe he would be happy with it."

Noll turned to Thomas, but did not meet his eyes.

"I was there when they took him," Noll said.

"I know."

"Hiding in the woods like a frightened hare."

"You already told me that."

***

"I watched Habsburg soldiers take him to the ground and beat him without mercy. He fought back, and it took forever. I had all the time in the world to act, to help him, but instead I watched like a child seated on the ground in front of a puppetry troop."

Thomas said nothing.

"If I had given myself up—".

"You would now both be dead," Thomas said. He stood the great ax upright and drove its butt-end against the ground. "Most men would have done the same as you."

Noll shook his head. "Not Pirmin. He would have waded into the midst of an army to save a friend."

"Pirmin was not most men. Do not compare yourself to him. Ask forgiveness from God, if that is what you seek. But do not look for it from me."

Noll turned away once again to stare at some far point down the valley. Thomas bit back the urge to say more. He was not one to waste words. In his experience, words never changed a man's intentions, stopped wars, or brought friends back from the dead. Perhaps Noll felt the same, for he continued to stare at that far-off point, as though Thomas was no longer beside him.

"What will you do now?" Thomas asked, finally.

Noll's blue eyes came alive when he looked at Thomas, but not in a warm, inviting way. They were the color of a cold mountain stream running over a bed of rocks, which, near the surface, were polished smooth. Those in the dark swirling waters below, however, were jagged and dark.

"I mean to finish what we started. The Habsburgs will attempt to take back their fortress, but we will see them broken against their own walls."

"I trust you have the men to do this," Thomas said.

"I will have. When the time comes."

Thomas doubted that, and he could tell by Noll's voice he was not fully convinced himself. Thomas had seen the walls of the Altdorf fortress and knew how many men it would take to man them against a siege.

But what did it matter?

"Very well," Thomas said. "Then I will stand on your walls and fight against Leopold's men."

Noll blinked. His mouth opened but no words came out at first.

"We would welcome your sword, Thomas. But I must admit I am surprised you would fight for me."

Thomas shook his head. "Not for you. I said I would stand on your walls, but I do not fight for you. It is best we get that in the open."

Thomas watched Noll's teeth clench and a tremor run the length of his jaw. He held his tongue for some time before he spoke.

"Very well. No matter the reason, I accept your offer," Noll said.

What choice do you have? You are in the deepest pit of your life, and you know that the only way out is to climb upon the backs of many a dead man.

Noll was brave, Thomas admitted. There was no denying that. But he was also young and rash, and had yet to experience the darkness of a bottomless pit.

"While I remember," Noll said, as he turned to go. "There is a merchant in town that has been asking after you."

"I know no merchants."

Noll shrugged. "Said he came from Zug and would be staying at the Altdorf inn should I see you. Whether you meet with him or not, is no concern to me. The fool tried to sell me spices, of all things. What use do I have of spices?"

Spices?

Noll left Thomas standing in the cemetery, leaning on Pirmin's giant ax. Thomas decided to pay his respects to Pirmin once more, and then, when he was ready, he would go to the inn to meet Maximilian.

A sadness came over him as he thought about how much Pirmin would have wanted to join them.

***

The Altdorf inn was filled to capacity when Thomas arrived that evening. With Noll's army attracting so many men and women from the neighboring villages and farms, the innkeeper and his staff were wearing ruts in the floor trying to keep up with food and drink orders. Thomas stood inside the door and scanned the twenty or so tables crammed into the low-ceilinged room. Smoke hung trapped between ceiling beams, and the smell of both sweat and old ale made his lip curl. He found himself wishing for the spotless oasis of order that was Sutter's place in Schwyz. He and Vreni knew how to run a traveler's house.

"Cap'n, over here."

Ruedi had his arm raised a half dozen tables away. A stocky form sitting across from him twisted on his bench and looked over his shoulder. Max, his neatly trimmed beard grayer than Thomas remembered, waved and his mouth spread into a grin. As Thomas weaved his way over to the two men, he realized that a woman also sat with them.

Max stood and grabbed Thomas in a rough embrace. "There he is! Been looking all over for you," Max said. "Some said you were dead. Others, you were in prison. One said you got yourself a woman and moved away when they burned your ferry," Max said. He looked at Thomas sideways as they sat down. "Was pretty sure that fellow was spinning a tale, though."

"You look good Max," Thomas said. "Judging by your clothes, you managed to set up a little shop in Zug after all?"

"Little shop? Look at him," Ruedi said. "Another few years and Max will own that town. I hear he has so much extra coin he makes loans to the nobles."

Max shook his head. "Now, I would not say that. Usury is a sin after all."

"It is at that," Thomas said.

"You mean you would not admit to it," Ruedi said.

"My money is made from pepper, believe it or not. I thought turmeric would have been my future, but it seems the noble households cannot get enough of plain black pepper. Apparently, nothing hides the flavor of rotting meat better—"

Ruedi cut him off by introducing Thomas to the woman sitting beside him.

"This here is my sister, Margrit Burkhalter. That damn Norseman knew what he was talking about."

Perhaps five years younger than Ruedi, she had dark hair and gray eyes.

Thomas bowed his head. *Burkhalter... was that Ruedi's last name?* Thomas realized he had no idea what his true name was. Ruedi *Schwyzer* was all he had ever known him as. And the same went for Max. They were all *Schwyzers.*

"Pleasure to meet you, Captain," Margrit said. "These

two boys have been talking non-stop about you and your friend Pirmin. Enough to make a lady blush. If one happened to overhear, that is." She was a handsome woman, and she looked Thomas straight in the eyes when she spoke. He had no doubt Pirmin would have found her attractive.

Max and Ruedi fidgeted when she mentioned Pirmin's name and she caught their sidelong glances to one another.

"What," she said. "A friend leaves this world and suddenly you have to stop talking about him? You think he would like that?"

Max grinned. "No, he most assuredly would not."

"Well then," Margrit said. "I look forward to hearing more stories about the man. But another time. Got to get home to the family. Some people may be able to waste their day with their head in a mead barrel, but I am not one of those."

So Burkhalter was most probably her husband's name. Maybe someday Thomas would ask Ruedi what his real name was. But then again, maybe not.

Once Margrit had left, Thomas managed to flag down one of the inn's women. Tired and bored, she listened to Thomas while juggling a tray in one hand and three pitchers in the other. He asked her to bring him wine and whatever food the kitchen was serving that night.

With Margrit gone, the three men sat in silence for a moment, not quite sure where to begin. Max was the first to speak.

"Glad to see you made it out of that mess, Thomas. Ruedi told me what Gissler done." He shook his head. "Never would have believed it."

"And I would be in a prison cell in the Aargau if it were not for Ruedi," Thomas said.

"I doubt that," Ruedi said. He turned away and examined something crawling up the wall.

"You will be glad to hear I still have your Genoese war bow," Thomas said.

This got Ruedi's attention and he turned to Thomas. "Well, do you now," he said, twirling one of the braided ends of his forked beard between his fingers. "Did not expect to see that one again, to be honest."

"What are your plans, Thomas?" Max asked.

Thomas shrugged, but said nothing.

"People are scared in Zug," Max said. "The Habsburgs have tripled the soldiers in town and they been building barracks and supply houses."

"Is that why you came?" Thomas asked. "To warn us that the Habsburgs are going to invade? That is old news around here I am afraid."

"I been up to the fortress and I saw what Melchthal and Stauffacher are doing up there." Max shook his head. He leaned over the table and lowered his voice. "They have no idea what is coming for them, Thomas. Zug is being turned into a base camp for a real army. Judging from the structures so far, I would say upwards of eight or nine thousand men."

Ruedi also leaned in. "I asked Max to help me get Margrit and her family out of Altdorf. You should come with us."

As soon as he heard Ruedi say he intended to leave Altdorf, Thomas let out a breath. Tension slipped away from his shoulders and he reached a hand behind his head to rub his neck. The moment he first heard Max was in Altdorf, a gnawing fear had begun to fester inside him. He was worried Max and Ruedi had decided to join Noll's army and was relieved that they had made more sensible plans.

"Travel on the roads is restricted, these days. Even to merchants," Max said. "But I have made arrangements to get a small group of people safely to Berne. We have room for another three or four people if there is anyone you would like to bring along."

Before Thomas could answer, the inn woman dropped three cups of mead on the table and a bowl of something that could have been brown porridge, with chunks of black meat in it.

"Armin says he is too busy to water down a new cask of wine right now. So mead is all we got," she said.

"That will do," Thomas said, grateful for the interruption.

She turned and was about to leave, but Thomas touched her arm. She spun on him and all three men swayed back on their bench seats.

Thomas pointed at the bowl of food. "What is this?"

She leaned over and peered at it like she was seeing it for the first time. "Porridge. With meat. What do you think it is?"

Thomas nodded. That was good enough for him. The woman leaned her wooden tray on one hip and stared at Thomas.

"I was there, you know. The day you bled those Habsburg boys up on the hill." She nodded in the direction of the Altdorf fortress. "Some people talk and say how you best not have done that. How we will all pay for what you did. But I was there, and I seen how you tried to help Seraina. She pulled out my first baby, you know." Her voice lost its calloused edge for just a moment. "You did a good thing that day."

A waving customer caught her eye. "Finish what you got, first!" she shouted across the room. She started walking away, but after a few steps she called back over one shoulder, "Just wanted you to know why you got extra meat. But do not expect it every night."

Max wisely waited until she was out of earshot before he laughed. "Now that is a woman," he said. "But I am afraid she would chew a man like me up and spit me out like so much gristle." He scratched his beard with one hand. "But Margrit on the other hand, now she might be more my taste. Just how good does she get along with her husband these days, Ruedi?"

Ruedi took a sip of his mead. "I been working on a new crossbow bolt," he said, ignoring Max and looking only at Thomas. "It has two, side-by-side, rusty broadheads on its tip. I call it the *plum-picker*."

"Have you tried it out yet?" Thomas asked.

Ruedi shook his head. "Just waiting for the right time."

Chapter 9

ENCIRCLING THE FOUR Venetians, nearly five hundred men sat on the ground. They were silent and attentive, perhaps some of them nervous, for none of them knew what to expect from a training session lead by the flamboyant outsiders. It was a cloudless, late autumn morning, and though the ground frost had retreated under the morning sun, the air still had the bite of winter to it.

Thomas sat on a stack of stone blocks at the sunniest end of the courtyard, far away from the center ring. He pulled his cloak tighter over his shoulders, and then abruptly changed his mind and took it off. He folded it several thicknesses deep and sat on it.

How did they do it?

He shook his head at all the men lounging about on the half-frozen ground, many wearing thin, sleeveless shirts, and watched the man called Giovanni Pomponio put on a display of swordsmanship. Thomas had lived with the men of the valleys and mountains for almost a year, and though they kept their feelings to themselves for the most part, Thomas felt he could often read them now. A wince here, a shake of a head there, the complete silence in the square; these were all indicators of a crowd in awe.

Today was the official start of training for the "Confederate Army of Free Men" as Noll had officially named his volunteers. The local judge named Walter Furst, and old Werner Stauffacher of Schwyz, known more for being the husband of Gertrude of Iberg than for any particular doings of his own, had opposed the idea. They wanted to simply call the army the "Eidgenossen", an old way of referring to those who had sworn *The Oath*.

Thomas had learned in the last few days, that the oath they referred to was some written pact made twenty-five years previously between the people of Uri, Schwyz, and Unterwalden. Each member community swore to uphold their ancient laws and to come to the aid of one another if they were threatened by an outside force.

Thomas suspected that they had envisioned that threat would more likely be from bandits, or some minor lord looking to take advantage of unprotected peasants. But Noll had pulled out the original document and had inflamed the passions of the locals by claiming *The Oath* may have been drawn up before his time, but there was no doubt it was created for just such a moment as today. Now, he said, was their one chance to throw off the yoke of their Austrian overlords, and with the support of Walter Furst and Werner Stauffacher, the three communities rallied to his words. Word spread quickly, and men began to trickle in to Altdorf, and the *Confederate*

Army of Free Men was born.

An appreciative murmur shot through the crowd. Pomponio had just demonstrated a disarming technique on one of his men, and now basked in the crowd's attention.

The Venetian was a man of excess. He wore a red vest over a cream-colored blouse of silk, and breeches that fit so well, Thomas had no doubt they must have been tailored. But, as grand as his clothes looked, especially compared to the simple farmers and foresters seated before him, Thomas noted the fabric was thin in places and the colors faded from too many washings. Though he was far from an expert in fashion, Thomas had been around enough nobles and high-born merchants to recognize the outdated styles of yesteryear. However, when looking at the Venetian, most people would never notice these things, for they would inevitably find their eyes drawn in by Pomponio's outrageous hat.

It was a blue, wide-brimmed piece that could have been cut from half the felt. With several brightly dyed feathers thrust through its green and turquoise hat-band, it flopped around like a living thing, yet somehow managed to remain on his head while he lunged, parried, laughed, and mocked his opponent.

Pomponio dismissed his current adversary and beckoned to another one of his men, a dark-haired, younger man with a smooth complexion and wide shoulders set atop a narrow waist encircled with a purple sash. His long, oiled hair was pulled back from his face and gathered behind his head with a length of white lace.

"Salvatore. Lend us your strength for a moment if you would."

Salvatore took his mark across from Pomponio and raised his sword in front of his face in a salute.

Pomponio raised his own long, narrow blade. It was a fencer's weapon, with a basket guard that served to protect his hand.

"Attack," he said.

Salvatore immediately bellowed out a loud war cry, which induced flinches from the first few rows of onlookers, and then he thrust straight ahead at Pomponio's mid-section. Pomponio stepped forward and met the attack with his own hair-raising yell, and smashed the young man's sword away with a powerful, straight-on block. Then, he drove Salvatore back the way he had come with a strong series of thrusts and attacks. The young man back-pedaled furiously, parrying as best he could, until he stumbled under the assault and fell to his back.

Pomponio put a foot on the man's chest and gently rested the tip of his sword under his chin. He looked into the crowd. "The man is dead, no?"

The comment produced some chuckles from the crowd. They were beginning to warm up to the Venetian.

"Although my technique was effective, it was ugly. Very ugly." Pomponio stepped away from his opponent. He leaned over and placed his hands on his knees to catch his breath. "You see how tired I am? You see what ugly technique can do to a man? If I must fight like this all day, like the common soldier is taught, I am soon exhausted." He removed his hat and wiped his forehead with the sleeve of one arm. "Come evening, even if I survive the day, my *bella* waiting for me at home, she will be very disappointed, no?"

The laughter came much easier from the villagers

now.

"If a man practices swordplay solely with the intention of besting an opponent, that man is missing the point. A dancer must train hard to make his craft appear effortless. Should it not also be so with a master swordsman?"

He smoothed one of the feathers from his hat and then carefully placed it on the ground behind him. "Seeing is believing. Let us try."

Without being asked, Salvatore bounced up to his feet and slashed the air with his sword. The other three Venetians drew their own weapons and spread out.

"We have you now, you Venetian fop," Salvatore said. His voice rang out clearly, easily carrying to every set of ears in the courtyard. A few men laughed, some only smiled, but all sat up a little straighter to get a better view.

Pomponio waved his sword arm in a graceful circle and carried the motion through into a bow. Then he straightened up, and with another arc of his sword, settled into a relaxed, upright fencing stance.

"Very well," he said. "Please, attack."

As one, the four men screamed and charged Pomponio. He deflected the nearest man's sword and slid behind him, while ducking under another's wild swing. He reached out with the flat of his blade and tapped the first man on the back of his head.

"Dead!" he shouted. The man cursed, gave a quick bow, and retreated out of the circle where he sat cross-legged on the ground. He rested his chin in both hands, looking more than a little dejected.

The others continued to come at Pomponio with powerful-looking attacks, but the swordsman weaved and spun about them, deflecting blows only when absolutely necessary. He grinned and laughed and twirled like the only man present at a ball of princesses.

"Dead!" he said to another, who groaned and backed out of the fray.

He parried an attack, and touched the man's heart with his slender blade.

"Dead!"

Only Salvatore remained. The anchor-shouldered man charged, and Pomponio slipped to the side. He whacked the man on his buttocks with the flat of his blade, and Salvatore jumped and let out a squeal.

"Cut! But, not dead," Pomponio said, grinning and shaking his head. Salvatore roared and raised his sword over his head. He brought it crashing down toward Pomponio's head, but when the blow fell it struck only hard dirt. Pomponio stood to the side of Salvatore with the tip of his blade touching his neck.

"Dead," he said. "Oh, so very dead, no?"

One villager had become so engrossed with the battle that when Pomponio dispatched the last man, he could no longer contain himself. He shouted and began clapping. Others also forgot all sense of inhibition, and they too let out a few whistles. The mood spread like wildfire and within seconds the entire crowd was caught up in cheers for the Venetians.

Pomponio took his bows and then held up his arms for silence.

"This is the Pomponio way. My friends and I will teach you my methods, and in a few short months each and every man here will be the equal of five Austrians!"

There were some doubtful looks exchanged throughout the crowd, mostly amongst the older faces, but they were by far the minority. To the young men of Altdorf and Schwyz, the flamboyant Venetian represented hope.

"So today, my students, your first exercise is to go into the forest and find for yourself a training sword. This is no mindless task. Put careful thought into its selection, and treat it as you would your best friend. We meet back here the day after tomorrow to begin training in earnest."

Thomas had seen enough. He pushed himself to his feet, picked up his cloak off the rock, and almost walked straight into Seraina. He hopped to one side to avoid hitting her and put too much weight on his still healing leg. He grimaced and Seraina reached out to steady him.

"Oh, I am sorry Thomas. I do have a habit of startling you," she said.

"It is my own fault," Thomas said. He stood up straight and tried his best to ignore the tremors of pain running through his thigh.

"I could start wearing a bell, I suppose," Seraina said.

"I would not oppose that. At least until my injuries have fully healed," Thomas said. The truth was, he was recovering amazingly fast. Whether it was thanks to Seraina's skill, or simply God's Will, he could not be sure.

"Well? What are your thoughts?" Seraina asked.

"I... think you saved my life," Thomas said. "In fact, I am sure of it."

Seraina cocked her head and gave him a puzzled look. "Not about that," she said, and nodded toward the center of the courtyard. Pomponio and his men stood talking with Noll. The villagers were filtering out of the courtyard since there would be no more training for the day.

"I wish to know what your impressions are of the men Noll hired to train his army."

Thomas shrugged. "I think this Giovanni Pomponio puts on a good show."

"He does at that," Seraina said. She stared at Noll and the Venetians. "But I wonder if he is truly capable of teaching farmers and goatherds how to use a sword."

Is anyone?

Thomas kept the thought to himself and looked at the sky. Thick clouds were gathering, blowing in over the Alps, where an hour before there had been nothing but blue.

***

"The day after tomorrow? What is wrong with tomorrow? Or even this afternoon for that matter," Noll said. The Venetians had been in Altdorf for six days, and they had yet to hold a single training session for Noll's army. But they had not missed a single night of drinking at the Altdorf inn, compliments, of course, from the Confederate Army of Free Men.

Army.

The word still sounded strange to Noll's ears, even when spoken in only his inner voice.

Pomponio sighted down the length of his sword, looking for nicks. "One must learn to conquer haste, Master Melchthal, lest it conquers you, no? That is the Pomponio way."

Noll crossed his arms. "What about not keeping your side of a bargain? Is that also the Pomponio way?"

Salvatore heard Noll's comment and made to step forward, but Pomponio put his hand on the taller man's broad chest.

"Easy now, my friend. If you are unsatisfied with my methods, I give you back your gold. We return to Venice and I shall go back to teaching at my famous school, where I have students from the families of nobles and kings begging me to impart even a small piece of my fighting style. It is no problem."

"Just how much time do you think we have? The Austrians will be here next summer and our only hope is to create an army from nothing," Noll said.

Pomponio nodded and placed his hand on Noll's shoulder. "I hear what you say. And it can be done. But we must mold these villagers of yours into fighting men, and to do that we must treat them like iron. We heat them, little by little. Then pound out their imperfections, and then we heat them some more. Only when they are ready, do we dare thrust them into water. It is a process that cannot be rushed, no?"

Noll looked into Pomponio's eyes. "The day after tomorrow then. But no later."

Pomponio smiled. "You carry too many worries for one so young. Let us carry some of them for you."

Noll spun and walked away.

Chapter 10

TWO OF NOLL'S BURLIEST men dragged the shackled and weakened form of Berenger Von Landenberg from his prison cell out into the frigid courtyard. When they let go of his arms, he groaned and dropped to his knees. He squinted against the direct sunlight and attempted to shield his eyes with his manacled hands.

Walter Furst, Werner Stauffacher, and his wife, Gertrude of Iberg sat at a simple table in front of him. To their right stood Noll, shaking his head. Seraina leaned against a boulder in the background holding the boy Mathias on her lap. She cringed when the men brought out Landenberg. Noll recognized the pity in her eyes, but he could not understand it. Landenberg was a monster, and the world would be a better place without him.

"Stand up," Noll said.

Landenberg blinked and turned his head in Noll's direction, but did not make any attempt to push himself to his feet. Noll nodded to his two men. "Make him stand," he said.

They each grabbed an arm and lifted the overweight Vogt unceremoniously to his feet, as if he weighed no more than a child. Landenberg's legs shook, but before he could collapse, his captors steadied him.

Walter Furst, the once Habsburg appointed Justice of Uri, cleared his throat. Today, he did not wear his black cloak of office. All three of them seated behind the table were dressed in the normal, loose-fitting garb of peasants who worked the land.

"Sir Berenger Von Landenberg, we the Council of the Eidgenossen, find you guilty of all charges. Do you have anything to say before we pass sentence?"

Fueled by his hatred of Noll, the Vogt summoned up a small burst of energy, enough to spit in the young man's direction. Noll did not bother moving, for the small ball of phlegm stopped far short of his boots.

"Missed again," he said.

"Your time will come! All of you, your time is near. Heed my words you godless, peasant gecks! Soon this place will be thick with soldiers cutting off your heads and having their way with your rotting corpses."

Landenberg had to break off his mad sputtering due to a series of coughs. Red-faced, and exhausted by his brief tirade, his chest heaved as he glared at the three people seated in front of him.

Noll too looked to the table. "Anyone wish to recast their vote? I still stand behind a hanging."

Furst shook his head. "That is in Landenberg's hands now."

Landenberg's eyes widened. Apparently, the thought that he might be executed had not yet entered his thick skull. "You cannot hang me. It is not within your rights!"

Gertrude spoke up. "As of this moment, we have every right. For we have decided that we will no longer be subject to the laws of the Holy Roman Empire. Or the Habsburgs. We, this council, will be the final stage of justice for all of Schwyz, Uri, and Unterwalden and will recognize the authority of no other court. Now, do not speak again unless you have our leave."

Landenberg looked from face to face, his skin was suddenly pale.

"What Gertrude says is true," Furst said. "However, we are determined that this court will not be unjust. Therefore, today you will be presented with two choices."

Noll rolled his eyes. Who ever heard of giving criminals choices?

"The first choice, is a quick and painless hanging. Someone will pull on your legs to ensure that it is so," Furst said, almost cheerfully.

Landenberg's mouth twitched. "What is the second choice?" he asked.

Stauffacher spoke up. "You will swear the *Urphede*."

"What is that?" Landenberg said.

"You must swear an oath that you will never return to these lands upon pain of death."

"And what happens to me if I take the oath?" Landenberg asked.

"You will be allowed to go anywhere you like, so long as you never set foot in Uri, Schwyz, or Unterwalden ever again. If you do, your life will be forfeit."

Noll could not help himself. "Does not a simple hanging sound so much better?"

When Landenberg spoke, he could not get the words

out fast enough. "I swear to never return. I choose the oath! I swear it," Landenberg said.

"Of course you do," Noll said. He addressed his next words to the council. "And I swear to see Sir Berenger Von Landenberg delivered safely to Habsburg Castle."

"Noll, I do not think we can allow that," Furst said.

"He is my prisoner. My responsibility. That is the *least* the Council should allow."

"He has a point," Gertrude said. "Someone must escort the Vogt off our lands, and who better for the task than Noll Melchthal? No one knows better than he where our lands begin and where they end."

"You might as well hang me now as allow this highwayman to slit my throat on the road to Habsburg!" Landenberg said.

Furst glanced over at Gertrude and Stauffacher. Something passed between them and then he turned back to Noll. "Do you swear you will do all in your power to deliver him unharmed?"

"Define *unharmed*," Noll said.

"Alive, then," Gertrude said.

"That I can do. I swear it on my father's good name."

"A father you have not visited in years," Stauffacher said.

"How does that concern you?" Noll said.

"Henri is a friend. A blind friend who spends far too many evenings alone," Stauffacher said. "I know for a fact that he would more than welcome a visit from his wayward son."

"You know less than you think," Noll said.

"The whole lot of you are mad!" Landenberg shouted.

"Gag him," Gertrude said. "He has had his say."

The two men complied and within seconds Landenberg's shouts were reduced to muffles.

Noll called Mathias and the boy bolted over to him. "Pack me some food and water for the road."

"Will you need horses?" the boy asked.

"No. I will go on foot. It will be safer that way." He glanced over at Landenberg. "But our fat friend will never make it. So get me the most ornery, skittish mule you can find."

Mathias grinned and saluted. He was off running before anyone could say another word.

Noll took no chances. He pushed deep into the forests and traveled only on seldom-used game trails. If he had been alone, he would have stayed closer to the main roads, but with Landenberg draped over the mule, grunting at every jostle, he could not risk being heard by one of the frequent Habsburg patrols. Noll was well aware of how human sounds had a peculiar way of echoing through the trees and off of boulders, and carried much further than most people realized.

He kept Landenberg gagged for the entire two-day trip. He had sworn to deliver him alive, after all, and he was not sure he would be able to keep his word if the man were allowed to speak. He had tied Landenberg on his stomach, with his face hanging over the mule's backside. So long as Landenberg had the strength, he could keep his head up and mostly avoid the mule's swishing tail. But, once his neck muscles gave out, his head bounced in and out of dark places, competing with the flies.

Noll kept up a constant stream of chatter to make up for the Vogt's relative silence. He spoke of all the times he had raided Landenberg's camps, the tricks he had played on his men, the various occasions when Landenberg had almost captured him, but always failed.

"Who would have thought it?" Noll asked. "That day you had my father's eyes cut out, that a few short years later you and I would enjoy a stroll through these woods together. As traveling companions…" He gave his head a shake.

One of the mule's hooves slid off a moss-covered rock and he stumbled. Landenberg's head smacked against the animal's flank several times before the mule regained its footing.

"Yes, it will sadden me greatly to have to part. But I suspect the mule will be happy enough to get your head out of its arse."

***

"My lord…"

Leopold looked up from his soup to his wife seated across from him. Three servants stood nearby but, in the manner of all good servants, were almost invisible. In fact, the best members of Leopold's staff were people whose names he did not even know. They were the best of the best, yet relegated to a life of obscurity.

He set his spoon down. One of the older men stepped forward and removed it.

"Yes, my dear?" He looked up, but Catherine's eyes still unnerved him. They were simply too far apart, and he found it impossible to share prolonged eye contact with her. He glanced away, under the pretense of reaching for his serviette.

Somehow, a clean spoon had appeared on the table.

Remarkable. Which one of you was it?

"My lord. I am with child."

Leopold realized that, with the proper incentive, he actually could look his wife in the eyes. Albeit one at a time, and with a slight head twist.

"Why, that is wonderful," he said. "Have you spoken with my physicians?"

"Of course, my lord. And they insisted I be the one to tell you."

Leopold made a mental note to have a little talk with them both. He hated surprises. Even good ones.

He picked up his new spoon and dipped it into his soup. But he did not put it into his mouth. Instead, he dropped it once again on the table, making a small splatter.

"And have you had the child divined?"

Catherine's head bobbed. A curt, enthusiastic motion. But nothing more. Apparently, she would have him drag it out of her.

"And... what do they think it is?"

The spoon was gone, but the splatter remained. He caught the older servant in the act of placing a fresh spoon beside the bowl. As he put the utensil down with one hand, the other wiped up the small splatter with a square of cloth concealed in the palm of his hand. Leopold had almost missed it.

"A boy, my lord."

"Fantastic!" Leopold said, slapping his palm onto the table.

Catherine's eyes widened, but not even one of the servants so much as blinked.

"I must admit, that is how I felt when they told me as well, my lord."

"This is cause for celebration," Leopold said. He waved to the servants. "Get rid of this broth. Bring us some meat!"

"You seem pleased," Catherine said.

"Of course I am. This is a special day. My first child," Leopold said.

Catherine nodded. "I am glad to see you happy, my lord. For some women, that in itself would be enough."

Uh-oh. Something is coming….

Leopold glanced down for a spoon to stick into his soup, but remembered he had just had them both taken away. He shot an angry glare at the nearest servant.

"I have tried to make you happy, my lord, in the short time we have been married. Do you think I have been a good wife?"

No soup, no spoon. Where is that meat?

"Of course. There is no man more fortunate in all of Austria," he said.

Catherine paused, and sat up straight in her chair. "I am not content. I wish to do more. For both the House of Habsburg and the Duchy of Savoy. My father always told me I had a keen sense for politics, better than any of his sons. He did not raise me to be a royal nursemaid."

She punctuated her outburst with a curt nod, and stared straight ahead at Leopold.

If Leopold had had a spoon in his hand at that very moment, he definitely would have dropped it.

Well, well, well. What have we here?

He leaned back in his chair and looked at Catherine, carefully, wondering how he had missed this side of her.

"And what exactly is it that you can do?" he asked.

She did not avert her gaze, and surprisingly, this time Leopold found himself in no hurry to look away.

"Many things. If you would but share with me some of the problems you encounter in your role as Duke of Styria and Further Austria, I am sure I could be of some help. You try to do too much yourself, but you are only one man, after all."

"Very well. I need money."

"Money?" she said it like it was a subject she had never given much thought.

"Yes. You know. Gold, silver, bronze. I would not even turn away copper at this point, although, if you can manage it, some nice florins or gold bezant would be preferable."

"And what need do you have for all this?" Catherine asked.

Leopold laughed. "Have you not noticed the new barracks being erected in the woods? Come spring I expect to have thousands more mouths to feed. Of course they are mostly infantry, so it will not take much. But, by summer, the Archbishop's knights will arrive. Knights, and their equipment, make short work of any man's coffers."

"But it is the Archbishop's responsibility to maintain his knights and provide funds for them while in the service of the Crown, is it not? And I saw the chest you brought back from Salzburg."

"Oh, yes. That chest. Well, it only looked big," Leopold said. He may as well have thrown it in the Salzach river for all the good it did him.

"I see," Catherine said. She looked at her hands, her slender fingers twisted about one another like a bird's nest. She raised her head. "I believe I can help. Give me some time."

Leopold almost laughed, but a part of him believed

her. Or wanted to believe her.

"That would be lovely," he said.

"In the meantime," Catherine began, "In light of recent developments, I trust that you will no longer see a need to send your gorilla to our bed? I fear the posts have weakened, and I am not sure they can withstand his weight any longer."

"Of course. I will tell him to cease his visits immediately."

Leopold smelled the meat before he saw it. Steaming beneath his nose was a generous portion of braised lamb, served atop a freshly baked trencher made with white flour. He saw the black specks, and a grin spread across his face. It was the latest culinary craze, and like most people who could afford it, Leopold could not get enough.

Pepper, lots and lots of pepper.

***

Evading Habsburg patrols lengthened the journey far more than Noll had anticipated. It took them the better part of four days to reach the Kussnacht, and another hour of traveling after dark before they finally heard the sounds of Habsburg Castle. Minutes later, light from torches on the outer walls peeked through the trees. Noll tied the mule to a bush and checked Landenberg's gag was still in place. The Vogt's eyes were closed from exhaustion, but he was still very much alive. He did not even wake when Noll slapped his face to crush a mosquito.

Seeing the man helpless before him, a man that only a few short years ago Noll had sworn to kill if given the opportunity, was not as satisfying as Noll had always dreamed it would be. He should slit the Vogt's throat now and be done with him. Noll knew that if their roles had been reversed, Landenberg would have executed him without a second thought.

Damn the council.

But he could not bring himself to do it. The last few years had not only been about bringing justice to the man who had maimed his father. They had been about fighting the system that had condoned it. And that system would still exist even if Landenberg was no longer part of this world.

Noll turned toward the castle and slid off into the woods to get a closer look. After climbing a short distance through the brush, he could make out the front gate. Several guards milled about.

Perched on top a hill, Noll imagined that the multi-floored keep within its walls commanded an impressive view of the surrounding farmlands, but overall, the castle itself was nothing extravagant. Its original design had been one of function rather than form. The road leading up to its main gate was steep and straight. At one time, there would have been no trees on either side of the road, but over the last few hundred years the castle's owners had grown lax with their defenses. Forests had reclaimed large parts of what had once been killing fields.

The castle was no fortress. But it did not need to be one, for who in their right mind would dare attack the hereditary home of the Habsburgs? Noll had never heard of anyone ever laying siege to the castle. Which could have been because of the political strength of its owners, but just as likely due to its remote location and the relatively poor lands surrounding it. In other words, no one wanted it.

As he crept closer through the woods, Noll allowed himself to fantasize about marching his own army up the road and storming the front gate. The thought of taking Habsburg Castle put a smile on his face and he covered his mouth with one hand, on the off chance that the white of his teeth reflecting torchlight might give him away.

Even if it were possible, he quickly dismissed the thought. What would he do once he had it? The place would be completely indefensible. *But what a blow it would be to Leopold!*

It was less than an hour past full dark, so there was still plenty of activity near the front gate. Workers were leaving for the day. Some carried axes and shovels, others lead oxen hitched to empty wagons. A dozen soldiers, with the red lion of Habsburg emblazoned on the chests of their tunics, marched forth and relieved the current guards spread along the wall near the front gate.

Noll became aware of an excessive amount of noise and light coming from within the outer walls. Curious, he moved away from the main gate and found a tall oak tree not far from one of the side walls. He climbed, moving slowly in the darkness, and after several minutes he turned his attention back to the castle. There, suspended high off the ground with his arms hooked around two branches, he had a view of the courtyard all the way up to the front steps of the inner keep.

What he saw made him want to jump down from his perch and run. The only thing that stopped him was he had no idea where he would go.

He counted a full score of new buildings in various states of completion. Most were long, rectangular structures that Noll knew only too well, for he had seen them in every Habsburg-controlled town he had ever visited.

They were soldier barracks.

Hundreds of tents surrounded these incomplete buildings, and armored men milled around cooking fires that lit the grounds like it was a full moon night. Noll had never seen so many soldiers in a single location. His mouth went dry and images of his own minuscule army of farmers, boys, and old men slapping one another with wooden swords, mocked him.

As soldiers wandered in and out of the light, Noll identified the red lion of Habsburg on many a chest, but far more bore the black eagle of the Holy Roman Empire. Even though his brother was embroiled in war against Louis the Bavarian, Leopold had still managed to call in Empire forces.

Noll felt the beginnings of panic set in.

The panic became a wave of vertigo and the dark night became darker still. He hugged the tree until it passed and he could see clearly once again. He took a deep breath and gazed out over the multitude of fires.

Perched in his fragile hiding spot, the reality of the situation overcame him. Did he think he was in a struggle against only Habsburg tyranny? Had he not considered Leopold would use all the resources he could muster, including those of the vast Holy Roman Empire?

Noll had assumed the German princes would be too preoccupied with the war for the crown. They would have enough problems of their own and would not pay any attention to a small uprising in a remote alpine town.

He tried to tell himself that. But he realized the truth was he had given the matter very little thought before attacking the Altdorf fortress. He had been driven with a righteous anger. Anger at what Leopold had done to Pirmin and what he was about to do to Seraina. He did not give a moment's thought to how his actions would affect the people of Altdorf.

He had simply acted without thinking. Just as he had when he smashed the fingers of Landenberg's tax collector. That day had cost his father his sight. What would the people of Altdorf have to pay for his latest rash act?

Noll made the hazardous climb back down and then crept his way from shadow to shadow back to Landenberg's tethered mule. He led the beast and its semi-conscious cargo to a spot on the road that could not be seen from the castle. Without a single wisecracking comment to Landenberg, he slapped the mule and sent him trotting toward the front gate.

***

"Please forgive the intrusion my lord," the oldest servant said. He acknowledged Catherine at the other end of the table with a deep bow. "My lady."

"What is it?" Leopold said, putting down his eating knife.

"A disturbance, my lord."

"I could tell you as much," Leopold said.

"At the front gate, my lord."

"Does it warrant interrupting my evening meal?" Leopold asked the question but he already knew what the man's answer would be. He was an impeccable servant and would not dare bother his lord and lady with something mundane.

"I believe so, my lord."

Leopold glared at the man, and although he avoided Leopold's eyes with his own, he continued to stare straight ahead without flinching. Leopold stuck his knife into the table and left it there, quivering.

"And I believe you," Leopold said. Then he turned to his wife. "Excuse me, my dear. I will not be long."

He stood and Lady Catherine also put down her utensils and pushed away from the table. "I shall accompany you," she said.

Leopold was about to protest, but remembering their earlier conversation stopped himself.

"Very well."

He walked around to Catherine and offered his arm. "Shall we?"

***

Hunched over in the darkness, less than fifty paces from the main gate, Noll regretted asking Matthias to bring him the jitteriest mule he could find. The animal had trotted up to the gate well enough, but when the guards approached with their torches, he spooked and would not allow anyone to get near. The soldiers called out others, and they came brandishing more torches, which only made things worse. Soon a dozen men chased the mule back and forth in front of the gate, and the animal became so frantic he began snapping at hands as they reached for him.

There was movement at the gate again as soldiers stepped out of the way. They lined up, forming ranks, and Noll was surprised to see Duke Leopold himself stroll forward. He stood with his hands on his hips and watched as the wide-eyed mule charged between the soldiers, evading all attempts at capture.

Leopold shouted something to a huge, gray-bearded man at his side, who snatched a spear from the hands of a surprised guard and stepped forward. When the panicked animal next came toward him, he thrust twelve inches of tempered steel behind his foreleg, puncturing his lung but missing his heart. The mule let out a sound that began as a horse's high-pitched whinny but died off in a breathless donkey's bray. He bounded away from his attacker and walked stubbornly for twenty seconds with the spear's butt-end dragging on the ground, and Sir Berenger Von Landenberg still tied to his back. Then the mule stumbled and his front legs began to give out.

Noll closed his eyes as the animal let out a last strangled cry and crumpled to the ground.

"Arnold Melchthal!"

Noll's heart pounded in his ears. He looked up to see Leopold striding directly at him. It took every last bit of self-control Noll possessed to resist the temptation to flee. He knew an animal flushed from cover was as good as dead.

"Or is it Thomas Schwyzer? Perhaps both of you hide within earshot?"

Leopold stopped walking and his head slowly turned as he scanned the dark woods.

Noll reminded himself to breathe. Silently.

When Leopold next spoke he looked into a section of forest fifty yards up the road from Noll's actual location, which was now less than ten paces from the Duke.

"No, I doubt very much the Hospitaller is here," Leopold said, shaking his head.

If only I had a crossbow.

"It is just you, *Noll*. That is what your friends call you, is it not?"

Noll fixed his eyes on the dead mule, for he did not want to look directly at Leopold. It was a hunter's trick that every old-timer swore by: you can only get close to your prey if you avoid looking at it directly. Prey knows when it is being watched.

But who, in this instance, was the prey?

At that moment, staring at the dead mule, Noll did not feel like a hunter. He shook his head in disgust. His idea of a joke had cost the animal its life.

More soldiers flowed out of the gates. Their yellow tunics bearing the black eagle seemed to light up the road. These were the hardened fighting men of the Empire; professional killers that knew no other trade. They were not part-time farmers or millers patched together to form a militia.

"I know why you hide," Leopold said. "I do not fault you for it. It took a brave man to come here tonight."

Leopold turned away from Noll and began walking to the gate as soldiers hurried to his side. Before they reached him, he turned back one last time.

"I will see you soon. Enjoy the night, Arnold."

Leopold disappeared amongst a sea of torches. Seconds later he was back inside the walls.

Noll sat shivering in the dark for a long time before he dared to move. He did not feel like a brave man.

Chapter 11

SERAINA WATCHED NOLL PACE circles around the only tree within the walls of the Altdorf fortress. The last of the day's sun had fled, leaving the two of them shivering in the pre-darkness of night.

"You were right," Noll said. "I admit it. The Venetians have no interests but their own at heart."

Seraina did not answer. What could she say that would not agitate Noll further? He had been stewing and miserable ever since he returned from delivering Landenberg to Habsburg Castle.

She put the hood of her cloak up and tested the air with her breath. It was cool, but no mist formed.

"Perhaps we should go in," she said.

Noll stopped pacing and leaned against the tree.

"I would rather not. I spend too much of my time inside as it is," he said. "The place feels like a crypt."

Seraina knew exactly what he meant. She too could not shake the ill feelings she held for the Altdorf fortress. And it was not just because of her vision. The massive stone structure, with its high walls meant to hold out the world, was a constant reminder of how her people had been subjugated by outsiders for centuries. It began with invading Germanic tribes from the north, then the Romans from the south. And now, the Habsburgs, on behalf of the Holy Roman Empire.

"The men like the Venetians well enough," she said. "I watched several training sessions while you were gone, and they seem to be learning."

"I am sure they work hard enough. I have no qualms about that. But most of them have yet to touch a real sword. Pomponio has them tapping at each other with sticks all day long. At some point I have to see them properly armed."

"Was there nothing in the armory?"

"A few blades. Some spears. But no more than a hundred in all," Noll said. He leaned his head back against the tree and looked up into its almost leafless branches.

A sadness tore at Seraina as she looked at Noll. He did not know it, but he had much of the Old Blood in his veins, and the way he naturally sought comfort by pressing himself against the tree proved it. Seraina had done the very same thing herself many times as a little girl. Gildas would often find her sitting in the shadow of one giant oak in particular, picking at clover. Somehow, he always knew where to find her, and what to say to ease her troubles.

Seraina stepped in and took Noll's hand. At her touch, Noll looked up and, for the briefest instant, the creases on his forehead and around his eyes smoothed over. Seraina saw the same handsome, self-confident, young man who had startled her six years ago by swaggering out of the woods into her camp; his presence unannounced by neither the wind nor the rustles of the trees. He was a child of the Weave, and Seraina had recognized him immediately.

She made it her purpose to protect him, then, and to guide him along the complicated paths the Great Weave had in store. And that was why, as she watched his face harden once again, and dark worries cloud his eyes, she could not help feeling responsible for his pain.

He had been the cocky son of a well-to-do farmer, a freeman, when she had first met him. For the first time, she wondered where Noll would be now had she not come along. Would he have struck Landenberg's collector when he tried to take the family's ox? She thought back and tried to remember what she may have said that would have prodded him into action on that fateful day. She could think of nothing. And everything.

"Seraina…" Noll said.

She looked up and realized Noll had moved closer. Very close. He took her hand off his arm, eased her toward him, and before she knew it, he was kissing her.

It was a strong kiss. Not forceful in any way, but it was the action of a man who knew what he wanted and was not afraid to let anyone know. Seraina felt her lips, and her body, respond.

She opened her eyes. *When had she shut them?* She let go of his strong hands and forced her arms between their bodies.

"Noll, no… I cannot," she said, leaning away.

He wore a half-grin. The old Noll had returned. "You just did," he said.

He made no move to back away and his blue eyes were as warm as Seraina had ever seen them. She stepped back, creating some space to breathe.

Seraina shook her head. When she spoke her voice was firm. "I have told you before that we can never be together. Not like this."

The moment was gone, if there had ever truly been one, and Noll sensed it. He threw up his hands.

"Why not?" he asked. "And do not tell me it is because I am this *Catalyst* you are so fond of preaching about. I am not sure I even know what the word means! There is no mystical hand guiding my actions. I do what I think is right—nothing more."

"That is precisely what makes you special," Seraina said. "For very few people have the courage to do what they know is right. It is not important for you to understand what being a Catalyst means. It is enough that you are."

"I am a man. *That* should be enough." He slid down the tree and sat on its roots. "What exactly is it that you want from me? If anything." He looked up at her. "You drive me mad. Do you know that? I look into your eyes and I have no idea what you are thinking. It is like gazing into the green waters of a bottomless lake."

His words stirred a memory in Seraina. The recent conversation she and Gildas had had when he left her and Thomas.

"...and so was I. Happier than at any other moment in my long years. And when I look at you now, it gladdens me to see that green lake reflected so clearly in your eyes. Somehow, you have preserved the same wonder and innocence as back then, but like those waters, I see the strength of steel as well."

Her breath stopped.

Noll sensed something, for his eyes narrowed. "What is it?" he asked.

"I see the strength of steel as well!" she said.

Noll cocked his head. "What are you talking about? When you say things like that I—"

Seraina cut him off. "Noll! Stop talking and listen to me. I think I know where we can get swords for the men! I cannot believe I did not see it until now."

Noll crossed his arms. "You do know how to change a topic. I will give you that," he said.

***

Thomas had leaned a few cut saplings against the warm outside wall of the forge to construct a simple roof over his head. The open-ended shelter was not high enough for him to stand in, but it provided more than enough space to spread his bedroll. As long as someone kept the forge burning, it would serve Thomas all winter. If it became colder, all he needed to do was close off the ends with skins to retain more of the forge's heat.

Thomas lay under his blankets and looked up at the patchwork roof. It was dark, but flickering torches nearby allowed him to see enough to make him cringe at the shoddy workmanship. A child could have built a similar structure. Perhaps he should have tried to make it more elaborate.

Of course, why would I bother?

It could have been a good permanent home… for someone. But as far as Thomas was concerned, it need only last until the Austrians came. After that, he did not care who took over the space.

"You have made quite the cocoon for yourself, ferryman."

Thomas jumped at the sound of Noll's voice. Every

muscle in his body seemed to contract and lift him a hand's width off the ground.

Damn him. The man treads on cat paws.

"Sorry. Did not mean to startle you."

"Was just falling asleep, is all," Thomas said, his pulse beating out of control.

He sat up and looked over his shoulder to see Noll crouched outside the lean-to. Torchlight glowed behind him, basking Noll's face in shadow. He picked at a stone on the ground and tossed it away, then plopped down to sit cross-legged. Thomas could not tell where he was looking, but he had a feeling it was the ground.

Trapped, Thomas thought. He prayed the man had not come to ask forgiveness again for what happened to Pirmin. He turned around and pulled himself out of his warm blankets to sit facing Noll. The cool autumn air soon had him reconsider. He pulled a blanket over his shoulders.

"Something on your mind?" Thomas did not want to ask, but the sooner Noll said his piece, the sooner he could go back to his bedroll.

"Seraina," Noll said.

That was not the answer Thomas had expected.

"What about her?"

"She has to go on a journey. It will take a couple days and I would ask you to go with her. To look after her."

"She has done well enough until now, without me looking after her. Or anyone, I suspect."

"Just the same," Noll said, scratching at the dirt with one hand. "Will you do it?"

Of course he would, Thomas thought. But he hesitated with his response. It was not like Noll to ask a favor of someone like this.

"Why not go with her yourself?"

"Because she wants you," Noll said.

"I spoke with her today and she mentioned nothing of—"

"Damn it, Thomas. You do not make this easy. Will you do it or not?"

Thomas nodded. There was nothing he would not do for her. Even if she had not saved his life. Thomas realized that Noll probably could not see him nod in the darkness.

"You know I will," he said. "Anything else?"

"I want you to take command of the Army of Free Men."

If Thomas was surprised at Noll's first request, he was doubly so at this last one. He did not answer for a long time, and the two men sat in the darkness with silence hanging between them. A few scattered bits of conversation from nearby cooking fires drifted up to them, but the words were gibberish whispers by the time they reached Thomas and Noll.

"I cannot," Thomas finally said. He found his hand holding a pebble he could not remember plucking off the ground.

"You mean you will not," Noll said. There was a bitterness to his voice but Thomas did not feel that it was meant for him.

"They would never follow me."

"They would if you were backed by Furst, Stauffacher, Gertrude, and myself."

Thomas shook his head. "You are the reason they are all here, Noll. They follow you. I think the fools have come to believe in your cause more strongly than you do."

"Be careful, ferryman. No one believes we would be better off out from under the Habsburgs than I do."

"Then why this sudden back-stepping? Why give up control of your own army?"

"Because if I lead them into battle, not one of them will live through it! There. Is that what you wanted to hear?"

Thomas remained silent. What could he say? For perhaps the first time, he completely agreed with Noll Melchthal.

Noll took a deep breath and when he spoke again his voice was quiet and under control.

"I have been to Habsburg," he said. "I saw the army Leopold is building and I counted at least three thousand men. Hardened soldiers. Not a farmer among them, I suspect."

"It is early," Thomas said. "The ranks could swell to triple that just before they march."

Noll became quiet and Thomas regretted saying what he had. But it was the truth. Leopold would gather a few infantry about him now as a precautionary measure, but horses would be too expensive to keep all winter. His knights would flock to his banner at the last moment. If the sight of simple infantry had unnerved Noll, what would he think when faced with fully armored knights mounted atop steel-clad war horses?

"I am in this to the end," Noll said. "One way or another I will make a stand. And I will do everything in my power to give the men and women who side with me a fighting chance. Even if that means relinquishing control of my army. I am wise enough to know when I need help."

"And foolish enough to ask me for it," Thomas said.

"There is no one else," Noll said. "You are the only one."

"And what would you expect of me?" Thomas said. He felt his heart quickening and his face flush. "I do not have God's ear any more than the next man, and the truth is, without His help we will not hold Altdorf. It does not matter who leads the defenses. You saw Leopold's army yourself. He has the finest fighting men in Christendom at his disposal. What do we have? A partially built fortress with not half enough men to defend its walls."

"You speak as though the battle has already been fought. If you feel our cause to be such folly, why do you stay?"

"I do not have to explain my actions to you or any other man," Thomas said.

Noll stood and brushed off his breeches. "No, ferryman, you do not. But do not expect any special treatment if you intend to stay on as part of the Army of Free Men."

Thomas turned his back on Noll and began to slide under his blankets. "I have asked for nothing so far, and I do not expect that to change," he said.

Noll grunted and turned to leave, but whirled around at the last moment. "And do not discount your countrymen so easily. We are more resilient than you know."

He tried to leave again, but after only a step, he stopped and leveled a finger at Thomas. "And one more thing! If you hurt Seraina, I swear, I will come and kill you in your sleep."

Thomas blinked and sat upright. *Why in God's name would I hurt Seraina?*

Noll appeared to stomp away in the darkness after that, but try as he might, Thomas could not hear a single footfall. He rolled himself up in his blankets and pressed his back against the heated wall of the forge.

He was warm and comfortable, yet sleep was a long time coming.

Chapter 12

THOMAS AND SERAINA took the main road north to Brunnen, and when they came to the site of Thomas's ferry, they stopped to rest. Thomas's tent still stood, and when he poked his head inside he was surprised to see his belongings still there. That is, the few things that he had salvaged from the burned out remains of his cabin.

He changed into a fresh tunic and strapped on his belt knife. He also added another blanket to the bedroll he carried slung over one shoulder. The days were still comfortable enough, but the nights were not getting any warmer.

When he ducked back out of the tent, Seraina had covered a boulder with a cloth and spread out some cheese and black bread.

"You had best eat something," she said. "Soon we should stay off the road as much as possible, so you will need your strength."

Thomas spoke little during the simple meal, and when they were done, he stood, eager to be away. His eyes settled on the nearby woods for a moment. There were memories here: a forest missing four score of trees, cut, limbed, and peeled by Pirmin and himself. The work had taken them all spring and part of the summer.

"You can come back here," Seraina said, mistaking his pause as a sign of him not wanting to leave. "You can rebuild the ferry. The people of Schwyz would gladly help." She spoke quickly, her words full of hope.

A ferry. It had been a childish dream, nothing more.

"Altdorf is not your fight, Thomas, and Noll has more than enough men. After we get the swords for them, you can come back here. Rebuild. The people will need a ferryman."

He looked at the yellowed end of a cut stump.He saw Pirmin laughing, as the tree that used to be there fell in the opposite direction Thomas had intended, and crushed their cooking pots.

"We shall see," Thomas said.

Seraina started, and looked to the road. Thomas followed her eyes and saw what she was looking at: two people walked toward them. After a moment, Seraina relaxed and waved.

"It is Sutter and… Mera, I think," Seraina said, shielding her eyes against the sun.

The innkeeper and his daughter joined them for their simple meal. But Thomas had lost what little appetite he had. He kept staring at the heavy packs Sutter and Mera carried.

"Where are you headed?" Thomas asked.

Sutter glanced out over the lake. It was Mera who answered.

"We are on our way to Altdorf. Father has decided to join Noll's army and I insisted on going too. Someone has to feed them all." She gave her father a stern look.

Thomas and Seraina looked at one another. "This is the very thing you said you would not do," Thomas said.

"You are right that Noll could use your help," Seraina said, directing her words at Mera. "But Altdorf will be a very dangerous place to be when the Austrians come. No one will be safe."

Thomas sensed she was trying to keep her voice calm. Something that he should do as well, but he could not.

"Turn around right now and go back to your inn, Sutter. Altdorf is no place for you. And definitely no place for a father to allow his daughter to go," Thomas said.

Sutter glared at Thomas. "You think I do not know that? You have no right to tell me how to protect my own family. Once Leopold has an army in Altdorf, do you really think he will leave Schwyz alone and unscathed?"

"And you think Noll's army can stop him? You are a fool," Thomas said.

"My father is no fool!" Mera said. "He believes in Noll and his cause. As do I."

Sutter put his hand on his daughter's shoulder.

"But what about Vreni? Who is helping her look after the inn?" Seraina said.

Sutter grunted. "What inn? It is no more than a large house that eats firewood these days. Leopold has all but shut down the roads to simple travelers, and he has put out the word that merchants are to bypass Schwyz. Vreni is staying at her cousin's farm."

"Then you should both join her there," Thomas said.

Sutter stood. "Come Mera. It is time to be on our

way."

"I am sorry I yelled at you, Thomas," Mera said. "But if we do not help Noll, who will? He needs us."

Thomas stared after them as they left.

Seraina touched his arm. "Do not worry. I will talk to them both when we get back. We still have time to convince them to leave Altdorf."

Thomas did not hear her. He was thinking about what Sutter had said, how he thought Leopold would march his army on Schwyz once he had taken back the Altdorf fortress. Thomas knew Sutter was wrong. Leopold would not do that.

He would go through Schwyz first. And it would burn.

Thomas and Seraina walked in silence. They left the road and entered the forest, passing an ancient mound of moss-coated stones only a few steps from the modern path. The remains of an old wall, or structure, built by a people whose time had long since passed. A few minutes later, they came upon a similar pile of rubble, and then a half hour later, another.

"Are we on some kind of an old roadway?" Thomas asked.

Seraina nodded, but kept walking, weaving her way unerringly through the trees and clumps of underbrush.

"People think the Romans brought us roads and civilization," she said. "Yet our Celtic warriors were feared for the use of their one-horse war carts. You tell me, how could we have horse-drawn carts with no roads? They may not have been as straight, or hard-packed as the Romans built them, but they worked well enough."

"Those stones, then, they were walls," Thomas said.

"Yes. Built to keep the Romans out of our lands," Seraina said. "Unfortunately, they did not work."

Against a vastly superior force, walls rarely did, Thomas thought. They only postponed the inevitable.

They passed another mound and a chill went through him as he imagined what it would have been like standing behind that barricade as legions of Roman soldiers, perhaps the most fearsome fighting force in history, came marching toward them. The legionnaires were career soldiers, disciplined and drilled better than any army before them. Their javelins would have come first. Then an unstoppable red wall of interlocked shields, their short, wide-bladed swords thrusting straight ahead at anything that came in front of them. It would have been a spectacular sight.

He crossed himself and whispered a quick prayer for the dead.

The Celts never had a chance.

They slept along a remote stretch of the Great Lake's shoreline that night and set out again at dawn. It was a dazzling, blue-sky day and the sun reflecting off the lake had even Thomas removing his cloak after only an hour of walking. Seraina became quieter as the morning wore on, and she stopped several times to gaze into the woods or look out over the lake. Thomas did not interrupt her periods of silence, for he could tell by the occasional smile, or shake of her head, that these were personal moments for Seraina. Memories of a simpler time, perhaps.

Eventually, in early afternoon, they came to a small tree-lined bay with a clear view across one arm of the water to a rugged line of white peaks that seemed to float on the very lake itself. Seraina dropped her pack on the pebbled beach. Then, without a word, waded in without removing her sandals. She stood with her hands on her hips and stared out over the emerald lake, oblivious to how the water lapped at the hem of her dress. As her auburn hair played in the breeze, and the sun danced off the mountains, water, and Seraina all in equal measure, Thomas sat where he stood, unable, or unwilling, to take his eyes off the scene in front of him.

And then she began to take off her dress.

"Uh… ," he had no words in mind, but thought he should at least try to make some noise in case she had forgotten he was there.

She turned and stepped back onto the beach, slipping one arm out of her dress and revealing one creamy, lightly freckled shoulder and the strap of her undergarment.

"This is it! I am sure of it, Thomas!"

Her green eyes flashed in the sunlight and the brilliance of them, combined with the shimmering lake behind her, made Thomas's mouth go dry. She laughed, shrugged her other shoulder free and undid her belt. She stepped out of her dress and kicked it high up onto the shore.

Like a siren in some old sailor's tale, she beckoned to Thomas from the water's edge wearing nothing but a thin, white shift that the sun's rays transformed into pure gossamer. The image was soon shattered, however, when she ran into the water and began splashing around, screaming and cursing at the coolness of it. She let out another yelp, took a big mouthful of air, and plunged beneath the surface.

The world went silent.

Seconds, shaped like minutes, passed, and Thomas felt the dryness of his mouth spread to his throat. He stood up and covered his eyes against the sun's glare.

As he took a step toward the water, Seraina bounced up a short distance away, her hair was slick against her head and her mouth opened wide as she took in a deep breath. The water was only waist deep, and the fabric of her shift was plastered tightly to the contours of her body. While that image alone would have been enough to fully occupy any man's mind, Thomas found his gaze drifting to what Seraina held in her hand high above her head: a very long, and very old, sword.

With an enthusiastic shout, Seraina lobbed the sword with both hands toward Thomas, and disappeared under the water again.

By God, Mary, and all the angels in Heaven, what is going on?

He managed to move his foot aside just in time as the sword clattered up the beach to where he stood. He looked down. It was a sword, all right. Ancient, and covered with a good deal of rust, but it was a sword.

He looked up as another shout came from Seraina, and another sword spun through the air toward him. This one did not have near as much rust on it. In fact, it looked like someone had just drawn it from a well-oiled scabbard.

By the time the third sword hit the beach, Thomas had his shirt off and was unlacing his breeches. Seconds later, he was screaming as the cold water took his breath away.

Seraina laughed and splashed her way toward him.

"We found them!"

With a shriek of pure joy, she grabbed his hand and

pulled him after her through the frigid water.

When they were done, the beach was filled with swords, like pieces of driftwood strewn about after a storm. Thomas was blue when he came out of the water, and his fingers could not work flint and steel, so Seraina had built a small, sheltered fire amongst the trees. Thomas had put his clothes back on and gave Seraina his blanket, which she wrapped about herself while her own clothes dried next to the fire. By the time darkness set in, they had finished a quick meal of melted cheese on toasted bread with berry jam.

Seraina was still high from the afternoon's events and she talked non-stop.

"How did they get here?" Thomas asked, when he could get a word in.

"I cannot say for sure, but Gildas used to tell me stories of how some people would collect them after battles and hide them. Some tribes burned their dead, and they would often throw a warrior's sword in a lake or river, as a way to maintain balance. And by not destroying the sword, it would be waiting for him to reclaim when he was reborn."

"But how is it that they are in such good condition? The first few were quite rusty, but most of the others need only a slight filing and their edges honed."

"It is the silt in this particular part of the lake," Seraina said. "If they are buried under even a thin layer, it will protect them for centuries."

Thomas stood and put two pieces of wood on the fire. He was still cold and would have given anything for a drink of Max's kirsch.

"The question is, how do we get all of these back to

Altdorf?" Seraina asked.

"I have given that some thought. How far are we from the Kussnacht? Specifically, the shoreline at the bottom of the road where I found you and Gissler?"

Seraina's face darkened for a moment. The memory of being held prisoner in a cage wagon bound for a session with Leopold's inquisitors would do that to anyone, Thomas thought.

But then she looked up. Her eyes widened, the whites of them clearly visible in the firelight.

"You think the boat is still there?"

"How did you know I had the use of a boat?" Thomas did not recall telling her how he had overcome Leopold's guards, with Ruedi's help, and stolen the small sail boat.

"How else could you have gotten to me so fast? Surely they would have found it by now. Unless you took the time to hide it."

"I was in something of a rush, so no, I did not conceal it very well. But I had some good speed when I ran it aground. It is a little further in the trees than one would normally expect to find a boat." *Some very good speed. Ungodly even.*

Seraina smiled, like she had heard Thomas's thought.

"We can hide the swords here, and try to find the boat tomorrow," she said. "Then, you can put me and the swords ashore near Altdorf and you can take the boat back to your dock. It will be your new ferry." She said it all matter-of-factly, like it was the most obvious of plans and had already been decided.

Well, it had not been decided by everyone.

"I mean to be in Altdorf when Leopold comes," Thomas said. "I think you know that."

Seraina turned her head and stared at the fire. "You cannot," she said.

I cannot?

Thomas felt a laugh building inside. But it was a cruel, mocking thing and he refused to let it escape. "And why not? You heard Mera. Noll needs every sword he can gather." *And even then....*

Seraina turned on him. "Because you cannot!"

She turned to stare at the fire once again and spoke to the flames. "I have seen something. Something terrible, and I do not pretend to understand it. But I believe if you are in Altdorf when the Austrians come, you will die, Thomas."

"A lot of people will die. We are beyond that now," Thomas said.

She pulled her knees up to her chin and looked over them at Thomas. "I know what you are doing," she said. "You have given up, and this is your way of taking your own life."

"That is a sin," Thomas said. "And a ridiculous thought."

"Is it? So you feel Noll's army has nothing to fear. The Austrians will crash against the Altdorf fortress and be thrown back like drops of rain from oiled leather. Is that what you think, Thomas?"

The dark laugh that he had so far kept in check, finally crawled out of his throat. "We will be slaughtered to a man! Leopold will reclaim his precious fortress and take up where he left off. Nothing will have changed. That is what *I* have seen."

Thomas stood and began feeding pieces of wood into the fire. He refused to look at Seraina, so it came as a surprise when he felt her hand on his arm. She moved her head so he was forced to look at her.

"No. That is not what the Weave has in store for us. You must believe me—that much I have seen and I know to be true." Her voice cracked. "It is you, Thomas. You that I fear for. Please, I beg you. You have everything to lose by being part of this."

Thomas gripped a stick of wood so tightly his forearm muscles cramped, but he could not let go. He tried to turn away but her small hand found the left side of his face and pulled him back to look at her. Somehow, the heat of her hand penetrated even through the childhood scar.

"Promise me," she said. "No, you must swear. Swear to your God, that you will not stand upon the walls of the Altdorf fortress."

As he watched her defiantly blink away the tears threatening the corners of her eyes, he knew then that she could have asked him for anything, and he would have given it to her. An image of Sutter and Mera came to him. They would be in Altdorf now, or close to it. Along with hundreds of other people Thomas did not know the names of, but people he had come to recognize all the same. Like the woman in the inn who had given him extra 'meat' in his porridge. When the Austrians finally did come, the lives of these people would be irrevocably changed for the worse. And that was the best case scenario.

He knew it was madness, but he would have to accept Noll's offer.

"I swear…" he said.

Seraina let out a breath and a soft sigh at the same time, and while the sigh was still on her lips, she pulled Thomas's face down to hers and kissed him. Thomas flinched at first, but the kiss lingered. Thomas had never known anything so soft in all his life. The wood in his hand dropped to the ground, and not knowing what else to do with them, he put his fingers to the side of her face.

Seraina pulled away from the kiss and smiled at Thomas, perhaps to suppress a laugh. She took his hand from her cheek and guided it slowly down the side of her body, all the way to the small of her back. Even though she had the thick wool blanket wrapped around her, the sensation of his hand sliding down over her ribs, skimming the side swell of her breast, and settling at the hollow of her lower back, filled Thomas with an urgent need to feel her pressed along the entire length of his body. He encircled her with both arms and pulled her in tight. Their lips found each other again.

Thomas opened his eyes. She had misunderstood him. His oath was not what she thought. He placed his hands on Seraina's shoulders and gently broke the embrace. She stepped back, a puzzled look on her face.

"I did not swear to you because I wanted to… well… this—,"

Seraina cut him off by reaching out and putting her hand to his lips.

"Oh, Thomas. How could a man who has seen so much of this world, have experienced so little?"

She took Thomas's hand and kissed it. The combination of the moistness of her lips and the cool night air set his palm on fire. She stepped back and, with a smooth roll of her shoulders, let the blanket slide off and fall to the ground. The firelight flickered across her nude body, turning her skin the same auburn shade as her hair for a split second, before plunging it back into shadows.

"Tonight, I think it is time to change that," she said.

He had been searching for a way to tell her he had decided to accept Noll's request to assume command of the confederate army. But when Seraina stepped in and kissed his neck, and he felt the warmth of her bare skin against him, all such thoughts fled from his mind, and he made no effort to reclaim them.

He was, after all, merely a servant of life.

Chapter 13

SERAINA AND THOMAS CROUCHED in the thickets and watched as three Habsburg soldiers sat in the sun pulling at pieces of dried meat for their midday meal. A small, single-masted boat bobbed a few yards offshore. Its sail was down and a long bow line tied to a nearby tree was the only thing stopping it from drifting away. Looking at the amount of ash burnt in the campfire pit, Seraina felt they could not have been here for more than one, perhaps two, nights.

If the boat had been grounded high up on the shore, as Thomas had said, then it were these soldiers who had slid it back into the water. If only she and Thomas had come a day or two earlier, Seraina thought. The boat would now be theirs.

She turned to tell Thomas to crawl back through the brush, but he was already standing. He turned his belt around so the long dagger was at his back. She whispered his name and he looked up. He put his finger to his lips, and then motioned for her to stay put. Before Seraina could stop him, he began walking noisily toward the soldiers. Trees bent and slapped at him, while twigs snapped under his boots.

Just when she was sure things could not get worse, she heard Thomas call out, startling more than one bird out of its nest.

"Hello at the camp!"

Seraina winced and dropped to her belly. She had been about to tell Thomas that they did not need the boat. They would find another way to transport the swords.

No one needed to die.

"Have you got a spare bit of that for a fellow traveler?" Thomas said, pointing at the dried meat in their hands.

There was a pause. Then one of the men answered. "Sorry, friend. This is the Duke's food and we have no right to give it to every beggar that comes along."

Seraina inched forward on her elbows until she had a clear view. The three soldiers all stood. Two were focused on Thomas, but the other had his hand on the handle of a dagger tucked into his sword belt. He was older, more experienced if not higher in rank, and he swept the forest on all sides with a suspicious gaze. Seraina held her breath when he looked right at her. But, after only a second, his eyes moved on, and he remained ignorant of her trembling only a few strides away. She mouthed a silent thank you to the trees for protecting her yet again.

Thomas stood in front of the men now; the dagger hanging off the back of his belt clearly visible to Seraina but hidden from the soldiers.

"Please, me lords. I would not ask, but I have been

out here lost coming on three days now. With nothing but bark to fight the rumbling in my belly."

"Why are you here?" one of the two younger soldiers asked.

Thomas swayed on his feet. "Looking for a goat that run off. Please, just a strip of that meat and I will be on my way." He shuffled closer.

"You do not look like a goat herder to me. Now, get back, or you will have more than a rumbling belly to worry over."

The soldier stepped forward and raised his hand. Thomas hunched over and put one arm up in a feeble attempt to ward off the man's blow. Whether or not the soldier actually intended to strike Thomas was something Seraina would never know, for the man suddenly screamed out in pain. He remained rooted in place while his piercing cry shattered the forest stillness. Seraina finally understood the reason for his lack of movement: a dagger was sunk up to its handle in the soldier's foot. Thomas had slammed his weapon clean through the man's boot. The steel blade had pierced the top of his foot and exited through the leather sole, staking him to the ground. Thick blood crept over the dirty leather, making it glisten.

The older soldier began drawing his long dagger but, before he could get it all the way across his body, Thomas stepped in and, using both his hands, redirected the deadly tip into the man's mouth. It slid in at an angle, piercing the man's soft palate and continuing up through the base of his brain. He died instantly, but his legs kept him standing for a few seconds longer, until the blood drained out of them and he collapsed like a rotten tree.

Seeing the steel go into the man's mouth brought

_aina's mind she had hoped to forget. She _, frozen in place, like the trees were pressing her _o the ground. Thomas bent over and tore his dagger out of the screaming soldier's foot, and then the woods went quiet when Thomas stood and slashed the man's throat.

Blood splashed across the third soldier's clean-shaven face, making him close his eyes. He was young. Much younger than the other two. He stumbled back, and then tripped over nothing but fear. He fell to his back, but quickly flipped over and began to scramble away on his hands and knees.

Seraina remembered her vision of Thomas in a tunic dripping with red, and as she watched him walk behind the young man trying to crawl to safety, she found the strength to push herself up off the ground.

"Thomas, no!"

She shrugged off the trees' attempts to hold her back, and threw herself at Thomas as he wrapped one hand in the man's hair and pulled his head back, stretching the softness of his throat toward the sun.

"Thomas…" She folded herself around Thomas's dagger arm and called out his name again, but softer this time.

He looked at her. His eyes were cold and distant at first, but they began to soften the harder Seraina squeezed his arm.

"You cannot kill him," she said.

His eyes narrowed and blinked, like she had told him something truly ridiculous.

"I must," he said. "There is a checkpoint fifteen minutes from here. He will bring a dozen men before we are even half loaded."

Seraina looked at the young soldier. Thomas still held

him with one strong hand twisted in his hair. The boy was less than twenty, and the way his chest heaved with deep, frenzied breaths, reminded Seraina of a wounded deer who knew the hunter would be along soon enough.

"There is rope on the boat. We could tie him," Seraina said.

Thomas scowled. "We may need that rope. And even if we did not, we owe his kind no mercy. Not after what they did. And what they stand to do."

Seraina stepped forward. "There is another way."

"You do not know his kind like I do," Thomas said, shaking his head.

She let go of Thomas's arm, slowly. "Trust me," she said.

He stared at her for a long time but, eventually, he relinquished his grip on the boy's hair and stepped back.

A boulder at the soldier's back was the only thing that stopped him from scrambling away. He pressed himself against the stone and looked from face to face, then pleaded in a rattled voice. "I swear I will not utter a word of what I saw. If you let me go, I swear it."

Seraina saw the dagger in Thomas's hand twitch, so she stepped between the two men before it was too late. She crouched in front of the soldier at eye level.

"Do I have your word you will stay exactly where you are? To not move until someone comes looking for you?"

"I swear. On the Virgin Mother, I swear it."

"He lies," Thomas said, moving forward.

Seraina stopped him with a glare. "Trust me," she said.

She reached down and gripped the boy's lower leg with both her hands. He tried to pull it away, but she tightened her hold.

"You too must trust me," she said. "If you wish to live."

The boy looked at Thomas, hovering close behind Seraina, and at the naked blade he held, and went very still. He nodded.

Seraina probed above his ankle with her fingers. She slid one hand along the larger bone of his lower leg; the mother bone. Beside it was the child bone, which was slender, and much smaller. Together they nurtured one another and were capable of supporting a great deal of weight.

With a deft twist of her hand, Seraina stretched the bottom of the mother bone away from its base. The young soldier yelped and pulled his foot away.

"What are you doing to me, witch?"

Saving your life. And ours.

Seraina stood. "You are fine. But do not try to stand for at least twelve hours. The mother bone will need time to re-align herself."

He eyed her while he flexed his toes and rolled his ankle. Seraina knew he felt no pain. He had only been surprised by the odd sensation of Seraina shifting his mother bone.

She turned to Thomas. "We can go now."

He stared at her and made no move to sheath his knife.

"Trust me, Thomas."

"You keep saying that," he said.

"And I will continue saying it until I see by your eyes that you do." Seraina pointed to the boat. "Prepare for cast-off, ferryman."

Thomas shook his head, but he returned his blade to

his belt.

"*You* are the ferryman?" the boy said. His eyes went wide. "The outlaw that attacked the Duke and shot his man?"

Thomas gave no response, but kept one eye on the soldier while he untied the boat's bow line and pulled it closer to the shore.

Seraina picked up a water skin and placed it next to the boy. "Remember. Do not attempt to stand until this time tomorrow."

They pushed out into the lake and Thomas busied himself with setting the sail. Soon, the trees on the shore obscured their view of the soldiers' camp, but they were still near enough to hear the boy's pain-choked scream.

Fool, fool, fool. I warned him.

Thomas jerked his head up at the sound.

"What happened?" he asked.

Seraina shook her head sadly. The foolish boy had tried to stand. But with his mother bone pulled out of line, only the child was left to support the boy's entire body. It would have snapped in half with even a fraction of that weight.

"I told him to trust me," she said.

Chapter 14

THOMAS AND NOLL SAT at a table near the inn's entrance. They leaned their backs against the wall, with untouched mugs of mead before them, and waited for Pomponio.

"When he comes, I will do the talking," Noll said.

Thomas nodded. He would not have it any other way. He had no desire to exchange words with the likes of Pomponio. Thomas looked around the tap room. It was more crowded than he would have liked. The evening rush had just begun, and three women and a man ferried drinks and trays of simple food between the kitchen and tables.

Noll's knee bounced non-stop and every time the door opened he looked up. Thomas rested his hands around his clay mug and stared at it. Inside was a plum mead, and it had a reddish tint that reminded him of Seraina's hair at dusk. Mind you, since their return from retrieving the swords, almost everything Thomas looked at reminded him of Seraina. He looked at the mead again, and this time was tormented with the memory of how her naked body had glowed under the soft light of their campfire.

He was about to take a sip when the door opened. Noll's knee stopped bouncing. A second later the shadow of Pomponio's ridiculous hat fell over Thomas's mug. As the shadow grew, Thomas's annoyance grew into an irrational anger, and he was surprised to find himself gripping the mug tight enough to turn his fingertips white.

"Master Melchthal," Pomponio said in a booming voice. His Venetian accent stood out, and several sets of eyes from neighboring tables looked their way. He stood for a moment, allowing curious onlookers to get their fill, and then sat down across from Noll. He was accompanied by all four of his fellow Venetians, and once Pomponio had settled himself, they also took up spots across from Thomas and Noll.

Thomas looked up to find Salvatore's broad shoulders at eye level. The man plunked his elbows on the table and began cleaning his fingernails with a long dagger, studiously oblivious to all around him.

Pomponio held up a hand to get a server's attention, but Noll stopped him before he could shout his order.

"Any drink will be coming from your own purse tonight," Noll said.

Pomponio lowered his arm slowly. He turned to Noll. "That was not our agreement," he said.

"That agreement is no longer in effect," Noll said. "In fact, consider it terminated. Your services are no longer required. You and your men have until tomorrow morning to gather your belongings and leave Altdorf."

The Venetians did not look the least bit surprised at

Noll's words. Pomponio smiled and shook his head sadly.

"Master Melchthal," he said. "Your men are just now beginning to learn the fundamentals of the sword. If we leave, all their training will have been for nothing. Next summer, when the Austrians come, they will make very short work of your... *army*."

Noll stared at him. "They will be ready," he said.

Pomponio leaned back and put his hands behind his neck. "So you say. But tell me, who will train them? You?" The disdain in his voice matched the contempt in his smile, and Thomas found himself crushing his mug once again. But if the Venetian's attitude bothered Noll, he did not show it.

"No. He will," he said, nodding toward Thomas.

Both Pomponio and Salvatore looked at Thomas like he had just snatched the last piece of meat from a communal trencher. Salvatore stopped fussing with his dagger, and with a slow, deliberate motion he placed it on the table in front of him, between himself and Thomas.

"Are you sure that is wise?" Pomponio said to Noll while staring at Thomas's face. "This man is obviously a soldier. Perhaps even a decent one. Although, not good enough to avoid at least one man's steel, no?"

All the Venetians got a chuckle out of that. While they laughed Thomas lifted his mug to his lips and took a long drink. The mead no longer had the dark auburn hue of Seraina's hair. The liquid appeared much redder now.

Pomponio dismissed Thomas with his eyes and turned back to Noll. "But a common soldier is no replacement for a sword master from the most famous school in Venezia. You do your men a disservice if you choose him over us, Master Melchthal. I fear you will regret it."

Noll cast a sidelong glance at Thomas. "You may be right. But all the same, I want you gone by morning."

Pomponio let out an exaggerated breath. "Very well. You negotiate strong, my friend. Tell me what you are paying this mercenary and we will work for merely double his fee, though we are ten times the talent. A better bargain—"

"Thomas! By God I never figured to find you in the first tavern I stuck my head in, but here you are!"

A small, wiry man, dressed smartly in a blue and red vest, walked toward the table. The sword swinging at his side seemed to be too long for him, but somehow it never dragged on the ground or impeded his movement. His hair was pulled back neatly from his face and glistened with oil. Hoop earrings dangled from each ear and his clean-shaven face beamed as he shouted in Thomas's direction.

Thomas blinked.

Anton? Where had he come from?

Thomas had been so preoccupied with the Venetians he had failed to see Anton come in the front door.

"Thought for sure I would have to spend the better part of a day tracking you down," Anton said. He gave a quick nod to Noll and the Venetians and then stepped over the bench and squeezed himself in between Pomponio and Salvatore. A normal-sized man could never have accomplished the feat, but Anton was much smaller than average.

"Planned on coming in here for a quick drink, or three, and see if anyone knew you. But by the Grace of Mary, who is the first person I set eyes on?" He looked around the table and grinned, then slapped his hands down flat. "Well, I have accomplished more today than I thought to, so let us get some drinks. You lot look like you could use one as well."

"Hello Anton," Thomas said, knowing full well he would just keep on rambling if Thomas did not say something. He fought back a smile at how comical his friend looked squeezed between the two scowling Venetians.

Pomponio's scowl turned into a laugh, albeit one with very little true humor behind it. "Is this another of of our replacements? One of the wandering folk is it?"

Anton smiled at first, but then Salvatore said, "She smells good enough to eat."

"What is that scent?" Pomponio asked. "Something from your sister's caravan?"

"Orange blossoms," Anton said quietly. He no longer smiled and Thomas could see his eyes beginning to hood over.

"Of course it is," Pomponio said. He turned to Noll. "Really, Master Melch—"

Anton drew back his arm and elbowed Pomponio in the side of the head. He jumped up off the bench and stood calmly by with one hand resting on the handle of the sword at his belt.

"Not sure if you was insulting me on purpose, or not, but thought that would be the fastest way to find out," Anton said.

Everyone at the table froze. Pomponio, with his eyes clenched tight, gave his head a few shakes and rubbed his temple. Then, he slowly pushed himself to his feet. "This gnat has a sting, no?"

Salvatore and the other Venetians relaxed as

Pomponio took up a position across from Anton. Salvatore licked his lips. He pointed at Thomas.

"No one moves," he said.

He inched his hand close to his dagger laying on the table, and turned sideways on his bench so he could see Pomponio, as well as keep one eye on Thomas and Noll.

Pomponio faced Anton and slid his narrow-bladed sword out of its scabbard. There was a shout from a nearby table and people fell over themselves to give the two men some room.

"Before I teach you today's lesson, I would have your name," Pomponio said.

"Aye, you would," Anton said. "If I was of a mind to give it to you."

Pomponio grinned. "Well, my rude gypsy friend, let me introduce *myself*. I am Giovanni—"

Gissler was the fastest man with a blade Thomas had ever seen. But no one was quicker than Anton when it came to moving unarmed. One moment he was standing relaxed with his hand resting on his sword handle, and the next he seemed to materialize beside Pomponio. Perhaps, because Anton had never drawn his weapon, Pomponio's mind had failed to recognize him as a threat. Or, maybe Anton was simply too quick. Whatever the reason, Pomponio had a puzzled look on his face when Anton seized his wrist, forced the point of his sword against the wooden floor, and then stomped on it. The thin blade snapped like second-year kindling. Anton then twisted Pomponio's wrist back against itself and there was another snap, followed by a scream as Pomponio dropped to his knees.

"Do not much care what your name is," Anton said, and then brought his knee up into Pomponio's face.

Strange, Thomas thought, how a man's screams never reveal even a hint of his accent. Pain sounded the same in any language.

Salvatore's hand snaked out for his knife. It fumbled blindly, once, twice, before he tore his eyes away from Anton kicking Pomponio on the ground. He turned just in time to see Thomas drive Salvatore's own dagger into the back of his hand, pinning it against the table. His screams became the new loudest sound in the tavern.

Keeping one hand on the dagger handle, Thomas leaned over and grabbed a handful of Salvatore's thick hair. He slammed the man's head into the table and then pressed his cheek into the hard surface so that he could see his hand skewered in place. Like lava, blood seeped out of the wound and ran down the sides of Salvatore's hand. And when Thomas leaned the blade to one side, it very well could have been lava seeping into his flesh the way Salvatore screamed.

Thomas allowed the blade to stand up straight, and Salvatore quieted down. His eyes were still clenched shut, however, and tears streamed down his cheeks.

"Do not move," Thomas said. He spoke to Salvatore, but he fixed his eyes on the other two Venetians who were still seated across from Noll.

"I think he means you two," Noll said. Their eyes looked at their master being pummeled on the floor, across at Thomas resting his hand on Salvatore's bloody dagger, and then at one another. As one they held up their hands to show they were unarmed and intended to stay that way.

Noll eased himself away from the table and walked to where Anton had just delivered one last knee into the moaning form of Pomponio. Rivers of blood ran from his nose, one corner of his mouth, and from cuts around his eyes. One side of his face was purple and had already puffed up to almost twice its original size.

Noll drew his own sword and put it against the Venetian's throat. Pomponio moaned.

"Dead," Noll said. "Oh so very dead, no?"

***

Noll decided to keep the Venetians' horses in exchange for an open clapboard wagon pulled by two nags. While Thomas, Anton, and a dozen of Noll's men stood nearby, Pomponio's men loaded him and a still-groaning Salvatore into the back. Noll tossed Pomponio's hat into the back of the wagon and it hit Pomponio in the face. He grimaced as he was forced to move his broken wrist, which he held tightly against his chest.

"I will have men following you with crossbows. If you stop before the top of the pass, I have ordered them to shoot," Noll said.

Pomponio's face was beginning to bruise over and swell from Anton's beating. He mumbled at Noll through his stiffened jaw.

"The Austrians will see you get what you deserve. Come summer, I will be drinking to your demise, young Melchthal."

Noll cut him off by slapping one of the horses. The wagon lurched into motion and both Salvatore and Pomponio grunted in pain. They watched in silence as the slow moving wagon crawled up the road, heading toward Saint Gotthard's Pass.

Before it disappeared from sight, Noll turned to

Thomas.

"We should discuss the training regimen. The next session was scheduled for the day after tomorrow by Pomponio. Unfortunately, the men have already been told, so we will have to stick with that. Too bad."

Thomas nodded. Noll was about to hear something else he would not like.

"On that day, we will need to make a list with every man's name on it. And they will have to mark it. If any man misses training he will be punished. And I want to know exactly how many men we have and what weapons or armor they bring with them."

"Fair enough," Noll said. "Then what?"

"We will divide the men into units. Half will participate in martial training and the other half will work on constructing the defenses," Thomas said. "They will switch every two days."

"That is a sound plan. The men will learn better in smaller groups. Tell me what sort of structures we will be working on so I can line up tradesmen and tools."

"The fortress wall," Thomas said.

"It is finished already," Noll said. "You want to add to it?"

"We must tear it down."

Noll laughed. "What? And rebuild it thicker? Higher?"

"No. Just tear it down. But try not to damage the materials too badly. We may need them."

Thomas began walking away.

Noll was no longer laughing. "You jest."

Thomas stopped and shook his head. "We have no hope of defending that structure. No sense leaving it standing for the Austrians to use against us in the future."

"Are you mad? It is a fortress! The only one we have, I might add. It represents the greatest victory we have ever made over the Habsburgs. "

"The only one, actually," Thomas said.

"I refuse to give it up. I will find the men to defend its walls."

Thomas stepped in close. He kept his voice low so no one could overhear.

"Not with ten thousand men could you do that. And you have what, five hundred?"

One end of Noll's mouth lifted in a sneer, so Thomas continued.

"You know nothing of siege warfare. The Austrians would surround the fortress, cut off your food supply, bribe someone to poison your well, and wait. For months. Years even. Half your men starve, most of the others are so weakened with gut-rot they cannot even keep down dry bread, if they can get any. Eventually, you turn on one another. Begin eating your dead. In the end, you throw open the gates and beg Leopold to save you from your own men."

Noll pushed Thomas away. He ground his teeth and stared at the Hospitaller, but eventually, what Thomas said found its way through his anger.

"It is the only stronghold we have," Noll repeated.

Thomas held up his hands. "Then you defend its walls. But I warn you, it is a death trap. You swore you would not question me. That I could run this army how I saw fit. If you have had a change of heart, I would know it now."

After a long moment Noll gave a curt nod.

"Very well. We will tear it down. But know this. I

would slit my own throat before I would beg anything from Leopold of Habsburg."

Thomas let out a sigh. "I have seen stronger men than you fight over the boiled knuckles of a fallen comrade. Do not be so quick to preach of your convictions."

"Preach? Look who rants on about the end of the whole world like some crazy monk!"

Not the end of the whole world. Just ours.

Thomas was about to say more, but he noticed Noll's eyes were focused on something behind Thomas.

"Uh, oh. Here comes Seraina," he said. "And she does not look happy."

Thomas turned just in time to get her finger jabbed into his chest.

"I thought at least one man of god could be beyond lies!" she said.

She jabbed him again. "You swore to me Thomas. I should have known better than to trust the word of any man. Especially one brought up by the Church. And you," she turned and withered Noll with a furious glare.

"Me? What have I done?" Noll said.

"How could you ask him to lead the defenses? You know what I saw. You know what will happen to him if he stays in Altdorf!"

Her voice verged on hysteria. Thomas sensed she was about to run off, so he grabbed her arms and turned her toward him. "Seraina, listen to me. I did not lie."

"You did." She struggled in his grip and refused to meet his eyes.

"I promised I would not stand upon the walls of the Altdorf fortress when the Austrians attack. And that is a promise I intend to keep."

Seraina wiped at her cheek. She looked at Thomas, her eyes red-rimmed slits.

"How can I believe you?" she asked.

"Oh, you can believe him," Noll said, shaking his head like he could still not believe it himself. "For in a few weeks time those walls will be nothing but rubble."

She looked from man to man. "What do you mean? And do not bandy your words any more than you already have."

"We will leave the keep itself standing over the winter, so the men have shelter, but I intend to see that fortress destroyed," Thomas said. "Before it destroys us."

"But how will we defend ourselves?" Seraina asked.

"Now there is a fair question," Noll said.

"We will rebuild the line of ancient forts we passed on our journey together."

Seraina blinked and her mouth opened but no words came forth.

"You mean the overgrown rubble piles to the north of Schwyz?" Noll said.

Thomas nodded.

Noll turned a full circle and threw up his hands. "Now I know you have lost your mind! Those are ant hills and fox dens. They have not been *forts*, by any stretch of the word, for centuries."

"They will be once we relocate the stones and timbers from Altdorf."

"But how will a few hastily built forts be more effective than an already completed fortress?" Seraina asked.

Thomas drew his dagger, flipped it over in his hand, and crouched low to the ground. Using the handle, not the blade, he began drawing in the dirt.

"Leopold will come from the north and most probably take the town of Schwyz. From there he can resupply and march on to Altdorf. If we construct a series of stone barricades and wooden palisades above and to the west of Schwyz, we can fight a retreating battle from one wall to the next."

As he drew more lines and X's, his dagger handle picked up speed, as did his words. He took a breath to slow himself down. "If we stagger them properly, we will always be able to attack him from two sides and never allow either his cavalry or infantry to achieve proper formations. We could never hope to face the Habsburg army head on. Outflanking them at every turn is our only hope." He stabbed one last time at the ground and looked up.

Noll and Seraina's eyes were wide and they glanced at one another. Seraina smiled.

"I have no idea what you just said, ferryman, but you do draw a pretty picture," Noll said.

Chapter 15

AS THE MEN FILTERED into the courtyard, Thomas saw the puzzled glances, darting eyes, and hushed voices questioning one another about the whereabouts of the Venetians. They knew something had changed. As those few, who had been at the inn two nights before, eagerly shared what they had seen, the noise of conversation began to rise.

Thomas wondered just how far the story had strayed from the truth. Judging from some of the wide-eyed glances he and Anton were getting from men, he suspected a fair ways.

Noll picked up a horn and blew a lingering note that brought silence to the crowd.

"The Venetians are gone," he said. "They should have never been here in the first place. And that is my fault. I should have known better than to put my faith in outsiders. From this moment on, the ferryman will command this army and see to its training. Now, those who are still with us, line up and be counted."

No one cheered, or applauded, at the news, but not a single man left the courtyard. And throughout the day, at one time or another, Thomas would receive a back-slap or a 'well-done' nod from nearly every one of the five hundred men present, starting with a certain innkeeper from Schwyz.

The day wore on as Thomas, Noll, and Anton sat on a log with a never-ending line of men stretched out before them. With quill in hand, Thomas leaned over a sawed-off log end that served as a desk. Each man shuffled forward, stated his name, and answered any questions he was asked. Then Thomas would scratch his name onto one of several yellowed sheets of parchment that Furst had provided.

"Name?"

"Marti Rubin."

Thomas looked up at the young man. He had red hair and his fair skin was tanned and heavily freckled from spending a great deal of time outside. Thomas was sure he had already seen him today.

"Were you not already here?"

"No, sir."

Noll chuckled. "That was his brother. Marti and Sepp are twins."

Thomas shuffled through the parchment pages until he found the one with Sepp Rubin's name on it. Each page represented a unit that would train, build, and fight alongside one another. Many years ago he had learned that it was best to avoid having brothers on the same squad, but to never separate twins. They had an eerie way of reading one another's thoughts and did wonders for a group's cohesiveness.

He wrote Marti's name beside his brother's, then re-dipped his quill and held it out to the young man.

"Make your mark," he said.

Marti took the feather in his fist and stared at what Thomas had just written. "How do I know that is my name?"

"It is yours," Noll said. "And right next to it is your brother's."

Marti screwed up his face as he examined them side by side. His face lit up and a self-satisfied grin took over his freckled features. "Mine is prettier," he said.

"Because you are the better looking one," Noll said. "Now scratch your mark and move on. We have two hundred more to go this afternoon. Next!"

A young boy appeared. He looked hauntingly familiar to Thomas, but he could not quite place him, until he saw Vex, Pirmin's dog, beside him. The boy was the one he had seen at Pirmin's grave.

"Who are you signing up Matthias, you or the dog?" Noll asked.

"Who do you think?"

"Well, do not look at me. It is Thomas that you have to plead with," Noll said.

The boy, who was not older than eight or nine, turned to Thomas. "I want to sign up," he said.

"How old are you boy?" Thomas asked.

"Fourteen," he said.

Thomas narrowed his eyes. "Does this look like an army of liars to you?"

Matthias glanced over at Noll. "Could be," he said.

Noll laughed. "You will have your hands full if you take on this one," he said to Thomas.

"Why do you want to join this army?" Thomas asked.

"I am going to kill Duke Leopold."

Thomas could not keep the hint of a grin from taking over his face. Noll chuckled. Matthias looked back and forth between the two men. "I mean it! I do not care if you let me into your army or not. I am going to stick my sword in his neck and watch him bleed to death!"

The anger behind his words wiped the smiles from both men's faces and made them sit up straight.

"Why would you want to do that?" Thomas asked.

"He deserves it. He killed my friend."

"What was your friend's name?"

"Pirmin," Matthias said.

Even though he knew what the boy was going to say, it still took a few seconds before Thomas spoke.

"Leopold has killed a lot of people's friends," Thomas said. "But you are too young to be thinking of killing men."

"Yeah, I thought you would say something like that. Come on Vex."

As the boy turned away, Thomas said, "Can you ride?"

Matthias turned back and his distrusting eyes fixed on Thomas. "No," he said. "Well, I sat on an ox a few times."

"You will have to learn, then. I need a runner. Someone to deliver messages for me. Until you are able to ride, you will have to do it on foot. Can you run?"

His face lit up, the distrust in his eyes fell away, and he looked just like any normal eight-year old should. He pointed at Noll. "Almost as fast as him!"

"That will have to do," Thomas said. He looked around and saw Ruedi standing not far away oiling his crossbow. "See that man over there with the forked beard? Go ask him to teach you how to ride. But ask nice. If you do not, he may shoot you."

The boy nodded and hooked one arm around Vex's neck. "Come on, boy."

"And one more thing, Matthias. A good soldier never lies to his captain. A poor one often does. You choose which one you want to be."

Thomas could see the boy thinking as he led the dog away. That was a good thing. He had been forced to grow up too fast, but then again, so had Thomas.

The next man stepped up and placed his hand on Thomas's makeshift desk.

"Touching," he said. He was missing the top half of most of his fingers. In his late twenties, the man had thick arms but long, sleek legs that looked like they could carry him for days without any rest. His eyes were hard and restless.

Thomas recognized him immediately. He was the brigand leader of the band that had tried to ambush him and his men near the Gotthard those many months ago. The memory of that time was so far away from his life now, it seemed to belong to another man. He glanced at Anton. He too was eying the man curiously.

"Hello Erich," Noll said, his tone flat.

The man's eyes jumped from Thomas to Noll. He nodded and gave Noll an imaginary tip of the hat with his stumpy right hand. "Nice to see you Noll."

"Better here than on the road," Noll said. "What brings you to Altdorf?"

"The lack of soldiers," Erich said.

"Must be quite the experience for you. Being able to walk into a town without a Habsburg man trying to take your head."

Erich shrugged. "It might be something a man could get used to. But I do not need to tell you that."

"What do you want, Erich?"

He stared at Noll and his chest rose and fell. "A place for me and my men in your army."

Noll leaned back on his log. "How many men are we talking about?"

"Twenty-seven."

"You realize what we are doing here? You know this is not just some warm place to spend the winter?"

Erich nodded slowly. "Like I said. A man could get used to being able to walk free in this town."

Thomas put his quill down and spoke up. "I am afraid we cannot accept your offer."

Noll looked at Thomas like he had just bitten the head off a chicken. "Uh, Thomas... maybe we should discuss this? Sure, Erich is an outlaw, but who can fault someone for that? He just offered us twenty-seven men."

"Twenty-eight, including me. And this." Erich pulled a leather-bound manuscript out of a sack at his feet and dropped it on top of Thomas's pile of parchment.

Thomas struggled to keep the surprise from his eyes, but as soon as he saw the title, he recognized the book. It was Duke Leopold's *Malleus Maleficarum. The Hammer of Witches.*

"Where did you get this?"

"Found it a while back in a cage wagon in the Kussnacht. Along with the corpse of a man both you and I know only too well."

He held up his shortened fingers and ran his palm over their blunt ends. He directed his next words to Anton. "You did a fine job firing these. Healed up real nice. I suppose I should thank you for that."

Anton shrugged. "I have done better work. But I usually reserve that for people who do not try to kill me first."

Erich looked back to Thomas. "What do you say? I have some skilled men in my band."

"And that is one of the reasons I must say no."

Noll held his head with both hands. "Thomas, I can vouch for this man. As far as I know, he has never preyed on our people. His targets have always been rich merchants or travelers from far away lands."

"And me and my men," Thomas said. "I am sorry, but I cannot take the chance. His kind are easily bought and I will not expose our army to that risk."

Thomas pushed Leopold's manuscript back toward Erich. "I commend you for the change you are trying to make. And even though I suspect your intentions may be true, I regret I cannot allow you a place amongst my men."

Erich looked down at the book, his face pinched. These were obviously not the words he had expected to hear. "You let that waif join, but refuse skilled men?" He pointed and sneered at the manuscript. "Keep it. Put it toward the cause. You are going to need all the help you can get."

He spun on his heel. "Out of my way," he said as he pushed through the men behind him.

Noll said something to Thomas as Erich walked away, but Thomas heard nothing. His eyes, as well as his thoughts, were fixated on the book in front of him. He ran his fingers over the fine leather cover.

Malleus Maleficarum.

Leopold's choice of Latin made Thomas's hand curl into a fist and an image of Seraina being forced into a cage wagon flashed before his eyes. *Maleficarum* was the feminine form of witch, so the title presupposed that all witches were women. Otherwise, he should have used *maleficorum*, which could mean either a male witch or a female witch. Was it a simple Latin mistake on Leopold's part? From what he knew of the man, Thomas doubted it.

Thomas was still staring at Leopold's manuscript when the next man in line dropped a scabbarded sword on top of it. Scowling, Thomas looked up and saw nothing but forearms. He knew the man before he even saw his face or heard his rough, guttural voice.

"Add me to your list, you distrusting bastard, and make whatever mark you want next to it."

Thomas shielded his eyes against the midday sun. He was afraid this would happen.

"Hello Urs. I see you got yourself a new blade."

"That one is yours. I made it with your awkward form in mind."

Thomas raised his eyebrow at that and picked up the short sword. He freed it from its scabbard with one quick motion. The sun glinted off it so fiercely Thomas had to squint. It was a straight, double-bladed weapon that reminded Thomas of an ancient Roman gladius. But the cross-section of its blade was shaped like a diamond. It was thick near the simple curved crosspiece, but it tapered to a deadly point.

"An in-fighter's weapon," Urs said. "The four-sided design makes it stronger than anything I have come up with yet. It separates chainmail like a straw mat and will punch a hole through plate if given the proper encouragement."

Thomas took hold of the honey-colored wooden grip

and sighted down the finely honed blade. Urs was not one to exaggerate. If he said it could pierce plate armor, Thomas believed him.

"This is an interesting piece," Thomas said.

"I call it a *baselard*. Seeing as that is where I made it."

A blade from Basel. Urs had never been one for fancy names or frills in the weapons he designed. He was far too practical.

Thomas slowly guided the sword back into its scabbard. As good as it was to see his old friend, this was the last place he wanted him to be.

"This is not your fight," Thomas said. "But Max and Ruedi could use your help getting Ruedi's sister and family out of Altdorf. You should seek them out."

Urs shook his head. "Blood and ashes, Thomas. Who do you think told me you were putting together a rebel army in the first place? And they said I was to tell you to put their names on one of your lists, as well. Seems Ruedi's sister is refusing to leave her farm. They would have come themselves, but they know what kind of a bastard you can become once training starts, so they decided to spend their last free afternoon drinking."

He tapped his foot and pointed at the pile of parchment in front of Thomas. "And I mean to join them, just as soon as I see your quill finish scratching. So get on with it, would you?"

Chapter 16

IT HAD SNOWED in the early hours of the morning. A light skiff covered the still frozen ground, but with hundreds of men churning it up, Thomas knew it would be a field of mud before the end of the day.

He watched the men come through the gates in groups of five or ten with their training swords in hand; fathers, sons, brothers, friends, and more than a few wives and mothers leading the way with packs of provisions to see the men through the day. One minute the courtyard was empty, the next filled to overflowing. Was it his imagination, or were many of them newcomers, men not yet on any of his lists?

They took up places on the ground, forming a semi-circle around the center of the yard, in front of Thomas and Noll. Behind the two men stood Ruedi, Max, Urs, and Anton.

The murmurs of the group began to grow louder, until Thomas stepped forward and held up his hand. He waited patiently for silence. He looked out over the crowd and felt curious eyes on him and his men. He saw many grin and sit back, exchanging nods with their neighbors. They expected a show, like the Venetians had put on.

And they will get one. But no one will be smiling at the end of this day.

Thomas scanned all those seated, looking for one man in particular. He found him almost instantly, for he was not hard to pick out: Gruber, Hans Gruber. The young giant from the Fall Festival that Pirmin had wrestled in the Schwingen finals. He had become a hero that day by defeating Pirmin with a skilfully executed hip throw.

Thomas called him up. The men around Gruber slapped the man on his broad back as he stood and made his way to the front.

"Today will be devoted to bare-handed training," Thomas said.

Gruber removed his vest and rolled his massive shoulders. Thomas met the man, well aware that he must look like a sapling growing next to a giant cedar.

"What do you want me to do, Thomas?"

"You will fight one of my men," Thomas said.

Gruber nodded. "All right."

The first row of spectators had overheard, and Thomas could feel them vibrate with anticipation. He looked to his men, and nodded to Max. The gray-bearded man took a drink of water, removed his sword belt, and began to walk toward Gruber.

Thomas caught Gruber's eye, and as he backed away from the man, he said, "What you do here today will save lives."

Gruber's brows knit together as he began to puzzle

out Thomas's words, but he did not get very far, for without warning, a loud scream erupted from Max and he charged the bigger man. Gruber's eyes went wide and he backpedaled, but Max lunged forward and struck him in the soft hollow beneath his sternum. Gruber tried to cover up but Max shuffled forward, yelling and hitting him in the face and body.

Gruber realized he was having difficulty breathing and his body tensed as he struggled for air. Panic overtook him. Max smashed his nose with the palm of his hand and wrapped the other in his hair. He bent the big man in half and delivered a series of forearm strikes to the back of his head, shouting with every blow. By the time Max brought his knee up into the young man's face, knocking him to the ground, many in the crowd had averted their gaze or closed their eyes to shut out the bloody spectacle.

Gruber hit the ground and a sickly wheeze came from his mouth as his body struggled to get air. Max jumped on top of him and straddled his chest. He rained down more blows until Gruber's thick, flailing arms gave up trying to protect his head and fell limp to the ground.

"Enough," Thomas said.

Max pushed himself off the still form of Gruber and wiped the blood off his hands onto his breeches. He turned his back on the young man and walked slowly over to stand with the others.

Sutter and another man hurried over to where Gruber lay curled up in a ball.

Sutter put one hand on the young man's shoulder and his head snapped up to look at Thomas. "There was no need to hurt this boy," he said.

"There was every need!" Thomas shouted, and all

eyes fell on him.

"Look at him," Thomas said, pointing to Gruber. The man lay on his side, shaking. Soft whimpers came from somewhere beneath the huge arms still covering his head.

"He froze. His body shut down. To be *paralyzed with fear* is not just a saying. It is God's way of sparing us pain when we are about to die. When a lion begins eating you alive, there comes a point when you no longer feel the agony of crunching bones. Your breathing slows, your muscles no longer respond to your commands, and pain is nonexistent. God is merciful. When we are convinced we are about to die, God shuts down our minds and our bodies, so that our passage from this life can be eased."

Thomas drew his new short sword and pointed it at the crowd.

"The first time you meet a fully armored knight in battle, a man trained from birth to kill, you will wish he were just a lion. Your lungs will stop working, and you will freeze. Your muscles will betray you, your mouth will go dry, your sense of smell will play tricks. *But*, if you can manage to stay alive for a few seconds, and remember to breathe, God will know you want to live and he will give you back your body."

As he spoke he bent down and helped Sutter lift Gruber to his feet. The young man's face was swollen and bloodied, but he stood without difficulty. He dabbed at his red-rimmed eyes quickly with the back of his sleeve and looked at his feet as he straightened his clothing.

"There is no shame in being paralyzed with fear, for we all have felt it at one time or another. But we must learn to recognize it when it happens, and realize it is merely God's test."

169

"Today, you will fight your friends and brothers as if your life depended on it. Your goal is to paralyze the man across from you, and if I see any man holding back," Thomas pointed at Max, Ruedi, Urs, and Anton, "his next opponent will be one of my men. We will devote a portion of every day to this exercise until every single one of you has experienced this fear and pushed his way through it."

Thomas re-sheathed his sword. The crowd was silent. Men averted their eyes from Thomas's stare and glanced at each other nervously.

"Today," Thomas said. "I will teach you how to breathe. Tomorrow you will begin training with naked steel. Take your wooden swords home tonight and burn them. You will not be using them again."

***

Seraina stepped over the raised threshold into the keep's kitchen where a score of women and a few younger children were working hard to keep everyone fed.

"Seraina!" Mera called out to her from across a large cauldron of soup, its vapors rising up and mixing with the steam from many other pots to contribute to the mugginess of the warm room. She ran over and grabbed Seraina's hands. Her face was flushed.

"Where does the tally stand now?"

Seraina had been helping Mera and the other women in the kitchen most of the week, but she was so excited she found it impossible to stay indoors for more than an hour at a time. She kept making trips outside to check on how the training was going and to see how many new faces she could spot. She pestered Thomas constantly with questions about his lists.

"Another hundred and fifty have come from Schwyz so far this week," Seraina said. She could not keep her voice from rising. "Thomas says they are past seven hundred men now!"

Mera bounced once and gave Seraina a quick hug. "Noll was right to ask help from Thomas. People trust him and after he stood up to the Habsburgs last fall, there is no one in the valleys who does not know his name. Many more will come. I am sure this is just the beginning."

Despite her earlier doubts, Seraina had to admit that Noll had made the right decision to hand control of the army over to Thomas. Seraina was proud of Noll, for it must have been a hard thing for him to relinquish control like that. But that is what Catalysts did. They made the difficult choices, the ones no one else had the courage, or insight, to make. They were, after all, the agents of change.

Seraina smiled and allowed herself to get caught up in Mera's enthusiasm. Seven hundred men did not make an army, but it was a start. A very good start.

Chapter 17

ABBOT LUDOVICUS SAT in the library of the Einsiedeln monastery. The large space was cold, for it had no hearth and the stone walls did little to keep the winter chill outside. He did not particularly like working in the library. But its three arched windows, with glass of such good quality they were almost clear enough to see through, provided the best light of any room in the monastery.

Beside the Abbot, on the same table, three monks labored silently copying texts. Two of the men's fingers were stained completely black. But one of the three, a younger man whose eyesight had not yet deteriorated, held a half dozen delicate brushes in one multicolored fist. He hunched over his work protectively, like someone trying to start a fire on a windy day. He dipped his brush in a vial of red ink and with almost imperceptible movements, added color to one of a hundred regal-looking characters squeezed into the margins surrounding a page of flowing script. Watching the illustrator at work stiffened Ludovicus's neck and he returned his focus to the ledgers in front of him. Horse revenues were the highest he had ever seen this year, but ale sales were low. Suspiciously low. He would have to talk to the brothers about that.

The timber door squealed on its hinges and a monk entered the room. He stood beside the Abbot and waited to be acknowledged. Ludovicus finished adding the numbers he was working on and then did another calculation before he set down his quill.

"Yes?"

The monk cleared his throat. "There is a Schwyzer at the gate demanding to see you."

"Demanding?" Ludovicus turned back to his ledger and picked up his writing feather. "Send him away. I do not have time."

The monk hesitated. "It is the Hospitaller. The one who brought in the black."

This got the Abbot's attention and he placed the quill back down. With a groan he pushed himself to a standing position, being careful not to jostle the table.

"Tell him I will see him," he said. "Once I have finished lunch."

The Hospitaller was sitting on the snow-covered ground outside the main gate when Ludovicus emerged an hour later. He did not stand when the Abbot approached.

"Nice to see you again, my son. Thomas, was it not?"

"I want to buy him back," Thomas said.

"Who would you like to buy back?"

"My horse."

"Ah, yes of course. Forgive me. My mind gets addled

easily these days. Now, which horse was yours again?"

"You know well enough. His name is Anid."

The Abbot nodded after a moment. "Yes, I remember now. The Egyptian with the infidel name. We call him simply 'the black' these days. But I am afraid he is not for sale."

Thomas lifted a bag he held on his lap. "This will change your mind."

Ludovicus grinned and shook his head, the flesh below his chin swaying with the movement. "Perhaps. If it is filled with gold florins."

He could tell it was not filled with gold simply by the ease with which Thomas lifted it. Thomas lowered the bag back into his lap and undid the length of rope securing it shut. He reached in his hand and pulled a manuscript halfway out.

Ludovicus laughed. "I know to someone like you a book must seem a true treasure. But I have an entire library filled with those."

"Not like this one," Thomas said. He pulled the bag down some more. "Read the title."

Ludovicus stepped closer and put his hands on his knees to lend some support as he bent over. He began reading aloud.

"Malleus Malefic…" his words died out and his eyes widened. *By the Devil's breath, it was Duke Leopold's missing manuscript!* And it was no forgery. He would recognize Bernard's bold script anywhere.

"Let me see that," Ludovicus said reaching for the book.

Thomas pulled it away and closed the sack around it once again. "You bring Anid out and we will talk."

Ludovicus smiled. That book was worth ten infidel

stallions. The Schwyzer was about to receive another lesson in the fine art of commerce, although the Abbot doubted it would make him any wiser. For, like most peasants, the ferryman most likely lacked the capacity to truly learn anything.

They exchanged sack for reins simultaneously, watching one another like stray cats who had accidentally wandered too close. Ludovicus clutched the bag with Leopold's tome in it to his chest, while he watched Thomas step up to the horse and whisper something in his ear. As he patted the stallion's neck with one hand his gaze got caught on the animal's saddle.

"That is not my saddle," Thomas said.

"Our agreement was for a certain horse. I recall no mention of a particular saddle."

A knife appeared in the Hospitaller's hand and Ludovicus took an instinctual step back.

"This one is too long for an Egyptian's back," Thomas said.

He carefully sliced through the leather straps holding the saddle in place and let it and the under-blanket slide to the ground.

"You can keep it."

"Very well," Ludovicus said.

This deal kept getting better by the moment.

"I must say, I will be sorry to see him go. He is a magnificent animal. Does the heathen name you gave him hold any special meaning?"

Thomas raked his fingers through the black's mane to pull out a tangle. He grabbed a handful of hair and swung himself up onto Anid's back in one easy motion. He looked down at the Abbot.

"It means 'stubborn'."

"How fitting," Ludovicus said.

***

Abbot Ludovicus eased open one of the library doors with care. He did not particularly care about disturbing the monks working within, but he did want to avoid having them pester him with questions about how he managed to acquire Leopold's manuscript.

He slid into the room with the bag containing the book clutched beneath one armpit. He wound his way through shelves lined with books and scrolls until he came to a pedestal desk situated in the farthest corner of the library. His hands shaking, he reached into the bag.

What to do, what to do? Sell it back to Leopold outright? That could indeed prove lucrative, *if* Leopold ever paid him. No, it would be safer to approach the Duke and mention he knew someone who had a knack for acquiring lost objects… for a price of course. Playing the third party in this scenario would be much safer. Even being the Abbot of Einsiedeln would not count for much if Leopold got it in his mind that Ludovicus was in possession of something he wanted.

Ludovicus withdrew the manuscript and placed it on the stand before him. Biting his lip, he undid the buckles and flipped open *The Hammer of Witches*.

"No…" He shook his head in disbelief.

The interior parchment had been torn out and replaced with wads of sack cloth.

He scattered the worthless rags to the floor as he dug through them looking for even one page of text. But there was none. He reached the end cover and threw the last bit of stuffing against the wall in a silent fit of rage. He grasped the podium with both hands and ground his teeth together to keep from crying out. He stood like that until his temples throbbed and his jaw muscles ached.

Finally, he opened his cramped fingers and released the podium. He eased the cover of the manuscript shut and refastened its buckles. After a quick look around to make sure no one was near, he climbed a step-stool and shoved the book into the middle of a great wall of manuscripts and scrolls dusty with neglect.

Then he left the library, and this time, he slammed the doors on his way out.

***

As Seraina walked across the courtyard in the darkness to the forge building, snow fell on her in swirling, dry flakes. She had put away her dress for the season, and now wore breeches, lined with rabbit fur, and tucked into high-cut boots that hugged her calves like a second skin. She wore a similar looking fur-lined vest over her white shirt and draped over everything was her simple, greenish-brown cloak. Even though her hood was up, snow worked its way under and melted on her eyelashes, making her squint. She could have easily wiped the moisture away, but her mind was on other things.

The Weave was quiet. Seraina had not even heard a whispering from the wind, never mind a full vision, since she and Thomas had brought back the ancient swords.

Had she made a mistake? Perhaps the swords of her ancestors were not meant to be used for Noll's cause. But the Weave had led her directly to them. It had been so easy and felt so right at the time. Now, she had her doubts.

As she approached Thomas's lean-to she noticed the heavy end-flap was opened part way and a thin tendril of smoke escaped into the night sky. Thomas did not usually have a fire inside, for the forge furnace was always burning and provided more than enough heat through the common wall. But tonight it would be especially warm.

Thinking of the comfortable shelter, with Thomas waiting inside, drove Seraina's self-doubts to the back of her mind. Since returning from their journey together, she had spent most nights there with Thomas. During the day, they went about their respective activities: he training Noll's army, she applying salves and setting bones. Thomas broke the men down and Seraina stood them back up.

It had bothered Seraina at first, seeing her people hurt so often, but when she realized that Thomas felt just as badly, and was only doing everything he could to prepare them, she grew to accept their delicate balancing act. And when she spent each night in Thomas's arms, it felt so perfect, she was sure they were both doing exactly what the Weave had intended.

Seraina had never spent so much time in one man's bed. Sometimes, when she found herself longing for nightfall and wishing the hours of the day away, she wondered if she was falling in love. It was possible, she thought. But she could not be sure, for that was one path she had never traveled.

Seraina removed her cloak and shook off the snow before pushing the flap aside and crawling into the lean-to. Thomas sat at the far end feeding a small fire. He glanced up and smiled nervously for a second, before reaching down and pulling a piece of parchment off a stack beside him. He tossed it into the flames.

"What are you burning?" Seraina asked as she crawled over their bed of fresh spruce boughs and wool blankets.

Thomas held the edge of another page to the flame and watched it catch. "Lies and half-truths," he said.

"Did you write them?"

"No," Thomas said. There was a harsh edge to his voice.

She squinted at the markings on one of the pages. They were meaningless to her and she wondered why anyone would bother with written words when so few could decipher them.

"Then how do you know they are lies?"

Thomas looked at Seraina and his dark eyes softened.

"I just know," he said.

He reached out to touch Seraina's cool cheek and she leaned into the warmth of his hand. He kissed her on the lips and then she slid in close and rested her head on his shoulder. She watched in silence as he resumed feeding sheets of parchment into the fire.

***

Thomas stomped across the snow-covered courtyard to where Urs and Maximilian were talking in raised voices. A crew led by Sutter was cutting down the circle of tall flag poles nearby for firewood to heat the keep. They had all but stopped working, distracted by what looked like a disagreement on its way to becoming a full-blown argument.

As Thomas approached he heard bits of a

conversation that would not be good for morale if the men overheard.

"…shields will keep them alive," Max said.

"They cannot stop dropping their blades as it is. And you want to give them even more to think about?"

"Keep your voices down," Thomas said. "The men are looking."

Urs crossed his arms and grunted. "I will if you can talk some sense into Max."

Thomas took a second to glance over his shoulder at Sutter and his work party. They saw him looking and made a show of picking up their tools and resuming their respective tasks.

"Now, what is the issue here?"

"Max wants to equip the men with shields," Urs said.

"We do not have any shields," Thomas said. "So that is not likely to happen."

"Then we had bloody well better make some, Thomas," Max said, his voice once again escalating. "Or we are going to have a mess of dead farmers on our hands!"

Thomas gave him a moment to calm down. "Out with it. What is on your mind?"

Max paced a quick circle in front of Urs and Thomas and then stopped inches from them. He kept his voice low. "I cannot teach these heavy-handed farm boys and old men how to use a sword. If we had ten years, maybe then we could get half of them to a competent level. But not in a few months. We are wasting our time here."

Thomas looked to Urs. "Do you feel the same way?"

Urs still had his massive forearms crossed over his chest. He looked off to the side.

"It might help if they had the same length and type of

blades. We have piercers practicing slashing techniques and men with single-edged weapons learning back-cuts. There is no consistency, and we simply do not have the time."

They were both right. Thomas had known from the beginning that it would take a miracle to make an effective army out of farmers and shepherds. No matter how hard they worked.

He looked over and caught Sutter staring at him. The innkeeper turned quickly away and resumed chopping at the thick flag pole that a short time ago had displayed the Habsburg pennant. These men of the forests were a sturdy lot, and they had heart. But they would be up against professional soldiers, and even worse, knights. Men who had been swinging swords since childhood, their bodies growing to accommodate the blade. Armor and weapons would become such a natural part of them that they would limp and feel less than whole when unarmed.

You cannot teach a man something in a few months that another has spent his entire life learning.

Sutter stepped back from the tall pole and said something to the Rubin twins who were sawing another log into firewood on the ground nearby. They put down the two-man saw and walked to stand behind Sutter, then Sutter reached out with his hand and gave his pole a gentle touch. Nothing happened at first, but then it began to slowly fall, picking up speed as it went. It bounced once and shook the ground when its full length hit. One of the twins picked up his own ax and began chopping at another pole.

"Axes…" Thomas said. *How much time had he wasted?*

Urs and Max had started arguing with each other

181

again and had not heard him. Thomas left the two men and walked quickly over to the forge. He retrieved Pirmin's blanket-wrapped ax and carried it over to Sutter's work party. With Sutter and the twins looking at him with curiosity, he unwrapped Pirmin's ax.

"What are you going to do with that?" Sutter asked.

"Not me," Thomas said. He tossed it to Sutter, who caught it deftly in one hand. Thomas pointed to a fresh pole, thicker around than a man's waist. "Cut it down."

Sutter shrugged. "I can try. But the length of this handle is going to make it a tad awkward."

Max and Urs came up behind Thomas. "Are you thinking what I think you are?" Max asked.

Thomas did not answer, but his pulse quickened as he watched Sutter step back from the pole and line up his distance. He set his feet and swung.

The ax head went past the pole and the shaft clanged against the wood. The vibrations tore the ax out of Sutter's hands and it fell to the ground. Sutter shook the sting out of his hands and cursed.

Urs and the twins laughed.

"It was a nice idea," Max said, touching Thomas's shoulder.

Thomas held up his hand and pointed at Sutter. The innkeeper had already retrieved the ax and was readjusting his feet.

He swung.

The blade hit the pole with a *whump* that Thomas felt deep in his stomach. He swung again and Thomas felt the force of the blow in his entire body this time. A thick wedge of wood spun off into the air. Sutter kept swinging. He settled into a rhythm, his movements were fluid, graceful, and appeared effortless. Less than a minute later he pushed the pole over.

Thomas had spent all of last summer cutting down trees for his ferry, and he knew it would have taken him five times as long. And he would have been winded, probably exhausted. But Sutter's mouth was not even open. He was about to lay into the next pole when one of the twins convinced him to let him have a go. The result was similar. After a couple of swings to get the new distance figured out, the young man seemed to be finished in seconds. Urs and Max looked at Thomas with wide eyes and their open mouths slowly turned into grins.

"Not bad for an innkeeper," Thomas said.

Urs picked up one of the men's axes off the ground. He fingered the ax's head and held it up to his right eye. "This is good steel," he said. "Who sharpened this blade?"

The twin holding Pirmin's ax replied. "I did, of course. Who else is gonna sharpen my ax for me?"

"Not me, that is for sure," his brother said.

"What do you think Urs?" Thomas asked.

He nodded. "They can use their own heads. All we have to do is fashion handles. They will have to be wood, though. Do not have the time or material to make them out of steel like Pirmin's."

"If we melt down all the old swords, can you make spikes for the ends? Or maybe hooks?" Max asked.

"You know the answer to that," Urs said. "And by the way, you still owe me for shaping the sword that *you* carry."

"Well, you better make damn sure nothing happens to me, then," Max said.

Thomas no longer heard their bickering. He was too

focused on Pirmin's ax.

Chapter 18

IT HAD BEEN A MILD winter, or so everyone kept telling Thomas. But to a man brought up in the scorching sun of the Levant, he thought he would never be warm again. The long winter months had been almost unbearable, and Seraina often joked that he would have perished if she had not taken it upon herself to keep him warm. Although she said it in fun, he suspected it was closer to the truth than she knew.

When the season ended, and the snows receded, he felt reborn. Now that it was spring, he had planned to redirect all efforts from military training to working on the defenses. One cloudless spring morning he made his way to the training ground and was surprised to find it deserted. Puzzled, Thomas sat down, wondering where everyone was. A half hour later Noll walked up with a bucket in hand on his way to the well.

"Morning, ferryman. What are you doing here?"

"What do you think? Where is everyone?"

Noll scratched his head. "What do you mean?"

Thomas waved his arm over the empty training yard. "The men. Did we give them a church day?"

Noll laughed. "You really do not know? I thought we talked about this."

"About what?"

"Planting season. We agreed that we had to allow the men to return to their homes to get their crops in the ground."

"Oh." Thomas did recall something about that a couple months ago.

"Everybody has got to eat," Noll said.

"Well, how many days before they come back?"

"Days? We will be lucky to see any of them for at least a month."

"A month? Leopold could be here in a month!"

Noll shook his head. "No, he will not risk marching an army over passes still wet from the winter thaw. I suspect it will be past midsummer before we have to worry about any Austrians crossing our borders."

An entire month of training lost. This did not bode well, Thomas thought. Last week he had introduced the men to the fighting formations he had decided would serve them best. A variation of a Greek phalanx. He had divided his army into groups of one hundred men and arranged them in squares ten men wide by ten men deep. With their long-handled axes, or halberds as Urs called the new weapons, held before them, the square would prove difficult for cavalry to approach and with training, maneuverable enough to make them almost impossible to outflank.

At least that was his hope. The men had taken to the new squares well enough, but they were still too sluggish when they had to move and reform. It would require many weeks of drilling yet before they could be called proficient.

"What about their families? Perhaps the women and children could see to the farms," Thomas said.

Noll's face went dark. "And just who do you think has been feeding our army, and us, I might add, all winter? You really know nothing about the life of a farming family, do you ferryman? It is thanks to the men's wives and mothers that we have any army at all to train. It is they who have shouldered many times their regular burden so that their husbands and sons can escape farm work for a few hours every day, in the hope that their men learn enough to keep them alive."

Thomas felt suddenly foolish for making the suggestion. "And what about work on the palisades?" he asked.

Noll shrugged. "The roads are still too wet to move the material we salvaged from the fortress. We will not lose any time there."

Thomas knew Noll was right, although, he still could not help thinking they were losing valuable time. But what else could he do? If he did not allow the men to tend to their animals and get their crops planted, the Austrians would be the least of their worries.

"Very well. I need you to get word to the men then. We cannot allow them to forget everything they have learned thus far, so make sure that not one among them uses a short-handled ax for anything. If the job requires an ax, they must use their halberds. Can you do that?"

"Easy enough. Of course that might mean they will be gone for a month and a half then," Noll said, his cocky half-smile turning up the corners of his mouth.

"You look like you are happy about all this," Thomas

said. "Or are you just pretending because you know how much it bothers me to sit idle?"

"I would be lying if I said I was not looking forward to a month's break from your miserable drills. But I, for one, do not plan on sitting idle," Noll said.

Thomas's eyes narrowed. He did not ask for any more information, but Noll offered it freely.

"I will go to Schwyz and help out Sutter around the inn for a while," Noll said. That same half-smile found its way to his face again.

"You mean you aim to help out Mera," Thomas said, crossing his arms. He was not the only one who had noticed Noll and Mera spending a suspicious amount of time together over the winter.

Noll let out a nervous chuckle and looked away. It was the first time Thomas had ever seen him display even a hint of embarrassment.

Noll recovered quickly though, and held up the bucket in his hand. "Sorry, much as I would like to, I cannot stand around all day chatting. Chores to do, and all." He gave Thomas a crisp salute. "See you in a month, Captain."

As Noll walked away, Thomas shouted at his back. "You just tell Sutter that if he decides to chop off your head he has to do it with his long-handled ax."

Noll waved his bucket-holding hand but did not look back. Thomas thought it may well have been the first time he had gotten in the last word with young Arnold Melchthal.

When Thomas arrived back at his lean-to, Seraina was just coming out. Her traveling cloak was fastened about her shoulders and she wore a pack on her back.

"Going somewhere?" he asked.

Seraina offered up a weak smile. "I will be gone for a few days. I was just on my way to say goodbye."

"Would you like company? It seems I have lost most of my army for the next month and suddenly find myself with a lot of time on my hands."

Seraina shook her head quickly. Too quickly, it seemed to Thomas. "No, you should stay here and help Urs finish crafting the rest of the halberds. I will only be gone a few days."

Now Thomas was sure something was wrong. When Seraina first heard about his plan to melt down the swords of her ancestors, she was furious and had threatened to throw them all back in the lake. It had taken Thomas a long time to explain how the swords were not being destroyed, but just reshaped into weapons the men could actually use. After a while, she had accepted his explanation, but was never truly happy about it.

Thomas looked at her, but she avoided his eyes and busied herself adjusting the strap on her pack.

"Seraina."

"Hmm?" She leaned down and retied one of the laces on her boot.

"Look at me. Please."

Her hands stopped moving and she slowly straightened up. She lifted her head. Her green eyes lacked their usual brilliance, and the skin around them was puffy from recent tears.

"I have to go," she said.

"Is it because of your visions?"

She nodded. The movement of her head almost imperceptible. "I cannot remember ever having gone so long without one."

"I wish I could fully understand why they mean so much to you," Thomas said.

She shrugged. "They are as much a part of me as any of my other senses. And without them, I feel like I have hidden a piece of myself, but I cannot remember where."

"Perhaps it is a good omen that you have not had any all winter."

Seraina looked at him and her face turned pale. She shook her head. "No, Thomas. To lose one's sense of the Weave is most definitely not a good sign."

"And how will running away help solve any of this?"

Seraina was quiet for a moment, like she was considering her next words carefully. She placed her hand on Thomas's arm.

"I know this is difficult for you, but please try to understand. Never before have I spent so much time in one place, with so many people I truly care about. I think their voices have played a part in drowning out my visions. If, for a time, I could put some distance—"

Thomas felt a lump form in his throat. "You mean me. I am the cause."

She shook her head and Thomas saw regret flicker behind her eyes. "No, that is not what I meant. Not at all."

"Then stay here. With me."

Thomas held his breath and waited for her answer. But Seraina was not the only one who could see things, and he knew what she would say before the words passed her lips.

"I cannot," she said.

***

Seraina walked all day, setting a furious pace that left her exhausted with the approach of dusk. She built a fire near a small chattering stream and brewed a pot of tea to have with her evening meal. Later, she spread her bedroll in a clearing filled with lillies of the valley. She lay there for some time breathing in the sweet smell of the bell-shaped flowers and listening to the sounds of the forest before sleep came for her.

And with it, finally, a glimpse into the patterns of the Weave.

A mist came and went, leaving her standing in a lightly treed forest. The ground was flat, with warm summer sunlight breaking through the canopy of leaves far overhead. The soil smelled of midsummer, and the leaves rustling against one another in the wind were thick and green. And nestled amongst the sound of wind and leaves, were children's voices.

Screeching with glee, a small boy burst out of a thicket and ran toward Seraina. He had light brown hair and eyes so dark they could have been black. He was no older than four, but his legs seemed long, his little feet uncannily sure-footed as he tottered along the forest floor. A few steps behind, came a girl a couple years older laughing herself breathless. As she ran, her long, light-colored hair flashed in the dappled sunlight and she looked toward Seraina with emerald eyes.

Seraina's heart ached and she felt a cross between pure joy and pride bubble within as she stared at the children running toward her. And then she saw Thomas, and her heart lurched once more. He was older, his hair more gray than brown, but his face was somehow younger, and unlined. The years even seemed to have faded his scar. As he chased the children, *his* children, he wore a smile so beautiful, so filled with happiness, Seraina wanted to cry.

With her vision beginning to cloud with tears, Seraina knelt down and opened her arms to the children. The boy ran past without even glancing at her. The girl too passed her by, but unlike her brother, she gave Seraina a curious look that seemed to ask *Who are you?*

Seraina realized then that the girl's eyes were not emerald green, but a deep blue.

Confused, Seraina whirled in time to see the children jump into the arms of a woman Seraina had never seen before. She was blonde-haired and beautiful. Thomas joined them a second later, and encircled them all in a hug. The children shrieked, Thomas laughed, and the woman smiled.

Seraina had never seen Thomas look so happy. And she had never felt so much pain.

She turned away from the sight, but something forced her to look back. When she did, the woman and children were gone. Only Thomas remained.

He now wore a tunic that looked like it was knitted together from drops of blood. He stared at Seraina and his face creased over with anger. And then he spoke.

"You mean me. I am the cause."

Seraina sat upright in the darkness. The sound of her heart pounding in her ears drowned out the stream and the surrounding forest. She took in a long, deep, shuddering breath.

It was Thomas.

It had always been him. He was the one around which all others pivoted.

He was the Catalyst.

The Weave was reforming around his actions, his decisions. Not Noll's. The changes in the Weave all began when Thomas arrived. Seraina had misread the signs.

Noll *was* special—he was an *Adept*. That is what Seraina had sensed. He could have been a druid, with the proper training, but he was discovered too late in life. However, he was no Catalyst.

How could I have been so blind?

Noll had been locked in a back-and-forth struggle against the Habsburgs for years, with no one able to gain the upper hand. Then Thomas appeared, and within the short span of less than a year, they had driven the Austrians out of Altdorf, seized control of their fortress, and raised an army. When Noll was in charge, men had trickled in to join his cause, but the moment Thomas took control of the Confederate forces, men flocked to his banner. Just as Vercingetorix had united the tribes against the invading armies of Julius Caesar over thirteen hundred years ago. Vercingetorix had seemingly come out of nowhere to terrorize the Roman forces. So too had Thomas.

Though much smaller in scale, the timing was right; the parallels unmistakable. The Weave had returned to them a wayward son of the Helvetii destined to unite the people against an unjust foreign occupation.

Looking back it all made perfect sense. But Seraina had become too close to see it. She had become blind to the Weave's pattern because she stood in its center and was unable to view it in its entirety. She had done the one thing an Eye of the Weave must never do: she had fallen in love with the very Catalyst she had been put in this world to guide. Even worse, she had allowed him to fall in love with her, thereby putting the future of all her people at risk.

Who knew what choices Thomas would make for her alone, with no thought toward the greater pattern? His concern for her would make him deaf to the subtle calls of the Weave and he could miss his one chance to lead his people successfully through a period of great change. Perhaps he already had. Seraina could not know for sure.

Seraina had gained a lover. But in doing so, she may have robbed the Helvetii of their last chance for survival.

Vercingetorix.

Seraina tried to put the name out of her mind, but she could not. Some say it was the Druids who had failed him, as well. After a series of brilliant victories against the Romans, he was ultimately defeated and imprisoned by Caesar. For five long years he was kept in chains and tortured. Once he had been reduced to an empty husk of a man, the greatest general the Celts had ever known was paraded through the streets of Rome and then slowly strangled.

Seraina hugged her knees and dropped her forehead to her arms. The lillies of the valley flooded her nostrils; so wonderful to smell, but deadly poisonous if eaten.

By Ardwynna's Grace, what have I done?

Chapter 19

FRANCO ROEMER ATTEMPTED to blink away the sweat in his eyes but only succeeded in making them burn. His arms were stretched back over his head and his fingers clutched a net stuffed with hay. His farm was located near Landeck, a small Austrian village located on a lush valley floor and squeezed between scenic mountain ranges.

The load was not heavy, balanced as it was over his broad shoulders, but it was awkward. The heat of the midday sun combined with the prickling spear-ends of the dry hay made for an uncomfortable task. But it was the last trip of the day. That thought brought a grin to his bearded face, and the knowledge that his wife was making meat pies for dinner added a bounce to his step.

His destination, a small hay shed on the other side of the road, was within sight. Franco tilted his head and did his best to wipe his brow on his shoulder without upsetting his load. He stepped over the ditch and stumbled onto the road, almost losing everything. He swayed back and forth, lurched forward a few steps, one back, and forward again, all the while talking to himself.

"Whoa now, easy does it. Hang onto her Roemer… there we go." Just when he thought he had it under control, the bottom half slid off his back and the entire thing slipped out of his fingers onto the road.

"Merde!"

He grinned at his sudden exclamation and shook his head. He was not French. But his wife was, and the use of her word told him something that he already knew. She was on his mind, and the sooner he got this task over and done with, the sooner he could be sitting at his table with her and the children.

He rolled his shoulders and rubbed the back of his neck with one hand while he looked down at the net of hay; its golden strands splayed across the road like a maiden's hair removed from the coif. He thought of what his wife would say and laughed out loud, thankful she had not been present to witness his clumsiness. When he had brought her back from Neuchatel six years ago, his family and neighbors had been delighted. To them, all born in the German-speaking Alps surrounding Landeck, she was a foreign exotic. They chatted about her like she was a countess from Paris, even though everyone knew she was merely the daughter of a dairy farmer a few valleys over.

Still, in many ways, she would always be considered an outsider in the close-knit community of Landeck. Franco knew it was sometimes difficult for her, but she was a resilient woman who knew how to stand up for herself. Although the locals soon learned to fear her sharp tongue, Franco knew it could be just as sweet. They had three fine children together, and if Franco had his way he would soon make it four.

He knelt and began re-stuffing hay back into the net. A familiar tremor beneath his feet gave him pause, and he stopped to look up the road. Three horsemen, riding fast, rounded a bend in the road. He shaded his eyes.

Soldiers. The King's Eagles, no less.

Franco stood. As he considered diving off the road, one of the men pointed in his direction. It was too late. They had seen him.

Within seconds they pulled up in front of him, their horses slick with sweat. The animals snorted and their nostrils flared as they took advantage of the break in their pace to refill their lungs. Even before their sergeant spoke, Franco had a bad feeling come over him.

"You there. Tell me of the nearest stream, or trough, where we can water our animals."

Franco wiped his hands on his work-stained breeches. His damp tunic clung to his chest. He looked at the hardened, sour faces of each man in turn and decided he did not want any of them near his home. Or his family. He raised an arm and pointed down the road toward the town of Landeck.

"Landeck is only a few miles ahead," he said.

The sergeant's eyes narrowed. "Our animals are thirsty. Where do you get your water?"

Franco avoided the man's gaze and looked over the horses. They were tall, fine mounts. "They are thirsty, all right. But they will easily make it to the Inn River before they have need to drink. If you rested them, they would even make Salzburg if need be."

"Will they now?"

He nudged his horse forward, forcing Franco to take a step back. The soldier let go of his reins and allowed his horse to graze on the hay at its feet.

"Where is your home, man? These are the King's animals. They have more right to your land, and everything on it, than you do."

Franco made no attempt to answer. He kept his eyes down and focused on the sergeant's horse as it tugged at a few strands of hay caught in the netting.

"I ask again. Where is your farm? And do not lie to me or I will come back and pull out your tongue. And cut that twine, damn you, so my animal can feed properly."

Franco looked up. "Cut it yourself," he said.

A silence settled over the men like a wet blanket. Franco thought even the horse stopped chewing. The sergeant looked at his two men and laughed, but it sounded more like he had a pheasant bone caught in his throat.

Staring at Franco, the sergeant slowly drew his sword. The sound of steel grating against a leather scabbard rang through the air. He let out a tired sigh, like a man who had exhausted all reasonable methods of communication, and leaned forward to place the flat of his blade against Franco's shoulder.

"Take your time and consider your next words carefully," he said.

Franco looked up. He nodded. "In my life, I have suffered many beatings from men better than you," he said. "Mind you, I was a child, then." His lips spread into a grin. "So, I do not expect to get one today."

The sergeant's horse sensed a change come over his master and he jerked his head up from the hay. The soldier pulled back his blade and swung its flat edge at Franco's head. It was a quick, lazy swing, but it was unchecked and had enough force behind it to shatter the bones in a man's face. If it connected.

Franco dropped to the ground on his back, watching as the blade fanned through the air above. The sergeant tried to halt his swing, but he could not prevent the flat of his blade from slapping his mount's neck. The startled horse whinnied in alarm and gave a buck in protest.

Keeping his eyes on the horse's iron-shod hooves, Franco rolled beneath the belly of the animal and came to his knees on the sergeant's opposite side. He knocked the soldier's foot out of its stirrup, stood up, and grabbed the man's tunic. In one fluid motion he pulled the man toward him, hopped high into the air, and swung his leg over the stallion's back to land just behind the saddle.

The sergeant let out a surprised howl as Franco's momentum pulled him half out of the saddle. A lesser horseman would have been on the ground already, but the sergeant was a Royal Eagle, and Franco knew these men could ride. The sergeant dropped his sword and grabbed a fistful of the horse's long mane as he hung off its side and fought to keep his one leg hooked over the saddle. His foot quested blindly for the stirrup so he could push himself back up.

Confused and uncertain about who exactly its master was, the horse began turning in tight circles. Franco changed that by giving him a hard, open-handed slap on its rump.

"Hyah!"

The horse broke into a gallop, leaving the other two soldiers staring wide-mouthed after their commanding officer as he hung onto the side of his mount like a gypsy stunt rider. But his screams and frantic scrambling soon dispelled that illusion and revealed his lack of the wandering folk's talent with horses. The man seated behind him, however, was another matter.

Franco reached over the struggling sergeant, who continued to hold on with only one leg draped over the saddle, and took hold of the reins with one hand. He spun the animal in a tight circle and the sergeant cursed as he slid further over the side.

Franco laughed. He could not help himself. He guided the horse straight and slapped its rump again. It bolted ahead, and then Franco spun him again. As the sergeant's heel slid over the smooth leather of the saddle, Franco helped it along with a flick of his hand. The soldier's feet bounced once and then dragged on the ground, and his fingers gave up their grip on the horse's mane. He fell onto the road amidst a cloud of dust. Franco heard him cough once as he hit and then he began shouting.

"After him! He is stealing my horse!"

Franco hopped forward to sit in the saddle and kicked his horse into a gallop. He leaned low over the stallion's neck and stroked it as he raced down the road.

"He thinks I aim to steal you, old boy," he said into the horse's ear. It twitched at his breath. Franco reined in the horse and guided him with his knees to turn around.

"Steal you," Franco repeated, contempt heavy in his voice. He gave the stallion another pat on his muscular neck. "You are a good mount. Well-trained and strong." He pointed at the two riders coming toward them.

"The dun on the left fears you, my friend. Pay him no heed. But the black stallion thinks you are weak. Together we shall show him the truth." He gave him one last pat and sat up straight in the saddle.

"Hyah!"

The two soldiers shifted in their saddles when they saw Franco turn and begin galloping straight at them. They fumbled to draw their swords and kicked their own mounts into a full charge.

Franco leaned over his horse's neck and took up the slack in the reins. He guided his horse directly at the gap between the two oncoming animals, using pressure from his legs and hands to remind his stallion that Franco was the one in full control. He waited until the exact moment he could clearly see the features of the men's faces and then he wheeled his horse hard to the left, directly at the flank of the dun. The horse's eyes widened and he veered a step away from the charge, cutting off the large black and there was a moment of panic as both men fought to prevent their horses from colliding.

Franco shot past and immediately turned his mount. The soldiers, with their horses once more under control, spun to see Franco already bearing down on them. But it was too late for them to meet him with a charge of their own.

Franco pulled his leg over his horse's head to ride side-saddle a second before his horse rammed into the side of the black with its shoulder. Caught from the side and off balance, the black whinnied in fear as its long legs flipped out from under it and it fell onto its side. Fortunately, his rider had the presence of mind to throw himself clear just before the collision. But Franco could see the man had hit the ground hard and was showing no sign of movement.

The other soldier closed on Franco and stabbed at him with his sword. Franco slid down off his saddle to avoid the blow. Keeping his horse between him and his opponent, he ran a few steps beside it until he could pull himself back up into the saddle in safety. He turned his horse and charged the man's weak side. He was right handed and once inside the arc of his sword, the soldier's options were limited.

Franco caught the soldier's arm as he attempted a backhanded slash. He struck him in the face and then looped his arm over the man's elbow. Then, using both his arms in a scissors motion, he jerked the soldier's arm back into a painful shoulder lock. The Eagle screeched as Franco dragged him out of the saddle and threw him to the ground.

Franco lifted his leg over his horse's head and slid off the saddle. He picked up the man's sword and pressed it into the hollow of his throat. The King's messenger clutched his shoulder, his eyes wet with pain.

"Who are you?" he asked, grimacing.

Franco saw movement out of the corner of his eye, and he turned his head but kept the sword at the man's neck. The sergeant limped slowly toward them. His sword was in its scabbard and one hand seemed to be favoring the small of his back.

"Fool," he said. "Who do you think he is?"

He paused to work up a mouthful of phlegm, then spit it onto the road. Franco noticed it was tinted with blood. The sergeant looked at him and the muscles around one of his eyes twitched.

"This here is Franco Roemer. Commander of the Stormriders."

He glanced over to where the other soldier was trying to catch a fidgety black stallion.

"The very man we have been sent to find."

***

Leopold leaned back in his chair and dropped the messenger's parchment onto his desk. Even though he was alone, he suppressed the smile he felt building behind his lips.

He had feared the worst when a King's Eagle rode into Habsburg less than an hour before. He had a premonition that his brother had been captured by Louis. Or worse. But this... he had not dared dream it was possible.

"Husband? Am I intruding?" Lady Catherine stood in the door, her hands wringing one another in front of her. She too was pleased with something, but she was not as adept as Leopold at hiding it.

"Never, my dear," Leopold said. "Come in, come in. But close the door behind you." He suddenly felt generous.

Her brow creased and she did as he asked. She took a seat across from him, folding her hands in her lap. "You look happy. As happy as I have ever seen you I dare say."

Leopold could no longer keep the grin from his face. "Can I not hide anything from you?"

"Not a thing," she said. "Now will you let me know what pleases you so, or shall I tell you my own news?"

Leopold was glad she was here. The news he had received was simply too good to keep to himself any longer.

"I have received word from my brother," he said.

Catherine's gloved hand flew to cover her mouth. She spoke through it. "Has he defeated the Bavarian already?"

"Better, my sweet. He is sending me the Sturmritter. He has commanded their captain, Franco Roemer, to gather his knights and ride to our aid as soon as possible."

"Wonderful!"

Leopold put his hands behind his head and looked at the carved ceiling.

"I did not think it possible with him being at war. But apparently he sent Roemer and his men home for a break to get some rest before a major offensive he is planning. He suggested I use them when I invade the forest regions as a way to provide the men with a little exercise."

"Your brother is wise. Men like those of the Stormriders are not well suited to leisure. Did you know I met Captain Roemer once?" There was open admiration in her voice.

"I did not know that," Leopold said. A pang of jealousy shot through him and it took a moment for him to recognize the strange sensation for what it was. "When exactly was that?"

"It was before he had been promoted to Captain. He stayed with us for a half year and was swordmaster to my cousins..." Her voice trailed off and she had a far away look in her eyes.

"And what impression did he make?"

"Oh, a very good one," she said. "Sir Roemer is a true gentleman," she quickly added.

"He is a killer. And a very good one. There is no man more capable with a lance in all of Christendom. I hear he once skewered three men with a single charge. Spitted them all like pigs."

Catherine looked away and laced her fingers together. "Well, he was always a polite, well-mannered nobleman when I saw him," she said.

"He was the seventh child of a minor noble in Landeck. We would not even know the Roemer name if

Franco had not distinguished himself so on the battlefield. Some say his family's blood is more gypsy than blue."

"That might explain his eyes," Catherine said, and then bit her lip when Leopold looked at her.

"You had some news as well?"

Catherine nodded, and her face lit up. "I too received a message today. From my father."

"Oh?"

Catherine glided over to the door and threw it open. A man wearing the livery of Savoy stepped through. He kept his eyes straight ahead and his chin up. He exuded the haughtiness Leopold had come to associate with his wife's duchy.

Today, however, Leopold hardly noticed, for his eyes were drawn to the large strongbox the servant carried. He placed it on Leopold's desk and lifted the lid. It was filled to overflowing with gold florins.

"My father has agreed to finance your campaign to take back the Gotthard Pass from those treacherous mountain people," Catherine said, her excitement creeping to a higher level with every word.

Leopold stared at the box. And then at Catherine. She beamed like an angel. He looked back at the gold to make sure he had not imagined any of it. What a miraculous turn of events. First, the Sturmritter were his to command. And now this. He looked to the ceiling and searched for the right words to express his gratitude.

"You are wrong my dear," he finally said. "Your father has agreed to finance *our* campaign. Yours and mine."

The way her face glowed told Leopold he had found them.

Chapter 20

MIDSUMMER CAME AND went, and the Altdorf fortress was completely dismantled. Thomas moved his army's base to Schwyz in early fall, since the network of forts and palisade walls had been completed and permanently manned with lookouts for some time. He set up his tent and command center behind the walls of the largest one, which guarded the main road leading south from Austrian lands.

The Confederate army numbered some eleven hundred men, but Noll's resources told them Leopold had assembled over eight thousand. It was what Thomas had expected, but when Noll heard the news, he insisted on making the rounds personally to Zurich, Berne, and Lucerne to find out where the additional men were that they had promised. He had been gone more than a week, and Thomas found himself wishing he had not let him go. The Habsburgs controlled all the main roads now, and travel, even for someone like Noll, was exceptionally dangerous.

One day, while doing an inspection round of the forts, Thomas stopped by Sutter's inn. He knew the innkeeper himself would not be there, for he was on duty at the main palisade walls. But that did not bother him, for it was Sutter's daughter, Mera, that Thomas had come hoping to see.

She greeted him outside with a hug and ushered him through the back door into the kitchen. Before he could protest, a plate of cheese and thinly sliced meats appeared in front of him.

"Have you heard from Noll?" She asked.

Thomas shook his head. "Nothing yet. But I am sure he will be along any time now."

She forced a smile and nodded. "How is my father doing? Have you made a soldier out of him yet?"

"He has become quite the natural leader. The men have taken to calling him 'the Baron'."

Mera laughed. "That is the perfect name for him, I can tell you that much."

Her laughter died off when she noticed Thomas looking distractedly around the room.

"What is it, Thomas?"

He pushed up one of his shirtsleeves and then pulled it down again. "I was wondering… if you had seen, or heard from, Seraina, as of late."

"Oh, Thomas." A sad smile crossed her lips. "Not since you asked me last. Three weeks ago she stopped by for a few minutes to drop off some salves and ointments for the men, but I have not seen her since."

Thomas nodded, and studied the larder shelves.

"I am sure she will be back before you know it though. This is not the first time Seraina has disappeared. She just needs her time alone, on occasion."

Thomas looked at Mera and could tell by her eyes that she was just trying to be kind. She had no idea when, or if, Seraina would ever be back.

Thomas left Sutter's inn at dusk. He walked Anid around the farmers' fields and took the forest path that lead to the west road. As Anid stepped out of the woods onto the wider road, he whinnied and his ears perked up. Ten feet away, sitting on a rotten log with his chin in his hands, was Noll. He looked up and then slowly stood as Thomas approached. His boots and the hem of his cloak were covered in dried mud, and his normally clean-shaven face showed a growth of several days. There were dark circles under his eyes, and sweat stains covered his chest.

"I just came from the inn," Thomas said.

"I know. I saw your horse there." Noll's voice rasped as he spoke. "Any word on Seraina?"

Thomas shook his head.

"Why did you not come in? Mera has been worried about you."

"I have news, Thomas. Bad news. And it is not something I wish to burden Mera with."

Thomas slid down out of the saddle. He pulled out his water skin and tossed it to Noll.

"Drink some of that, first. I do not want you dying halfway through."

Noll tipped the skin to his lips with both hands. When the water flow began to slow down, he squeezed it with one hand, drank some more, and then sprayed his face off with the remainder. He lowered the depleted skin and looked at Thomas.

"They are not coming," he said.

"Which ones?"

"Zurich, Berne, Lucerne. All of them. None of them. Zurich and Berne I can understand. Leopold has no doubt made the guilds better offers. But Lucerne? They are right across the lake from us. We share the same waters! Yet they believe they can distance themselves from this? Are they mad?"

He shook his head and sat back down on the decaying log.

"There must be someone else," Thomas said.

Noll shook his head. "Even if there were, Leopold has all the roads and passes blockaded. No one can get through to us now. And it gets worse."

"How?"

"Have you heard of the Sturmritter?"

"I have," Thomas said.

"They just rode into Habsburg three days ago."

Both men went silent. Thomas had been hoping for another thousand men, for that would have nearly doubled their forces. Noll's news, however, did not come as a complete surprise. Stauffacher and Furst had been in negotiations for months now with the other cities. If they had truly intended to make a stand with Schwyz, Uri, and Unterwalden, they would have sent men by now.

Thomas reached into his saddlebag and pulled out some cheese Mera had wrapped in a piece of cloth for him. He carried it over and sat down next to Noll.

"The Sturmritter are men, just like the rest of us," Thomas said, handing the cheese over to Noll.

Noll nodded a 'thanks'. He unwrapped the cheese, stuffed a good portion of it into his mouth, and mumbled around it. "So where the hell is Leopold anyways? He should have been here last month. Why does he delay?"

Thomas shrugged. "Could be waiting for the final harvest to come in. That is what I would do."

"Well, most of it is in. The first snows could be here any day."

"Then I suppose it is time we made our final preparations," Thomas said. He patted Noll on the shoulder and stood back up. "See you at the wall."

"What, no offer to give me a ride?"

Thomas shook his head. "You are on your way to Sutter's. You and I both know that. If Leopold attacks before you get back, I promise to not let Matthias kill him before you show up."

"You are one mad ferryman, you know that?"

"I have had no ferry for a very long time, thanks in no small part to you. So why do you insist on calling me that?"

Noll grinned. "Because it makes you angry. And the angrier you get the better chance I think we have," Noll said.

Chapter 21

LEOPOLD HAD TO ADMIT Bernard was skilled at much more than just the use of a quill. Sculpting also seemed to be no small part of his repertoire.

Leopold's war council gathered around the wide table built especially for the detailed clay landscape that Leopold's chief scribe had built. Bernard had been out of sorts ever since the manuscript under his care had been lost when Leopold and Gissler were ambushed by Thomas Schwyzer, so when his lord told him he needed a very detailed map of the areas from Zug to Schwyz, Bernard had thrown himself wholeheartedly into the project. The result was a precise model of the two towns, complete with little wooden houses and stables. The surrounding countryside was also recreated from sculptor's clay, painted in life-like colors and complete with forests, mountains, and rivers.

It was so realistic, Leopold had trouble keeping his captains focused on the battle plans. The Habsburg Fool delighted in touching lakes and trees and then would hold up his finger for the dozen or so men in the room to inspect. And beside him, Landenberg also seemed to be infatuated with the model. He kept trying to peer inside the small windows of the buildings of Zug.

"Landenberg? Did you hear what I said?"

The Vogt straightened up. "Yes, of course, my lord. We overnight in Zug and then assemble at dawn."

Captain Roemer spoke up. "And from there we march straight on to Schwyz?"

Leopold nodded. "Most of us. Count Henri?"

Henri of Hunenberg had been quiet all night, Leopold thought. *Perhaps he suspected something like this was coming.*

"Yes my lord?"

"I intend to take the fight to them on two fronts. You will take your men over this pass," Leopold traced a line with his stick over the landscape, "and attack this village in Obwalden. The rest of us will take Schwyz."

The Count's eyes clouded over and he crossed his arms. He kept his eyes locked on the model and said nothing.

"And remember. Ensure every one of your soldiers has enough collars and rope to secure at least three captives. If any man comes back with fewer than that, he will forfeit two months of his salarium. Is that understood?"

There was some murmuring at that, as to be expected, but Leopold did not care at this point.

"Good. Then, if there are no questions I propose we adjou—"

The Fool's hand shot into the air and waved back and forth inches from Leopold's nose. "My lord Duke! I have a thought!"

Some of the men chuckled, a few rolled their eyes. But Leopold was feeling especially magnanimous at the moment. This night had been a year in the making. *Why not end the evening on a ridiculous note for the sake of morale?*

"You have something to add?"

The Fool stood upright and decided that was not enough. He hopped up onto a chair and turned a full circle, looking at every man in the room as he did so. There were more than a few smiles as the men tried to guess what the jester was up to.

"You have all given wise council tonight," the Fool began, his voice deep and solemn. "Very wise council indeed, on how to get into the lands of the mountain people. But my question is…"

He paused and turned a slow circle again on his chair, pointing at each man in turn.

"My question is… how do you intend to get out?"

The room was quiet for more than a few seconds, as men waited expectantly for more. But when it finally became clear that the Fool had nothing further to add, someone began laughing. Others soon joined in, and eventually everyone had at least a smile on his face.

Everyone except Count Henri of Hunenberg, and ironically, the Fool himself.

Leopold dismissed the marshals and lords and they wasted no time in retiring to their appointed rooms within Habsburg Castle. Within minutes, only Leopold and Klaus remained in the council room.

"You disapprove of my plan. I can see that. Admit it. Tell me what is on your mind, Klaus."

"You split our forces by sending Count Henri to attack from the Brunig Pass."

He paused, and would have been content to leave it at that, but Leopold waved for him to continue. So Klaus grunted, and pushed on. "He does not command many soldiers. I agree. But the ones he has are good fighting men, and well disciplined. He has got men that even fought against the heathen of Outremer. Next to the Sturmritter, they are our best soldiers. I would rather it be Henri's men at my back than those riffraff from Kyburg and Toggenburg."

Why Klaus, what an impassioned speech. For you. The last time I heard you string so many words together, I was seven, and you had just caught me sticking a handful of crushed glass under father's saddle blanket.

"Good. If even you, a man who has been at my side for my entire life, cannot see what I am up to then chances are no one else does either," Leopold said.

Klaus squinted and the flesh of his eyelids bunched up, making his eyeballs all but disappear. Leopold could not help thinking how it made him look like a newborn babe. Albeit, a large, hairy one with very little patience for fast-talking princes.

"You are right, of course," Leopold said. "Henri's men are excellent. It is Henri himself I find fault with. You see, I simply do not trust that he will do what I tell him. He has a perverse sense of honor and I think it could come to haunt him someday."

"If you keep sending everyone away you do not trust, your army is going to get very small, very fast," Klaus said.

Leopold chuckled. "Truer words were never spoken. Fortunately, we only need to keep this force together until the day after tomorrow."

"Yes, my lord. And I for one will not be sad to see it

disband."

"Oh, come now, Klaus. Enjoy it while you can. Did you find a suitable gathering ground south of Zug?"

"Aye, my lord. A farmer's field, about an hour south of the town. From there we will be able to form up into ranks and march into Schwyz."

"Does this farmer know what we intend to use his land for?"

"Damn rights. My lord."

"Excellent," Leopold said.

"And I told him to not be hiding any of his cows either, because I counted them when I was there."

"You need not have done that," Leopold said.

"The men will be hungry. We may need them all," Klaus said.

"Yes, yes. I realize that. But what I mean is, we will never be at that farmer's field."

A grin spread across Leopold's thin lips. He waited for Klaus to speak, but the old soldier just stood there, his eyeballs retreating further and further into the back of his head.

"Do you know why we are not going to use that field?" Leopold asked.

"It was a ruse. You wanted a mouthy farmer to tell everyone that we would be there."

"Precisely."

"But we will not be there," Klaus said.

"You are much better at this than you look."

Leopold walked back to the clay model of the lands surrounding Schwyz. He pointed to the road running south from Zug all the way to the village of Schwyz.

"As far as the farmer knows, and I am sure far more people are aware of it by now, our army will spend the night in Zug. Then, early the next morning we set out for Schwyz. We stop at this cooperative peasant's farm, break our fast, check equipment, form up into ranks and then charge the Schwyzers' little mud walls they have erected to protect their precious lands. Correct?"

"That is… or… was the plan, my lord?" Leopold gave Klaus a moment. It was not that he thought him to be a stupid man. Far from it. Leopold had been witness to, and the benefactor of, some very well thought out plans that the old veteran had concocted entirely on his own. But he was a plodder, and like most plodders, did not handle change well.

When Leopold saw the light flicker in Klaus's eyes, he continued.

"When we leave Zug, we will not go south. We will go east until we reach the far side of Lake Aegeri. Then we turn south, and take the paths below Morgarten."

"Morgarten?"

Leopold nodded. "The Schwyzers have been busy little builders, stacking up their wooden palisades and mud walls. They have managed to create a meager line of defenses that stretches from the Great Lake all the way to the western shore of Lake Aegeri. But that is where it ends."

"Bah, we would only lose a few men taking those stick walls," Klaus said. He had seen some of them and was not impressed.

"But why lose any? For every Austrian knight that falls off his horse and dies, years from now, there will be some ragged child sitting on the mud floor of his hut, listening to his grandfather regale him with tales of how he killed an honest to god nobleman."

Klaus shrugged. He saw the sense in Leopold's plan,

but clearly did not care what tales might be told after he was gone.

"But no one is to know any part of this plan until we are on the road and headed east out of Zug. Is that understood?"

"Yes, my lord."

It was simplicity in action, really. A scheme as old as violence itself. Make your opponent look somewhere and then run around behind him and slit his throat.

Leopold felt his eyes growing heavy. He sensed he would sleep well tonight.

***

He waited a full hour after he heard the men leave and the massive door slam shut. He had almost dozed off twice, but had kept from doing so by biting his cheek. The pain reminded him of what was at stake.

He knew he was granted certain liberties and privileges because of who he was, and who his allies were. But he was under no illusion that any of that would save him from Leopold's wrath. The Duke would not let all his preparation go to waste. If he knew someone other than his trusted Klaus had even an inkling as to what he planned, that man would not see another sunrise.

So, he breathed, and waited, and ordered his limbs to stop cramping. The cold from the flagstones pressing up against his back had stopped bothering him long ago. When he finally tested his muscles by rolling onto his side, blood seeped into all the unused parts of his body.

It burned. He gritted his teeth and welcomed the discomfort, for it meant he was alive. This too reminded him of what was at risk.

When he was ready, he flipped the skirting of the strategy table aside and rolled out from under it. In the darkness, he could still make out the shapes of clay mountains and hills upon the miniature landscape. One mound, in particular, stood out.

Morgarten.

As quietly as he could he walked to the door and, holding his breath, he eased it open enough to glimpse into the lighted hallway. Seeing no one, he slipped from the room.

The entire time, the bells on his shoes made not a sound.

***

Sir Henri of Hunenberg sat up in his bed. It was blacker than a pit of tar in his room, but he had no trouble wrapping his fingers around the dagger handle hanging off one bed post. He withdrew the blade silently and stared into the darkness.

A soft rapping came once again from the door.

Someone was… knocking? At this hour?

The tapping came again. This time it had a playful rhythm to it. Henri growled and threw back his blankets. He fumbled in the dark for his night robe. He tied it about his waist, thrust the dagger through his belt, and then made his way to the hearth. He blew a small flame back to life, enough to light a candle, and then went to the door. He unlatched it and eased it open partway, keeping his foot lodged firmly behind its corner. He had to hold his own candle up to see who was there, for the hallway was shrouded in darkness and his late night visitor carried no light of his own.

"You? I do not find this entertaining. What—"

The Habsburg Fool held his finger to his lips. His white painted face stood out in the flickering candlelight like that of a ghost. "Night is the best time to visit a Knight, my lord. May I come in?" His voice was little more than a whisper.

"What do you want?"

"Oh, I cannot tell you all of that." The little man leaned against the door jamb and traced curved outlines with his finger onto the heavy wooden door. "But I can tell you more than enough to make you happy you invited me into your room." He began humming quietly to himself, turning his attention back to the door and the finger artwork that only he could see.

Henri cursed, threw back the door, and beckoned the simple man inside.

Chapter 22

SERAINA STOOD AT the forest's edge, on the outskirts of Zug, and gazed out over a vast sea of soldiers erecting thousands of tents. Darkness was less than an hour away, so there was an urgency to their activities that gave the scene a frantic, disorganized appearance. She could have been standing right in their midst, instead of hidden in the shadows of a giant oak, and no one would have noticed her.

Above the shouts of men and the sounds of horses, far away, in the mountains above and to the south, she could hear the deep notes of alphorns as Noll's lookouts relayed messages from peak to peak. She wondered how long it would take for Thomas to hear the same notes she was listening to right now. How many horns would it take to pass on the alarm?

Seraina sensed something behind her. Relief and anger flowed through her, competing to see which would overcome the other.

"Hello Gildas."

Seraina did not turn around, but she heard the old druid exhale. After a moment he came to stand with her and share in the shadows of her tree. He wore a nondescript gray cloak, not his usual white one. It allowed him to blend into his surroundings more easily, Seraina thought, but it had not hidden him from her.

"There was a time when I could surprise you whenever I wished," Gildas said.

"And there was a time when I knew I could trust you to tell me the truth," Seraina said. She looked at her mentor, but he turned away from her and stared at the army setting up camp in the distance.

"Tell me you did not know Thomas was the Catalyst," Seraina said. She had meant it to come out sharp and scolding, but instead, to her ears, she sounded like a little girl. Still, it seemed to have the desired effect, for Gildas flinched at her words, and when he looked at her, his eyes overflowed with regret.

"I suspected, my child. Nothing more."

"Why did you not tell me? You should have said something before… before…"

Gildas took one of her hands in both of his and turned to face her. "I could not, Seraina. For I could have just as easily been wrong and *you* could have been right. I wanted to say something, I truly did. But to do so could have caused an unraveling of the Weave, with dire consequences neither one of us could have predicted."

"And what of this?" Seraina pointed to the Habsburg army, thousands of men strong, spreading out before them as they spoke. Cooking fires were beginning to pop up like fireflies in the night. "Perhaps this is one of the dire consequences of which you speak."

She looked at Gildas. "This could be a war of my

221

own creation. What if this is not the time for the Helvetii to fight back? Perhaps my people were meant to go into hiding and wait for another hundred years. If I have misread the Weave, thousands will die tomorrow and their blood will all be on my hands."

Seraina looked out at the fires again and tears broke free from both of her eyes. "I could not live with that," she said.

Gildas stepped in and put his arm around her shoulders.

"I too have misread the Weave, and you will again before this life is finished. No one can be expected to see all Her patterns, but do not be so quick to doubt your abilities. And besides. An occasional misreading of the Weave can have wonderful results."

He turned her head toward him and wiped her tears with his finger. "I think Thomas Schwyzer, Catalyst or not, would agree with me on that one."

Seraina rapped the old druid in the chest with the back of her hand. "How can you joke at a time like this?"

"Jokes should be strictly reserved for times like these," Gildas said, smiling. "Now, come here. Give an old man a hug and then we had best be moving on. Time is short."

Seraina made a show of resisting, but truth be told, there was nothing she wanted more. She would have stayed wrapped in the warmth of the old druid's arms for much longer, but he finally broke the embrace.

"It is time, Seraina."

"To the Mythen, then," she said, wiping her eyes once more.

Gildas nodded. "You go ahead. Someone must see that Thomas knows Leopold has reached Zug. I will stop by to warn him and then meet you on the mountain."

Seraina frowned. "I heard the alphorns, so I am sure they know by now."

Gildas nodded, knowingly. "You are most likely right. But since it is only an hour out of my way, I would like to make sure. Now go. The others will be waiting."

Chapter 23

IT WAS MID-AFTERNOON and Thomas was in his tent when the alphorns began. Seconds later, Noll ducked his head inside.

"You hear them?" Noll asked.

"How could I not," Thomas said. "What do they mean?"

"Leopold has reached Zug with a force eight thousand strong. Three thousand of them mounted."

Thomas nodded. It was no worse than they had been expecting. The Confederate forces numbered just over eleven hundred, with no cavalry to speak of. But Thomas had confidence in their defenses. The men had worked tirelessly at their drills. They would make Leopold's army bleed, of that he had no doubt. Whether or not it would be enough, that was another question.

An alphorn sounded again in the distance, and Noll looked in its direction.

"What do we do?"

"Make our rounds as usual. Check on the men, then

eat a good meal and go to bed as early as possible."

"That is it?"

Thomas shrugged. "We have done all we can. The waiting is over. We are in God's hands now."

It was an hour past midnight when one of the Rubin brothers woke Thomas. He spoke in an urgent whisper.

"Sir, you should come to the front wall."

He could not tell whether it was Sepp or Marti, but Thomas knew neither one of them excited easily. He shrugged off his blanket and convinced his sleep-stiffened joints to get him on his feet. Without pressing the young man for further details, he followed him to the front gate of the wooden palisade.

Ruedi, Anton, and the other Rubin boy were already there, standing on the narrow ledge built halfway up the wall. They all stared at something in the darkness beyond. Thomas glanced at the brother walking beside him, and again at the one on the wall. He still had no idea who was who. When Anton saw Thomas approach, he hopped off the ledge to give Thomas room to climb up.

"What is it?" Thomas asked, as he stepped up the three split-log stairs to the ledge.

"A rider," Anton said from below. "Probably their advance scout come to survey the defenses."

"Evening, Cap'n," Ruedi said as Thomas slid in between him and the Rubin boy. The bearded man had rested his war bow between two of the sharpened poles used to build the palisade. The string was drawn, and a black bolt sat in its groove, waiting to be unleashed. Ruedi's fingers tapped the stock of the weapon tenderly. "Just say the word, and we can all go back to sleep."

At first, Thomas saw nothing. There was only a sliver

of moonlight, but someone had already extinguished the nearby torches on their side of the wall, so he was able to separate out the shape of a man and horse from the darkness of the forest.

"He is too far out," Thomas said. "What is your count?"

Ruedi nodded. "The man knows his ranges. But I figure I could find him with six of every ten bolts. Nine of ten if you just want the horse."

Thomas shook his head. "Hold, for now." *Six of ten* was a very long distance in Ruedi's measuring scale. The scout would not get much useful information from that far out. Especially, on a dark night such as this.

"How long has he been there?"

Ruedi nodded toward the brother. "He spotted him first. Rubin?"

Apparently, Ruedi still could not tell the brothers apart either.

"At least fifteen minutes, by now," the boy said.

"Any sign of a flag? Maybe he has come to offer terms," Anton said.

Thomas was just about to say that he would not be accepting any terms offered in the cover of darkness by Leopold, when Ruedi nudged his elbow and pointed at the shadow on the road.

"Here we go," Ruedi said.

The figure began walking his horse toward them, its hooves echoed off the hard packed road, carrying far in the stillness of the night. He nudged his horse into a trot, and the echoes sounded like a drum roll.

"That is no messenger pony," Ruedi said. "The man rides a destrier." He hefted his crossbow and placed it against his shoulder.

The black figure's horse broke into a gallop and both horse and rider began to emerge from the night and take form. He sits the saddle well, Thomas thought, just as the man let go of his horse's reins and raised a crossbow to his shoulder.

"He is attacking!" the Rubin boy said.

Ruedi sighted down the length of his war bow, following the motion of the man and horse barreling toward them. They were almost within normal crossbow range now. Thomas scoured the woods, looking for others. But there was no one. What could he possibly hope to accomplish by attacking the palisade single-handedly? A young knight trying to make a name for himself? Thomas had certainly seen men do madder things.

"Cap'n…?"

Just as he was about to tell Ruedi to put him down, Thomas realized the man was not wearing armor. There was no glint of metal anywhere on him, and he shifted around much too easily on top of his war horse.

"Hold," Thomas said. "Get your head down, Rubin." He decided he liked Ruedi's efficient naming method for the brothers. The boy crouched over, but kept one eye high enough to see above the wall.

Still at full gallop, the attacker sighted down his crossbow, and, raising himself slightly in his stirrups to steady his aim, fired. The bolt thudded into the main gate of the palisade, and sent vibrations through the wood to where they stood. As soon as he let the shot go, he wheeled his charger around and galloped back into the night. Like the man, the hoof beats soon receded beyond the senses of everyone standing at the wall.

"Rubin," Thomas said. "Get me that bolt."

The boy did not move, but kept staring over the wall into the darkness. Thomas was about to tell him again, when he heard someone throw off the crossbar on the gate and pull it open. He leaned out over the wall and saw the other Rubin boy digging at the head of the crossbow bolt with his knife.

Maybe tomorrow he would figure out a way to distinguish between the two of them, but for now, Ruedi's system seemed to be working fine.

Seconds later, he came running back with the bolt in hand. Thomas jumped down and took it from him, then he and Anton looked it over in the light of a nearby torch.

"You think it might be a whistler?" Anton asked.

Thomas nodded, and held the bolt up to the light. "One that failed to whistle. Maybe a hastily constructed one." He found what he was looking for; he twisted the iron point and the head came off. The shaft of the bolt was hollow, and inside was a piece of parchment. He fished it out carefully with the tip of his dagger and held it under the torch. Now Ruedi and the two brothers also crowded around, craning their necks to get a better look.

The characters were slanted, the penmanship unskilled. Much like his own, really. It took him a couple of tries to fully understand what it meant. And when he finally did discern its meaning, he prayed he was wrong.

By the blood of Mary.

"What does it say?" Anton asked.

"Rubin! Bring Noll here. Now."

The two brothers looked at each other. "Which one of us, Sir?"

"Both! Carry him here if you must, but bring him now."

While he waited for Noll to show up, Thomas began arranging several lanterns and torches so that they bathed a wide circle of dirt in light.

"Someone get me another—"

"Lantern?" Gildas said. He held one out to Thomas on the end of his walking stick. "Will this one do?"

Thomas took a step back, and blinked. "Gildas? Where did you come from?" He immediately cast his eyes over the area behind the old man.

"She is not there, Thomas Schwyzer. You might as well stop looking."

Thomas was about to ask who he meant, but something in the old man's eyes would not let the words come out.

"Where is she?" Thomas asked.

"Safe. Is that not enough?"

A thousand questions burned in his mind, but they would have to wait. For just then the boys came back with a puffy-eyed Noll Melchthal lagging behind.

"Sleep did not find me easily, this day, ferryman. But I was finally dreaming of soft hands and the most beautiful woman I have ever seen, and the next thing I know, Sepp and Marti's callused paws are shaking me like an apple tree."

Noll looked around and seemed to notice Gildas for the first time. "Who is the old fellow?"

"Some names are worth knowing, Arnold Melchthal. But mine is not one of those," Gildas said.

Noll glanced at Thomas.

"He is right. Ignore him for the time being. We have more important things to worry about," Thomas said.

Gildas nodded. "Agreed. Now, read us the message."

With everyone gathered around, Thomas unrolled the small parchment. "First, let me say that I believe this to come from a man well-known to all of us that served in Outremer. And while we have not always seen eye to eye in the past, I trust that he would not lead us astray. We must heed his words."

"Someone from the Levant? Who?" Anton asked.

"Sir Henri of Hunenberg," Thomas said.

Ruedi let out a whistle. "Henri? Is he still alive?"

Noll scrubbed his face with his hands. "Very much alive. And he rides against us under Leopold's banner. Go on. Read the note. Then we can decide whether or not to trust the man."

"It is direct and wastes no time, much like the man himself," Thomas said. He read it out loud then, though he had read it so many times to himself already, that he could have recited it from memory.

Thomas,
Beware the paths of Morgarten.
H.H.

Thomas looked first at Noll and then at Gildas. Noll's face was suddenly pale. Gildas stared at the moon and shook his head.

"Where *exactly* is Morgarten?" Thomas asked them both.

Noll cursed, and since he seemed to be the first to recover, Thomas turned to him. "It is a mountain range. Far to the east."

Thomas held out a long stick and pointed at the ground bathed in the orange light of lanterns. "Draw it," he said. "Mountains, roads, rivers, hills, and forests. I need to know everything."

Noll snatched the stick from Thomas's hand. "And you will. I may not understand the scrawl of monks, but I can read the lay of the land better than a man's face."

I believe you can. But whether or not it will be of any use, only God can decide.

The more Noll scratched in the dirt, the clearer Leopold's plan of attack became.

"Where is the last of our palisades?" Thomas asked.

"Here," Noll said, drawing an 'X'. "Just west of Lake Aegeri. To the east, on the other side of the lake, stands Morgarten. Leopold will march his army south, between Morgarten and Lake Aegeri. Here," Noll put his stick in an area south of the lake, "lies the town of Sattel. Just before Sattel the trees thin out and the land opens up. It would be the perfect location for Leopold to spread out his men and form up ranks."

Anton shook his head more with every scratch of Noll's stick. "From there he will be able to storm Schwyz, while bypassing every one of our defenses." A knife found its way into Anton's hand and he threw it at the palisade wall. It hit with a thump and quivered in the wood. "All these walls we spent months building, all our drills—useless."

Ruedi shrugged. "Gave us something to do, I suppose. Better than standing around waiting."

Noll pointed at the southern shore of the lake. "Normally, this area would be too marshy to march an army through—," he said.

"But not in late fall," Thomas said, finishing Noll's thought. Leopold had put off his attack until now because he had been purposely stalling. Waiting for his bridge to form.

231

Noll nodded. "The ground has already begun to freeze some nights. It will be hard and dry."

They had all been deceived, but none felt the blow harder than Thomas.

Leopold had disguised himself as a brash, overconfident general who favored a direct assault, where his overwhelming numbers would give him the advantage. And Thomas, seeing no further than Leopold had wanted him to, fell for it. He clung to his first impressions of the Duke as a young man of privilege, with little military experience, because that was the only advantage he could find in a hopeless war. He had eagerly accepted the notion that the Austrian army's weakness was its leader, when, in truth, Leopold was its greatest strength.

Thomas had underestimated the enemy. And now all those that depended on him were about to pay the Devil's toll.

As Noll kept adding to the landscape around the mountain of Morgarten, Gildas placed his hand onto Thomas's shoulder.

"You could not have known," he said, his voice carrying no further than Thomas's ears.

He refused to look at the old druid, or even acknowledge his words, but something in them, or his touch, quieted his fears enough for him to think. While staring at the dirt map, he felt a slim hope emerge. He took the stick from Noll's hand.

"We must attack them as they are stretched along the shore of the lake, where they have no room to maneuver. If we hit them hard enough, we could drive them into the waters where their own armor will do most of our work for us," Thomas said.

Anton crossed his arms and arched an eyebrow at Thomas. "Charge an army that will most likely outnumber us seven-to-one? And that would be seven *soldiers* to every *farmer*."

"It could work," Ruedi said. "If we come down off those hills and hit them in the flank like that."

The Rubin brothers perked up and glanced at one another. Thomas could feel the hopelessness, which had surrounded them all only seconds before, begin to lift like a morning fog.

"I have to kill that plan before it goes any further," Noll said. He held out his hand and Thomas surrendered the stick. "Lake Aegeri is very small. And very far. Leopold will march from Zug at first light, meaning even if we leave right now, the bulk of Leopold's army would already be well past the shores of the lake by the time we arrived."

He made one last, definitive 'X' between Schwyz and the lower end of the lake. "They would catch us here, out in the open, with not a rock to hide under. Leopold's knights would ride over us like a field of wheat."

Noll put the tip of his stick into the flame of a torch. He pulled it out and watched it burn. "There simply is not enough time," he said. He blew out the tiny flame and a delicate column of smoke rose into the air.

The fog was back. Someone cursed.

But Thomas was not yet ready to give up on his plan. "What is this here?" He pointed to a mark on Noll's map.

"A fork in the road," Noll said.

"Where does this other road go?"

Noll drew again with the stick. "It is the old road to Sattel. No one uses it much any more because it is in such poor shape and takes twice as long to reach the town."

"Is it still passable?" Thomas asked.

"I believe so," Noll said. "A small hamlet, called Schafstetten, is located here, so I imagine they still use it. But they would be the only ones that I can think of. At any rate, it is little more than a rough path, so we will only lose time by taking it."

"But how much would it slow down a large army?" Thomas asked. "If we blockade the main road and force Leopold to take the old one, would it give us enough time to get our men into position on the slopes above the lake?"

"Possibly, but we do not have the time or the numbers, Thomas. First, we would need to create an impassable barricade, which is no easy matter. Then we would need to get a sizable force to Schafstetten to hold back the Austrian advance until the rest of our army can get into place. They would be on open ground and unprotected."

Gildas stepped into the lantern-lit circle and stood right on top of Noll's map. He spoke directly to Thomas, as though he were the only one present.

"The plan is a good one. But no need to waste your men creating a barricade. Leave that to me."

The men cast questioning glances all around.

"Uh, you are standing on my stick…" Noll said.

"The time for scratching in dirt is over, Noll Melchthal," Gildas said.

"Who the Devil are you?" Noll asked, raising his voice.

"He is a friend of Seraina's," Thomas said.

"Oh. Well, that explains a few things, but—"

"Can you really do it?" Thomas asked Gildas. "Erect a barricade by yourself?" *I am mad to even be asking.*

The old man nodded.

"Are you sure? I need to know for certain."

"Trust. That is all you truly need, Thomas Schwyzer. Nothing else," Gildas said.

Thomas let out a deep breath and stared at Gildas. Five thousand more men is what I really need, he thought.

Chapter 24

SERAINA CLIMBED IN TOTAL darkness. Eventually, the sun appeared upon the horizon, but its presence provided little comfort. In fact, she felt the lightening landscape was only time's way of mocking her.

She resisted the urge every few steps to twist and look over her shoulder far below in the direction of Zug. She knew she was too far away to see the Austrian army's base, but that certain knowledge did little to lessen her need to look. They would march soon, and weave their way through the mountain roads on their way to rid the land of the Helvetii. How many of her people could possibly survive?

She drove the thought from her mind, and instead focused on putting one foot in front of another. Her thighs burned, her calves cramped, and the elevation change was proving a challenge for her lungs. But she knew she must press on, for the others would be waiting. They would need her strength.

Finally, after what seemed like two eternities, Seraina

stood upon the summit of the Greater Mythen. She sucked in full mouthfuls of the thin air and turned in a slow circle, gazing in awe at the land below, with all its secrets revealed through the majesty of the mountain.

A tremor ran through her body and her eyes glistened with tears. There was power here; ancient and undisturbed for hundreds of years perhaps, but nonetheless it was here. She could feel it in the air, smell it in the thin layer of dirt dusting the solid rock beneath her feet.

Unlike the Greater Mythen's neighboring mate, this mountain had no trees on its summit; only rocks and scrub, and in its center a lone Christian cross three men tall. It was formed from two peeled logs, as thick around as her waist, notched and lashed together with cracked leather straps.

Seraina marveled at the willpower of whoever had hauled the logs up from the tree-line. It must have been a grueling and dangerous trip. But Christians were never ones to back down from the impossible. Thomas had taught her as much. They would have sensed the natural power in this place, just as the druids did thousands of years ago.

There were only a handful of the Old Religion's sacred sites left in the world, to the best of Seraina's knowledge, that did not have a church or cross built upon some ruins of a long forgotten people. Why should the fate of this place play out any different?

But those were concerns for another day. Another time. As of this moment, the past was not yet dead. The Helvetii were not just another memory, like so many others had become. Seraina swore that she would not let her people be washed away by the sands of time. Not while she yet lived.

With that vow upon her lips, Seraina walked toward the cross, and the twelve white-robed figures that surrounded it.

***

Leopold had been in his armor for less than half a day and already it chafed his neck and hips. He could not wait to get out of it. When this day was over, he swore he would not don it again.

What was the point anyway?

He had no intention of being anywhere near the battle, if there even was one. The leather collars dangling from his horse's saddle were for show. Nothing more. The thought of trying to slip a strap around a sweating, bleeding, Schwyzer repulsed him to no end. Although, perhaps he could attach a line to his horse and drag the peasants behind. That would be good for morale when they entered Zug on their return trip.

Far away, the sound of another mountain horn called out. Two long, mewling notes, like a calf calling for its mother. The horns had been sounding all morning. Ever since they set out from Zug. Leopold closed his eyes and shook his head, which was beginning to ache.

When he looked up he saw a man. A very old man with white hair. Preoccupied with his thoughts, he had not realized that Klaus had brought the column to a halt. He had one hand on the bridle of Leopold's horse.

"What is this?" Leopold asked.

"It is an old man blocking the road," Klaus said.

"Ah, thank you."

It was not actually the old man who blocked the road,

but rather, it was the score of felled trees crisscrossing it that made the way impassable. The old man just happened to be sitting atop that pile.

The old man wore a dull, colorless robe that may have been brown at one time. But his hair was white as bone and glistened when the sun's rays found it through the trees. He chewed on a long piece of grass and seemed to be completely unaware of the Austrians' presence.

***

As Seraina approached the center of the Mythen, the white-robed figures encircling the cross began to chant. Seraina recognized it immediately. It was a lesser verse, called *A Greeting to the Weave*, and was a precursor for more powerful incantations.

One of the figures, an older woman, her blond hair heavily streaked with gray, broke away from the circle and stepped toward Seraina.

"Blessed be the Weave, daughter." She touched her forehead and her heart, and smiled at Seraina.

Seraina bowed her head and held her right palm over her womb. "Blessed be the knowledge of the Weave as passed through the Elders," she said.

"Do you remember me, child?"

"Of course, Elder Orlina. Gildas and I stayed with you often when I was young."

The woman placed her hands on Seraina's shoulders. "I should have known. You never forgot anything as a child. Why should that have changed?"

"Thank you for coming," Seraina said, her voice cracking.

Emotion swelled into the back of her throat. She

looked at the circle of druids, the last of their kind, all come to help the Helvetii. As though they could read her thoughts, one by one, they turned and smiled at Seraina. They continued chanting. She recognized a few of the faces under the white hoods, but most were unknown to Seraina. The Weave only knew how far they had traveled to be here.

"Thank you…" Seraina said again.

Orlina shook her head. "Those who do the bidding of the Weave require no gratitude. We do what we do so that life can go on."

"Even though none of you are Helvetii?"

"We are all of the Old Blood, Seraina. We are all Celts. And today," she fanned her arm in the direction of the druid circle, "we shall all be Helvetii."

The chanting suddenly stopped. A cloud passed over the sun and a shiver that began in Seraina's stomach fluttered out through every limb.

"Come," Orlina said. "It is time to awaken the Mythen. We will need your strength, as you will have need of ours."

Orlina took Seraina's hand and led her to the edge of the circle. The druids there spread out to allow them room. Seraina looked at the base of the cross for the goat, for a ritual of this magnitude would need a sacrifice. But there was no tethered animal. Puzzled, she looked at Orlina.

The older woman pursed her lips and tried to smile, but her eyes crinkled with sadness. She gripped Seraina's left hand tighter, and the man on Seraina's other side took her right hand in his own. The other druids, likewise, grasped one another's hands, making a human chain around the cross. All save for two men opposite

Seraina. They stepped aside, and Oppid padded silently into their center.

What is he doing here?

"Oppid!" The wolf looked at Seraina when she called his name. His golden eyes flashed and he whimpered once.

By Ardwynna's Word, no….

Seraina tried to shake her hands free, but the druids tightened their grip. She looked at Orlina, who only shook her head and stared at Oppid. "Orlina, no, please…"

Orlina closed her eyes, and her chest heaved with a heavy breath. "The Mysts will not come without a great sacrifice, my child. Balance must be maintained."

Oppid sat down at the base of the cross, next to a large, flat rock that someone had put there for a very specific purpose.

The druids began to sing. The melody slow and mournful.

"No! There must be some other way. Not Oppid… please, Orlina."

This time it was the older druid's voice that cracked.

"No, Seraina. *Not* Oppid."

Then Orlina's words failed her, and all she could do was thrust her chin out to point in Oppid's direction. Tears streamed down her cheeks. She shook her head and began to sing. Her voice quavered, but soon it was picked up and carried by the sounds of the others.

Seraina turned her head, and for the first time, noticed what was placed on the flat rock at Oppid's side. Folded ever so neatly was the white robe of a druid, and placed next to it was a walking stick. A peeled piece of oak, crooked and polished smooth with memories.

She screamed, her legs gave out, and she tried to curl into a ball. But Orlina and the other druid holding her hands would not let her fall. She stood there and cried, her body writhing, and still they would not release their hold, or let her fall.

Oppid howled.

Seraina answered the wolf with a scream. And sometime later, still wracked with sobs, Seraina began to sing.

***

"You there!" Landenberg shouted. "What happened here? Who cut down those trees?"

The old man looked up and his eyes went wide, as though he had, until that very moment, been oblivious to the fact that an army thousands strong was less than fifty paces away.

"You came!" he said, pushing himself to his feet.

"What are you talking about? Come down off there," Landenberg said.

The old man chewed on his blade of grass, then pulled it out of his mouth and stared at it for a moment before throwing it away. Then he began walking down off the pile of trees, without once crouching or reaching out to balance himself by grabbing a branch. In a few seconds he stood on the ground, next to the exposed roots of a giant oak, and beckoned to the men to come closer.

"It is against the King's Law to cut down that many trees," Landenberg said.

The old man stroked one of the soil-covered roots next to him. "Do these look like they were felled with an ax, Vogt Landenberg?"

"If you know who I am, then you must know who this is as well." He gestured toward Duke Leopold.

"I do. And I have a message for your Duke," the old man said.

"Very well," Leopold said. "Go ahead. Tell me what you will."

The old man shook his head. "It is for your ears only, I am afraid."

Once again he gestured with his hand for Leopold to come near.

Leopold had already nudged his horse forward a couple steps before he felt Klaus's arm on his own. "My lord, it could be some form of trap."

Leopold blinked once and looked at Klaus. He was surprised that the two of them were already twenty feet away from Landenberg, Franco Roemer, and the other captains of his army. The old man beckoned again.

"Nonsense," Leopold said. "Look at him. He is even older than you. But accompany me if you must."

Leopold walked his horse forward. The old man smiled and began taking slow steps toward the two men. A strong wind blew at the old man's back, whipping his hair and beard about his face. He closed his eyes, and his lips began to move. Something told Leopold to stop, and he yanked back on his horse's reins.

"My lord? Is something—,"

The old man's arms shot up toward the sky and the very air around Leopold seemed to scream. His horse reared up on its hind legs, its nostrils flaring in fear, and Leopold felt himself catapulted out of the saddle. He hit the ground hard and the air burst forth from his lungs.

He could hear laughter. A mad, gleeful cackle that

ushered forth from the old man's lips. He stood there pointing and laughing at the Duke, while the wind swirled around the old man, plucking at his gray robe like dozens of giant fingers. Leopold pushed himself to his elbows. He wheezed and gasped, trying to coax even the smallest bit of life-giving air back into his body.

He became dimly aware of movement to his right. Klaus's horse ran by and mud from its hooves sprayed Leopold's face. The next thing he saw was the old man's head hitting the forest floor, the bloody stump of its neck picking up pine needles as it rolled. The laughter stopped and the woods went silent.

The headless body, however, remained standing with its arm raised and finger pointing at Leopold. Until Klaus yelled, and from his saddle, stretched out one of his long legs and kicked it over.

Klaus and several soldiers ran to the Duke, but Franco Roemer was already there, helping him sit up. Leopold's air returned, eventually, but the sunlight that had been streaming though the trees only minutes before, had deserted them completely. After a tense few minutes they had Leopold back in the saddle of a different horse. Leopold slapped at Klaus's hand as he attempted to steady his lord.

"Stop fussing over me! I am quite all right," Leopold said. He kicked his horse and began heading east, away from the deadfall.

The captain of the Sturmritter pulled up beside Klaus and asked, "What do we do with the old man?"

"Leave him to the wolves," Klaus said. Then he spurred his own mount ahead to catch up with Leopold.

Chapter 25

FRANCO FELT IT TOOK forever for their long column to scramble over the poorly maintained road. Mountain streams regularly crossed their path, some of them so wide that Leopold would have to stop the entire column and send a scout on ahead to determine the safest point to cross. But finally, shortly after noon, the trees opened up, and they sighted the rebel forces.

Leopold signaled his army to a halt. Two mounted men waited in the middle of a lush, green field. One caught Franco's eye immediately, for he was dressed in a red tunic with the distinctive eight-pointed Hospitaller cross on his chest. Behind them, Franco could see a long line of men crowning a hill far in the distance. Their clothes and armor were the dull, motley assortment of grays and browns common in peasant armies, but Franco saw a few more of the bright red tunics amongst their number.

"What is a knight of Saint John doing here?" Franco could not stop himself from asking.

"That is no knight," Leopold said. "Only a pretender. A blasphemer dressed beyond his station. Pay him no mind, Sir Roemer."

That was easier said than done, Franco thought.

"Forgive me, my lord, but the Hospitallers are the Pope's holy soldiers. My men will have reservations, you understand."

Leopold turned on him. "They are no longer Hospitallers. The Order has discharged them all. They are deserters turned mercenary, and now they have sold their services to a rebel army. Tell your men that."

Leaving the column behind, Leopold, Franco, Landenberg, and Klaus trotted out to meet the two rebels.

Franco kept his eyes on the Hospitaller the whole time. He had never met one of the Black Knights in a tournament. He found himself wishing Leopold was wrong about this man being a pretender. The prospect of facing a Hospitaller knight on the field, especially one in his full red battle tunic, appealed to Franco's competitive spirit. A shiver went through his lance arm. It had been a long time since he had felt that sensation.

He watched the Hospitaller carefully as they approached. By the time they brought their horses to a stop in front of the two men, Franco felt he had a fair understanding of the man's abilities. He had no doubt the Hospitaller would prove a formidable opponent when his feet were planted on firm ground, but he was no horseman. His mount, a beautiful, spirited animal with the chiseled features of a true Egyptian breed, stamped its feet and threw its head around. The man was constantly jerking his reins, trying to keep the horse under his control.

"Hello Melchthal. I have been waiting for this day," Landenberg said, his lips settling into a twisted smile. He breathed noisily through his mouth, and Franco saw saliva spray through the cool air when he spoke.

The young rebel leader remained composed and did not reward the Vogt of Unterwalden with even a glance. Instead, he looked directly at Leopold. With no preamble, and certainly no respect for the fact he addressed a Prince of the Holy Roman Empire, he began to speak.

"These are our terms. Turn around and march back to your homes."

"You grossly overestimate you own worth if you think—," Leopold began.

"I am not finished. Before you leave, your men will drop all their weapons and equipment on the ground at their feet. We shall accept that as a toll for coming onto our land unannounced."

Leopold laughed and shook his head. "Still playing the part of a thief I see, eh Melchthal?"

The rebel kept speaking. His voice calm and detached. "You may keep your horses, so that your stink does not remain in our valley any longer than necessary. However, Berenger Von Landenberg must be turned over to us to be executed for reneging on his oath."

Franco started at the young man's direct words. He could not decide if he was brave or simply stupid beyond reason.

Landenberg was the first to respond. "That is *Sir* Landenberg, you whelp." He seemed to be more concerned about the rebel not mentioning his title rather than the fact the peasants wanted to execute him.

Leopold's lips spread into a thin line. "You have no

idea how much I am going to enjoy this," he said. "Custom dictates I respond to your terms with a counter-proposal. Very well. These are *my* terms. Lay down your weapons and submit to be manacled by my slave handlers. You will be put to work in the quarries and mines until the Altdorf fortress has been rebuilt, to twice its original size, or until you die. Most assuredly, the latter."

It was the rebel's turn to laugh. "And you, Lord Leopold, still playing the part of the tyrant?"

Leopold held up his index finger. "I am not finished," he said, smirking. "Your wives and daughters will be given to my men as a just reward for faithful service to their Duke. They may submit quietly, if they prefer, but to be honest, my troops would much rather take the women against their wills. They are fighting men after all. And is not a savage raping the only way to cool the heat in such a man's veins?"

Leopold cast his gaze on the man at Noll's side. "How do you prefer to take your women, Thomas? Willing, or defiant until the end?" He looked around, mockingly. "And where is your witch by the way? I do look forward to seeing her again. It will be nice to catch up where we left off."

The Hospitaller's eye twitched, and because he had a long scar at its corner, the movement seemed to tug up one corner of his mouth. But he most definitely was not smiling. "She is far away from here. And safe. Which is more than I can say for your blasphemous manuscript."

Leopold's face clouded over. His horse turned its ears back, feeling his master's rage, but the Duke was quick to regain his composure. He pointedly ignored the Hospitaller and began to exchange more unpleasant words with Melchthal. Franco took the opportunity to look behind the men at the lay of the land and the opposing force. The rebels in the distance were spread out. Probably to give an exaggerated impression of their number. Franco estimated no more than fifty men stood on top of the hill. Perhaps that many again trying to hide behind it. Did they really think they were fooling anyone? They were armed with pole weapons of some sort, and the postures of more than half of them betrayed that they had seen the passage of too many years.

What were they armed with? Homemade spears? Pitch forks?

Franco shook his head. There would be little chance for glory in this battle. Something about the rebels' left flank caught his eye and he craned his neck to get a better view.

Just then the Hospitaller's horse whinnied, shuffled sideways, and then reared up on two legs. His master cursed and fought to regain control. Klaus spurred his mount forward in front of Leopold and had his sword half drawn, thinking his lord was under attack. However, it quickly became apparent that the rebel had simply lost control of his fiery mount. Klaus spit on the ground and backed his horse away. Franco was the first to speak once everyone relaxed somewhat.

"You have a fine animal," he said to the Hospitaller.

The man looked at Franco. His dark eyes stood out against his long facial scar like coal on snow. He nodded once, but offered no words.

"I would have you know that I intend to claim him when this battle is over. However, I will allow his return to you, if you can afford his ransom. Provided you are still alive, of course."

For some reason that Franco could not understand,

Leopold found his claim to be humorous. He laughed, leaning low in his saddle.

The scar-faced man cleared his throat. "If you have my horse, there will be no ransom paid. For I will be quite dead."

There was something about the way the man spoke that made Franco want to take a closer look at him. There was no false bravado in his words, nor did he utter an idle threat, like so many men tended to do in order to quell their own fears. The Hospitaller's horse fidgeted some more, shifting from side to side, like he knew he was the topic of discussion.

"If it should happen otherwise," Franco began. "And you find yourself holding the reins of my own destrier, I trust that you will afford me the same opportunity to buy him back."

When the Hospitaller spoke, his words were slow and deliberate. "We both know that will never happen. One way or another."

Leopold rolled his eyes and sighed. "If you two are finished sniffing out one another, I would like to call an end to these negotiations."

He performed an elaborate mocking bow aimed at the rebels. "It seems we have reached an impasse. Regrettably, the only alternative is war. Enjoy the afternoon, gentlemen." He squinted at the thick cloud banks rolling in. "Pity, it looks like rain."

Without waiting for anyone to respond, he wheeled his horse around and galloped back toward his army. Landenberg's face broke into a greedy grin. He raised his arm and pointed at the rebel leader, and then jammed his heels into his horse's side to take off after Leopold. Klaus, ignoring everyone, eased his mount away and walked after them, like he was in no hurry to be in anyone's company, friend or foe alike.

"I look forward to meeting you on the field," Franco said. He gave the Hospitaller a curt nod and trotted back toward his place at the head of the Sturmritter.

***

"I think that went quite well," Noll said.

Thomas scowled as he reined his horse around. "What are you talking about? You were supposed to stall. Use up as much time as possible. Not send them galloping out of here, enraged like a kicked nest of hornets!"

"Well, maybe you should have done some talking then. For my first war negotiation I think I did very well."

"Very well? You virtually demanded they surrender and allow you to execute an Austrian noble in front of them. What kind of terms are those?"

"What has gotten into you? You are even more miserable than usual. Or is this just how you act before every battle?"

Thomas pushed Anid into a gallop. They did not have time to stand about arguing. Noll shouted something at him and followed close behind.

Though it pained him to admit, Noll was right about one thing. Thomas was more miserable than usual. And that was because he had met Franco Roemer. He had looked into the Austrian's eyes and where he had hoped to see a cocky, self-absorbed knight, he had seen a leader. An intelligent, experienced warrior with the most skilled knights in the western world under his command.

He leaned over and whispered into Anid's ear. The stallion leaped forward leaving Noll and his mountain pony far behind. He hit the bottom of the hill at lancing speed, but halfway up even Anid could no longer maintain a full gallop.

Good, Thomas thought. As long as they stayed at the very top of the rise, even the Sturmritter could not hit them with a full charge. Still, he wished he had had time to dig in cavalry pits and stakes to further slow them down and force them to break formation. But there was not enough time.

Time. The Devil's mistress. First, they could not get enough of it, and now, they had too much. How far away was the rest of his army? How long before they would arrive? How long could less than a hundred men hold back the might of the Holy Roman Empire? Was this really the best plan Thomas could have come up with?

Perhaps he could have done better. If only he had more time.

He topped the rise and his men opened up their ranks to let him through.

"Matthias!" Thomas called the boy to him as he jumped out of Anid's saddle. "You ride Anid and lead Noll's horse back to the men furthest away. Can you do that?"

"I could. But, Cap'n, I might miss the fighting."

"Then you better ride fast and run back even faster. And tell the men to double up on the horses."

The boy hesitated and glanced at the reins Thomas held out.

"That is an order, son. If you want to be part of this army, you must obey orders. Is that understood?"

"Aye, Cap'n!"

Matthias snatched the reins from Thomas's hand and was in the saddle before Thomas had to say another word.

"They will be here. I swear," Matthias said.

Noll finally appeared, and Matthias had his horse's reins before Noll's feet touched the ground. A second later he was galloping over the grassy slopes toward Schwyz, the soft, moist ground silencing the hoof-beats. Within seconds the mist enveloped both boy and horse and there was no sign that either had ever existed. The other horses had already been sent back. Thomas was well aware that four more men would make little difference, but knowing the boy would not be here when the fighting began, allowed Thomas to breathe a little easier.

Thomas stood at the bottom of the hill, the side furthest away from the Austrian army. He looked at his own forces: half were assembled on top the hill, in full view, and the other half crouched low behind its base. They had rounded up every last horse and mule available and rode here at full speed.

Eighty-nine mounts. Eighty-nine men. Handpicked by Thomas himself. Thomas had set quill to parchment yet again, and created another list. He glanced around him, seeking the Religion's red war tunics, and found his friends easily enough. Ruedi, Max, Urs, and Anton; they were the only survivors from the first list he had ever created. Both lists had started out with a similar number of names, and he could not help but wonder at the irony of it all.

Who was he to choose? Were the lists God's work, or the Devil's?

He closed his eyes and let out a deep breath. He

reminded himself that on the other side of this hill, eight thousand Austrians wound their way toward them.

He felt a tap on his shoulder. Noll held out a water skin. "Better drink up," he said. "We might end up sweating a bit."

He grinned at Thomas, and more than a little surprised, Thomas found himself grinning back. Then Noll raised his voice so all the men could hear him. "That goes for everyone. If you have skins now would be the time to use them. Does not matter what is in them. No man in this army fights thirsty!"

Thomas took a long drink and was relieved that it was actually water, not wine. Cool, fresh water from one of the countless glacier-fed streams that quenched the landscape's thirst and kept the slopes covered in thick, green grass. Thomas thought of all the times he had gone thirsty over the years in the Holy Lands. Water was worth more than gold in Outremer. If he had possessed even a fraction of the water that now surrounded him, he would have been the richest man in the Levant.

He took one more drink and then he walked up the slope. Thomas took his spot between Anton and Max at the front of the square.

Seven men wide, seven men deep.

Behind him, in the second row next to Urs, Sutter called his name. Thomas turned and Sutter held out Pirmin's great ax. Its heavy head glistened with the wetness of the fog. Through the small cross cut into its center, Thomas could see the outlying buildings of the small hamlet of Schafstetten. And far in the distance, although he could not see it, in his heart he felt the church of Sattel watching over them all.

"The big guy would be 'right pissed' if he missed out

on this day entirely," Sutter said, his voice breaking ever so slightly.

Thomas took the ax. He was once again amazed at how light it felt in his hands. As he rotated the shaft in his grip, a sing-song Wallis accent sounded in his head.

"Do not fret none, Thomi. I would not make you carry it all by yourself."

The fog was building, and its moisture seemed to accumulate on Thomas's cheeks more than anywhere else. He drew a hand across his face and stared out at the enemy.

***

"Captain Roemer!" Klaus called out.

Franco left his place at the front of the Sturmritter and trotted over to join Leopold, Klaus, and Landenberg.

"Your commands, my lord?"

"I want that hill with a single charge," Leopold said. "I see no reason to waste any time here."

"My thoughts exactly, my lord," Franco said.

"And I want my knights to be part of it," Landenberg said. He squished his helmet onto his head and gave it a slap, which made it ring. Steam poured out of the breathing holes in its long, metal snout.

Franco looked at Leopold. "With all due respect, the Sturmritter can do it alone, my lord. Perhaps Sir Landenberg's forces can ride them down as they run."

"Not bloody likely," Landenberg said.

"Stop it," Leopold said. "There will be more than enough Schwyzers to go around before the day is out. But remember this: each of your knights carries shackles enough for three men. Our goal is to get workers. We kill no more than necessary. Is that clear?"

"What about Melchthal?" Landenberg said.

"Yes, by all means kill him. And the Hospitaller as well. For that matter, kill every man who stands on that hill defying us. An example should be made. But stop there. Is that understood?"

Franco could not see Landenberg's face behind his mask, but when he spoke he could hear pure joy echo in his words.

"Perfectly, my Duke."

"Now, Captain Roemer. Take your force in for a frontal charge, but at the last, wheel around and take them in their left flank. I would like to see how quickly they can move their formation".

"Yes, my lord."

It was the exact strategy Franco had himself been considering. Of course he would never have presumed to say anything unless the Duke had asked for his input. The front of the hill was too steep for a cavalry charge, but the approach to the rebel's left flank was much less so.

"Landenberg. You will follow after Captain Roemer has crested the hill, and attack directly from the front. That should scatter them to the winds."

"Yes, my lord!"

It was a good plan. Franco was beginning to grow a healthy respect for Leopold's war skills. Perhaps he deserved the nickname people were calling him recently: the Sword of the Habsburgs.

"Today, gentlemen, we will teach these rebels what it means to defy God's Divine Order!"

Landenberg drew his sword and cheered. Other knights close enough to hear Leopold also let out some shouts and raised their weapons.

It was a good plan, Franco thought again. But as he stared back at the hill and saw the Hospitallers in their blood-red war tunics, he did not feel much like cheering.

**

Seven men wide. Seven men Deep. To bide time, the square must hold.

Thomas watched the Sturmritter, perched atop their huge war horses, pull away from the vanguard. They came to a complete halt on open ground and remained motionless, like statues carved from mountains. Then, with their lances pointed straight up, they eased their mounts forward into a walk. Their timing and rhythm were impeccable; their movements exact copies of one another. Even the tall, blue feathers that crested each man's helmet seemed to sway in the wind to the same beat.

Thomas thanked God above that his forces commanded the high ground. Even still, it was intimidating to see such a perfect formation. A quick look at the men's faces around him, and Thomas knew his side was on the verge of losing this battle before it ever began.

He stepped out from the square and turned his back on the knights preparing to charge, and addressed his men.

"They are peacocks," he shouted. "Peacocks on horses, nothing more. They ride a fine show, but they cannot top this hill without their mounts stumbling. And once they do, their lances will be useless, and those plumed heads will be well within range of our axes."

He hefted Pirmin's ax into the air, and heard Urs let out a guttural holler. Max banged the flat of his sword against his own long-handled ax. They were used to these pre-battle pep talks. They knew the value of making noise to summon the battle furies and subdue fear. Fear that would otherwise rise up and consume even the bravest of men.

Anton whooped and other voices joined in.

Behind him, Thomas imagined the Sturmritter pushing their destriers into a trot. He did not look back.

"Those peacocks have come into our lands uninvited. Unwanted. And make no mistake, they mean to harm you and yours."

Thomas had to pause to let their shouts die down.

"Once they have killed you and me, they will march on Schwyz. After they have slaughtered your animals, burned down your homes, and raped your women, they will enslave anyone who manages to escape the initial butchering. Will you allow that?"

The men howled in outrage.

"Was any man here born to be a slave? Are you the fathers of slaves?"

"No!" Thomas clearly heard Sutter's voice over all others. Men slung the foulest of insults at the army before them, and screamed their defiance.

Thomas felt the ground shake with the approach of a hundred war horses. Still, he did not look back.

"I ask you again, because today you have a choice. Whereas tomorrow, you will not. Will you allow this?"

"NO!" The answer came as one deafening shout, as united as the Sturmritters' charge.

Thomas held up Pirmin's ax again and shouted, "And neither will I! God have mercy on their souls!"

The men went wild and waved their own weapons high in the air. Thomas turned in time to see the Sturmritter break into a gallop. They couched their lances, and as one, slowly lowered the deadly points until they were horizontal with the ground. Each man's knee brushed against the man's next to him. It was a perfect *conroi* in the making.

Thomas felt the earth tremble at his feet.

Chapter 26

ERICH SAT WITH HIS LEGS dangling over the edge of a small rock bluff. High above the Confederate army's position, he had a perfect view of the battlefield, so long as the clouds did not get any lower. Boots scraping on stone made him turn, and he saw the bald head of Reto push through the trees. He stopped well back from the cliff's edge, but tried to lean forward to get a better view.

That was the problem with men such as Reto, Erich thought. He wanted everything, but was willing to risk almost nothing to get it.

"Are the men in position?" Erich asked, turning back to the world far below.

"They are." Reto tipped a wineskin to his lips, swished the liquid around in his mouth, and then spit it onto the rocky ground to Erich's left. It stained the rocks there a rusty red. "But some of the men are grumbling. Been asking when they will get paid."

Erich pulled one leg up from the overhang and turned to look at Reto.

"You mean *you* have been wondering," he said. "Most of them have been with me long enough to know the answer to that question."

Reto took another drink as he stared back at Erich. "All right, then. I will not deny that. But I know I am not the only one."

"You will get your pay, along with everyone else. And the second you do, I want you gone."

"Some of the men might want to come with me," Reto said.

"You are welcome to any who do," Erich said.

He turned away and dropped his leg back over the ledge. As he did so, a fist-sized rock tumbled off into the abyss. He watched its long, silent descent until it disappeared from sight, and then Erich pushed himself to his feet. He stood there for a moment, with the tips of his boots hanging over the void, and watched as Leopold's cavalry began their charge.

It was time, he thought. Time to risk everything.

***

As per Leopold's command, Franco led his men thundering straight at the hill. The men on top formed into a tight square and braced themselves for a head on attack that would never happen.

Franco raised his lance, pulled his destrier in a tight, right hand turn and galloped toward the enemy's left, curious about what he would see waiting for him behind the hill. Sure enough, as his mount started powering up the gentle slope to the side of the hill, a loosely formed mob of rebels appeared before him. They milled about, and seemed surprised to see the knights bearing down on them from this direction.

He released his reins and, guiding his horse with only his knees, pointed at the group on low ground. They would have to take this group first, and then climb the hill for the second. He shouted the command to change targets and, like a great flock of migrating birds, the Sturmritter adjusted their course without a single falter in the warhorses' strides.

"Lances!" Franco commanded. The knights' weapons came down once again, their iron-tipped points aimed straight ahead. The small group of rebels, who only seconds before appeared to be on the verge of fleeing, formed up into a square with what looked like short spears held before them.

The maneuver bothered Franco on some instinctual level. He remembered the Hospitaller, and his beautiful, but poorly trained mount. Why would a man ride a horse into battle that he could not control? Especially, a man trained by the Knights of Saint John. Some of the greatest horsemen in the world had come from their ranks.

The answer, of course, was he would not.

Franco reached up his hand and threw open his helmet visor.

It had been a diversion. The Hospitaller was drawing all eyes to him, because there was something he did not want Franco to see.

The men hiding behind the hill, perhaps?

The warhorses of the Sturmritter bore down on the rebels at full speed, their hooves tearing up great divots of the soft, grass-covered ground. The enemies' faces began to take shape. Franco flipped his visor back down. Impact was seconds away. Only thirty yards of grass separated the Sturmritter from their targets.

Thirty yards of grass that did not stand?

It was cut, and as Franco stared at it, very wet. As though brought there from somewhere else….

"Bog!"

Franco drove his legs back, commanding his horse to stop, but the animal's blood was up. It was bred for war, and once at full charge, stopping was the last thing on its mind. Desperate, Franco grabbed the reins and yanked on them, pulling his mount's chin to its chest. He slowed, but not much.

Several knights shot past Franco, and as soon as their horses' front legs sank into the mud, he heard a series of sickening cracks and whinnies of terror shot through with pain. The momentum of their mounts' rear ends carried them forward and over, spilling riders and horses everywhere. Packed so tightly together, there was little the knights following could do but trample their comrades, or try to leap from their saddles.

Franco fought to stay seated and save his horse from breaking its legs as it sloshed through three-foot-deep mud and over slippery rocks. He thought he was going to make it to solid ground, when an out of control knight speared his lance deep into his horse's flank. The horse fell, and rolled, with Franco still in the saddle.

He lay there thinking he should get up, but the mud was warm, comfortable, and a great weight was on his leg. He felt quite content to remain where he was.

Until he heard a scream. And another.

He turned his head toward the sound, just in time to see a peasant swing a long, heavy ax into the head of one of his men as he attempted to stand.

Unlike the others, no scream came from his lips.

***

Thomas watched from the top of the hill as Noll's square charged the disoriented Sturmritter as they attempted to free themselves from the wetland marsh. Several were already on a firm piece of ground, and one of them blew a horn, summoning them all to that spot. They were recovering much faster than Thomas had anticipated. If enough of them managed to regroup, Noll would be in trouble. Thomas hated to give up the high ground so early in the battle, but the Sturmritter were far from finished.

"Square, left face!" Thomas shouted.

Every one of the forty-nine men lifted his ax to point at the sky and then pivoted to the left.

"Forward, slow."

As they began to walk, the first row lowered their axes to stomach height and the next row, slightly staggered from the row in front, aimed theirs slightly higher. The rest kept them pointed up.

"Three man front!"

The last three rows of seven men broke away from the square and ran to form a new front line beside the first. Thomas checked to make sure the line was straight, then he tightened his grip on Pirmin's ax.

"Forward. Full!"

Every single man let out a loud battle cry and the formation charged down the hill. They crashed into the knights, driving them back onto the marshy ground where their heavy armor became more hindrance than help.

Thomas pulled one of the few knights still mounted out of his saddle with the hook on the back of his ax and then speared him through the eye slits. He saw Sutter and one of the Rubin boys bring down another knight in a similar fashion. To his left, Urs exchanged blows with a knight covered in mud, but Thomas had to look away to bring his ax down onto a knight's arm as he attempted to crawl out of the marsh. Pirmin's ax slid into his armor's elbow joint and removed it cleaner than a surgeon's cleaver. He staggered back, screaming. A crossbow bolt appeared in his eye and he fell over. Thomas looked for Urs again. He was gone, but a dead Austrian knight lay on the ground.

The screams became fewer, the sense of movement less. Men from Noll's square appeared, and Thomas knew the Sturmritter would not ride again. The thought saddened him, but that did not stop him from bringing Pirmin's ax down upon another one's head as he tried to crawl away.

His feet felt wet. Thomas thought he might be standing in blood, but when he looked down the earth was hidden by a thickening layer of mist.

Then it started to rain.

***

Leopold's anticipation changed to confusion when he watched the Sturmritter go down. Then horror took over as he watched the two small squares of Schwyzers charge. A mist hugged the ground where they were, and blotted out some of the action, but the wind carried the screams of horses and men to his ears, leaving little doubt as to what was happening.

The Sturmritter, the finest knights in the known world, were being slaughtered to the man.

"God have mercy," Landenberg said.

Leopold turned on him. "Why are you still here?"

Landenberg did not seem to hear Leopold. He could not tear his eyes away from the axes rising and falling in the distance.

"Landenberg!"

"I, uh, I was waiting for Franco to appear on the hill. Only, he… never did."

"Get as many cavalry to the front as you can. We will hit them in the open, before they can climb back onto that hill."

Landenberg shook his head, his eyes still locked on the dying men in the distance. A riderless Sturmritter warhorse, its eyes wide and nostrils flared, trotted past him looking for a new herd.

"Hornman!" Leopold called out and a young man ran to his side.

"Yes, my lord."

"Call up the rear guard cavalry as well."

The young soldier put his horn to his lips. The sound echoed all the way down the mile-long line of Habsburg forces.

Leopold took a deep breath and looked to where the rebels were reforming into squares.

"Now that you have sprung your trap, Thomas Schwyzer, let us see how you manage the rest of us."

Chapter 27

"FORM UP! FORM UP!" Noll called out again.

So engrossed were his men with the grisly task of killing the last few armored knights flailing about in the marshland, that he had to run around and cuff several of them so that his orders registered. When they looked at him with eyes wild, but vacant, their blood-splattered features twisted, Noll hardly recognized them. He remembered Pirmin talking of how the battle furies could consume a man during times of war, and lend him strength. He watched the huge, but usually gentle, form of Hans Gruber run bellowing into mud up to his knees, grab a staggering knight by the plume on his helmet, and wrench his head around in a circle, throwing him back into the sucking muck from which he had just managed to free himself. He pinned the Austrian on his back with the butt end of his ax, and stomped on his helmeted head over and over, driving it deep below the water's surface. Gruber kept stomping long after the peacock feathers disappeared. Whether the man died from the crushing impact of the young man's blows, or drowned, Noll had no idea. But, he had long since ceased his struggles by the time Noll reached them.

"Gruber!"

He kept stomping until Noll shoved him from behind. The young giant whirled around and Noll jumped back, not liking the way Gruber leveled his ax in his direction.

"Gruber, what is wrong with you? Form up!"

The big man blinked. Noll had to yell again before the man looked around sheepishly and, seeing half of his square already standing in the field, began wading through the mud to join them. Thomas's complete square stood there already. Noll saw Max and Urs, moving around the battlefield, shouting at members of Noll's square to form up ranks. Their red tunics made them clearly visible amongst the earth-covered dead and dying.

A minute later, Noll stood in the front line of his completed square. He could not remember the last time his lungs had worked so hard. But he felt strong and eager for whatever came next. Intermittent shouts and snarls erupted from his men telling him that they felt the same way.

Noll looked at the enemy for the first time since re-forming ranks. At least two hundred cavalry trotted toward them. Another five hundred milled about in a disorganized mass at the front of the army, trying to get into some semblance of attack formation. Behind them, tightly packed infantry, and more mounted knights stretched along the road and disappeared around the bend.

"God Almighty," Noll whispered.

"Ruedi, Max," Thomas shouted. "Take up rover positions on Noll's square. Anton, you and I will be ours."

"Aye, Cap'n."

Ruedi, crossbow in hand ran to stand to the left of Noll's square, while Max, his sword drawn went to the right. Normally, they would have seven to ten rovers per square, fast men with swords whose task it was to dart in and out of the enemy ranks, doing as much damage as possible when the two fronts collided. But, Noll reasoned, since this was a stalling mission, Thomas must have decided he would rather have the squares themselves as strong as possible.

Noll watched Thomas walk to stand outside his own square. He put Pirmin's ax on the ground and drew his short sword and mace. Next to him, stood Sutter.

Semi-transparent tendrils of mist wrapped around Sutter's ankles, as though rooting him to the damp ground. He stared defiantly at the approaching Austrians, with his ax held before him and his face grim. He looked more like some mythical warrior than a middle-aged innkeeper. The momentary illusion was shattered, however, by the old, patched, and mended vest that his wife had made him years ago. The same one that he had worn to serve Noll many a mug of ale over the years.

"Sutter!" Noll shouted.

"Sutter!"

The innkeeper turned around slowly, looking for the source of the call. He saw Noll waving and gave him a curt nod and a half smile, which was worth a full smile from any other man.

"I want to marry your daughter!"

Sutter's eyes went wide and then narrowed in the

space of a heartbeat. Noll was suddenly glad he was separated from Mera's father by a score of armed men. He had not planned his words, but as soon as he said them he knew it was the perfect time, even as the men around him laughed.

"I mean when this is all over. And things have settled down a bit," Noll said.

Sutter's jaw clamped shut, and his eyes narrowed further.

He pointed at Noll. "Stay alive, boy. We will talk about this again."

Noll grinned. "That most definitely did not sound like a 'no'," he said.

"Time to get your feet back on the ground, Noll," Ruedi said, as the knights attacking broke into a charge. There were several flag bearers of Austrian noble families riding in the charge, but one in particular had caught Noll's eye: the red fist of Berenger Von Landenberg.

He tightened his grip on his own ax, and pushed all thoughts of Sutter and Mera from his mind. Out of his peripheral vision he saw Thomas rotating his mace arm to loosen it up.

"Squares, front face!" Thomas shouted.

The men in the front lines dropped to one knee, wedged their ax handle against their front foot, and pointed the spear tip of their weapons toward the enemy. The next line squatted and also stepped on the hafts of their halberds but remained standing. The next couple of lines completed the deadly wall by holding the points of their weapons parallel to the ground and over their comrades' heads. The men behind assumed a solid stance and placed one hand on the man in front of him to lend support, and to be ready to replace him when needed.

"Squares. Meet charge!"

This was no Sturmritter charge, Noll thought before the first horses hit them. Their front was not unified, and less than half of the knights attacking had lances. Most of them swung long swords that needed room to operate. And since the Schwyzer forces were so concentrated, the Austrians had to crowd together as they approached, cutting off a large number of the attackers. This forced them to slow down and follow behind the main force, waiting for their prey to run.

"Hold your ground!" Noll shouted as a horse penetrated three lines into the square before its rider was pulled from its back and hacked up by axes from the rear lines.

A swordsman slashed out and Noll saw Gruber recoil in pain, he dropped his ax and pressed his huge hand against his collar bone. Blood seeped between his fingers. Ruedi's crossbow clicked, and the young knight pushing into the square was lifted out of his saddle with a leather-fletched shaft punched deep into his breast plate. He fell under the hooves of the other knights pressing their mounts forward, trying to find an opening in the wall of axes. As soon as Ruedi fired, he ducked into the protection of the back lines of the square to reload.

Gruber found his ax. He hefted it up, and using it with one hand began pulling knights off horses like they were low-hanging apples. Once on the ground, the cumbersome armor of the knights was no match for the penetrating ax heads and the men who wielded them.

Another click from Ruedi's crossbow; another riderless horse crowding the front line. On the right, Noll caught glimpses of his other rover, Max. He seemed to be everywhere, with sword in hand, moving in and out of the square at will. Men, or horses, cried out every time Noll lost sight of him.

Noll had no idea how Thomas's square fared. Every time he tried to look he was confronted by a new enemy. He could see nothing but horses and knights' legs. He swung an overhead strike at a knight's thigh. His ax hit just above the knee, and even though it was covered in chainmail, he felt the end of the large leg bone crumble under the blow. The knight screamed, and fell forward, but managed to hold onto his horse's neck and break out of the throng around him. He went twenty feet before falling out of his saddle, and was promptly trampled by a riderless horse.

Within minutes, most of the horses immediately surrounding the square lacked riders. But the Austrians were so numerous, the horses could not escape. Terrorized, and many of them wounded, by the sharp spear points and the flashing ax heads, they stumbled around the outside of the square until they could force their way through the Austrians and gallop back to the main army.

Noll's arms were heavy, but he was not winded when the man behind him tapped his shoulder to initiate a line change. Noll dropped back, and Gruber stepped forward.

What is he doing behind me? That is not our regular formation.

As Noll stepped back he had to lift his leg over a body. One of his men. And another. The square held, but almost half his men had fallen. That was why Gruber was behind him, he realized.

He put his hand on Gruber's shoulder and rested his ax handle on the ground. He rolled his shoulder as best he could to relax the muscles. Gruber suddenly jumped. A long lance had been driven through his middle and stuck four feet out his lower back. Only Noll's quick feet stopped him from being skewered as well.

Gruber began to fall backward, but the point of the shaft stuck against the ground and would not let him fall. The big man looked around weakly. Noll leapt forward to protect him and maintain the front line. As he looked up, he found himself staring right into Landenberg's face.

The Vogt had a helmet with a metal snout, but his face mask was raised. Probably so he could breathe better, Noll thought. He pointed at Noll as he wheeled his mount around in a circle.

"I got myself a big one, eh Melchthal! And you will be next!"

Landenberg dug his heels into his horse's flank and barged through the other Austrian knights. Noll saw him heading straight to a lightly armored man with Landenberg's crest on his chest. He had three or four long lances, and held one out as the Vogt approached. Then, Noll had to focus back on the battle at hand. Someone had unhorsed an Austrian, and he rolled right in front of Noll like a sacrifice. He let the man push himself up to his hands and knees before beheading him. Then he stepped on his back while he used the hook on the back of his ax to help Sepp Rubin unhorse another.

Next to Sepp, working the front line with a borrowed ax in hand, was Ruedi. And next to him was Max. The rovers had taken up positions inside the square. The front line to be exact. This was not a good sign, Noll thought.

He risked a glance over his shoulder. There were only two rows of men behind him. Gruber was still standing, but the way his head and empty hands hung limp, Noll knew he could no longer count him.

The horses in front of Noll suddenly cleared, and for the briefest moment he thought the Austrians were retreating. But then, with his heart stuck in his throat, he realized that they had only pulled back to ready another charge. He saw Landenberg among them, lance in hand.

"Squares, form single! Seven men across, no rovers!" Thomas shouted.

The men pushed and jostled themselves into new positions. Noll found himself once again on the front line, touching shoulders with Thomas and Sutter.

"Square, forward full!"

Evidently Thomas too had had enough of defensive formations. Noll could not blame him. If they were going to die, they might as well die on the offensive. The men all seemed to agree, for the entire square raced across the open ground with renewed strength and war cries so terrible Noll wondered who was making them.

Landenberg tested the weight of a lance before handing it back to his squire and then took another one. He glanced over his shoulder, to see what the loud noise coming from the Schwyzers was all about, and had just enough time to lower his visor before the first charging rank was on him. He dropped his lance and drew his sword. Next to him, he saw his squire dragged from the saddle and his throat cut.

With no regard for maintaining formation, Noll pushed himself to reach Landenberg, cutting down everything in his path. But Sutter beat him to the Vogt. The innkeeper hooked his chainmail and pulled him half out of the saddle. Landenberg cursed and swung at Sutter's head, but he ducked and gave a final tug that pulled the Vogt down on top of him. The heavy man knocked the breath out of Sutter and he was slow to stand. As Landenberg stepped forward to thrust his sword into Sutter's guts, Noll hit the Vogt with the shaft of his weapon from behind and knocked him off to the side.

Landenberg turned and flipped open his visor. He smiled and his eyes lit up with mad intent, but he was too out of breath to speak. He swung his sword with both hands in an overhead strike at Noll's head. Still holding his halberd shaft before him, Noll lifted it and blocked the attack on the wood between his hands. Then he brought the bottom of the heavy pole across Landenberg's face. Spitting blood, Landenberg reeled back, but Noll kept his momentum going and, stepping forward, spun his ax over his head and sunk it deep into the side of Landenberg's head. His head bounced off his shoulder.

Noll shook as he looked down at Landenberg. His eyes, now as sightless as Noll's father's, stared up at the low clouds as the rain fell. It was hard to say what killed him first: the broken neck, or the heavy, flanged ax head lodged above his ear.

Noll felt rough hands on him.

"Noll, look!" Thomas said, facing him in the direction of the main army where at least five hundred more cavalry were readying to charge, and a long line of other knights were pushing their way up to the front through the ranks of infantry.

"No, there. On the slopes above."

Noll looked to where he pointed. A treeless slope. But a slope that was alive and in motion.

A score of giant logs, some of them covered in oil

and burning, bounced their way down picking up speed as they went. Leaving a trail of burning oil on the green mountainside, they smashed into the horses and men gathered at its base. The scene instantly turned from what was already a frenzy into a full-blown panic. Horses' legs were swept out from under them and broken, some men were crushed, others burst into flames by simply being too close. Then, behind the logs and trees came rocks; large, jagged pieces taller than a man but round enough to roll faster than a horse can run.

Thomas stared at Noll, looking as surprised as Noll had ever seen him. "Did you…," he began.

Noll shook his head. "That is not my doing."

In the distance an alphorn sounded. Then another far, far away. Seconds later, more horns blared, but closer this time. Much closer.

Noll laughed and clapped Thomas on the back. "But those! Those are our doing!"

There was no longer any fighting around the men. The survivors of the Austrian cavalry that they had charged were racing back to the main army. Noll was not sure that was such a wise choice of destinations. For there were a great many screams coming from the main force as over a thousand horses tried to avoid the falling rocks and logs. Spooked, they threw their riders and trampled anyone in their path.

Thomas was watching the same turmoil.

"Now is the time," Thomas said. "We have to turn them on themselves." He placed cupped hands to his mouth. "Form up!"

"Form up!" Noll repeated.

"Square, face forward!" Thomas said.

They began to march toward the head of the largest

army Noll had ever seen. Movement on the hillside caught his eye. A score of men were making their way down following the same route the logs had taken, shooting longbows and crossbows as they came.

No, not a score, Noll corrected himself. Twenty-seven men. Twenty-eight if you counted Erich. He grinned and could not help elbowing Thomas to make sure he saw them.

"Your outlaw friend has chosen a side, it seems," Thomas said.

"I never said Erich was my friend," Noll said. "But I must admit, I have never been so happy to see anyone."

Horns blew again, but this time one after the other in quick succession.

"Stauffacher is in place," Noll said.

Thomas nodded.

"Square, forward full!"

***

It was raining, yet Leopold's world was in flames. He stared at the demons coming down the mountainside on paths of fire. The acrid stench of burning soldiers and horse flesh clogged his nostrils. An arrow flew past his ear, but he did not notice.

"The Schwyzers are charging us my lord," Klaus said, drawing his sword. "We must move back into the ranks!"

Leopold's eyes remained focused on the mountainside and he seemed not to have heard Klaus.

"My Lord! We must leave. Now."

"What? No… that will not do… The men will think something is amiss," Leopold said. No sooner were the words out of his mouth than an arrow thudded into his horse's flank. She took it stoically, with only a short whinny, but then the pain came and she bucked madly until Leopold was thrown from her back.

"Leo!"

Klaus jumped down from his mount, but kept the reins wrapped around his hand so the horse could not bolt in the confusion. Men and horses were everywhere, and everyone seemed to be trying to go in the same direction. However, the road was too narrow, and neither the impenetrable forest on the one side, nor the steep hill on the other offered any alternative.

Leopold sat up, but his vision was blurred and he felt nauseous. He blinked and a bald-headed man kicked him in the face.

"Are you who I think you are?" the man said, his words echoed but Leopold was surprised at how they were so clearly audible with the shouts and screams of all those around him.

The man scrunched up his ferret-shaped face and his small eyes doubled in size. "Well, blackball me to—"

His blood was suddenly airborne and sprayed over Leopold's face, making the Duke squeeze his eyes shut. When he opened them, the man's body was on the ground; his neck cut half-way through from the rear.

Klaus reached down and grabbed Leopold by the scruff of his chainmail and hoisted him to his feet. Two more men brandishing swords appeared out of the fog. Klaus yanked Leopold behind him and pushed his horse's reins into his hands.

"Get on that horse, my lord, now."

Leopold heard the words but he could not move. He was not injured, but his feet seemed rooted to the spot. While Klaus fought for their lives, he found himself turning to look up the mountainside once again at the paths of fire. They were gone now, but they had been there only moments before. He was sure of it.

The demons had hid them, so none would know the truth. But I know....

Klaus ran one of the men through and jumped back to narrowly evade the other man's slash.

"Get on that horse!" Klaus yelled.

What horse?

Leopold again felt a tug on his chainmail, but this one was quick and from behind. The next thing he knew he was across a saddle on his stomach.

"I have him," Franco Roemer called out to Klaus. "Large groups of rebels are attacking all down the line!"

The mountains... they come from the mountains... and they are not rebels....

Klaus batted his opponent's sword aside and split the man in half with a two-handed overhand stroke.

"Get him out of here, Captain. I will follow as best I can."

Klaus managed to retrieve his horse's reins that Leopold had dropped and swung himself up into the saddle. Franco did not wait. He kicked his horse into a gallop and they weaved in and out of the press of men and animals crowding the road. Leopold thought his insides were going to explode, but as soon as they came to an open space, Franco stopped the horse and had Leopold sit behind him.

Klaus caught up with them. "Are you hurt, my lord?"

Is he talking to me?

"He seems fine," Franco said. "A little shaken, perhaps. But we can worry about that after."

On one particularly crowded section of road, fifty

mounted knights struggled to regain control of their destriers in the midst of a group of infantry. War horses did not fight together with infantry, so any man not riding a horse, was an enemy in their minds. The snorting animals, trained to lash out with their hind legs, were kicking and trampling anyone that came too close and there seemed little their handlers could do to control them.

Franco tried to go to the left of the road, but there was a deep creek, and the ground around it was too soft. He opted instead for the sloped, but firmer, area to the right. They had to duck under tree branches and scramble along scree, but they were able to bypass the troubled section.

"Hold on, Duke," Franco said as he made his horse jump over a large boulder, dripping and dark with moisture, to get back on the road. No sooner were they on level ground, surrounded by their own infantry, than a horn sounded.

Leopold jumped.

A split second later, on the slope above, hundreds of howling demons brandishing giant axes erupted from the mist-shrouded trees.

Leopold screamed and covered his eyes.

The Schwyzers attacked at several points along the Austrian line, almost half of which was still marching along the shores of Lake Aegeri. Their panicked cavalry proved useless in such cramped fighting conditions, and some say the horses killed as many Austrians as the Schwyzers did. But, if truth be told, it was the lake itself that was responsible for the deaths of more men than anything. Encumbered with their expensive armor, thousands of Austrian nobles died that day trying to fight in water, or flee through it.

Chapter 28

COUNT HENRI OF HUNENBERG and the captain of the thirty cavalry troops Leopold had sent along with Henri and his knights, sat atop their horses and eyed the village in the field below. It consisted of a dozen thatched-roof huts and a common building. The one street was empty; all doors were closed. The villagers had seen them coming a long time ago. Just as Henri had wanted it. But the captain, a career soldier of the Holy Roman Empire, was beginning to suspect that perhaps Henri was not quite up to the task Leopold had charged him with.

"Shall we attack, my lord?" the captain asked.

"No. Not until we have word from Duke Leopold."

"We received his orders, and his blessing I might add, when we marched from Habsburg," the captain said.

"And I have ordered you to await confirmation from the Duke. If that is not to your liking, *captain*, then I suggest you find another Count to take orders from."

The man fidgeted in his saddle, making the leather

squeak. "No, sir. Was just wondering is all."

Well, you will not have to wonder for very long, Henri thought, for in the distance he could see his messenger returning. Henri shielded his eyes to get a better look.

Something was wrong.

The man was bent low in the saddle, and his cloak billowed out behind him as he came at them full speed. His horse was foaming at the mouth when he pulled up before them.

"What is it?" Henri asked.

"The Duke's army, it is… it has been routed, my lord."

The captain let out a loud exhalation. "Come on, man. Talk sense. Routed by whom?"

The messenger looked at Henri. "It is true, my lord. The Schwyzers ambushed them on the shores of the lake. Thousands are dead, the rest are in full retreat."

"Who told you this?" Henri asked.

"I saw it with these eyes, my lord. The Duke's entire army scattered, running for their lives. I heard from one survivor, the Schwyzers are executing any man taken prisoner. Who could have predicted this?"

"What of the Duke?" the captain asked.

The messenger shook his head. "I saw no sign of him. They may have captured him. Surely the godless peasants would not execute a prince!"

Henri thought of Thomas and what he knew of the man. "You are wrong on both accounts. They are not godless, and yes, they are quite capable of executing a member of the royal family."

The captain turned to Henri. "This is dire news, but we should push on with our objective."

Count Henri stared at the man. "Take your men and return to your homes."

The captain looked at the defenseless village below. Henri could see him imagining the possible treasures that could be uncovered inside the simple buildings.

"I have been ordered by Duke Leopold to take this village," the captain said.

Henri shook his head.

"It seems Leopold no longer has any claim to these lands. But, as of this moment, that village is under the protection of the House of Hunenberg. You set one foot in there, and you will hang. The day is over, captain. This war is over. And if you set one foot in that village, your life is over."

Henri turned his horse and headed home.

Chapter 29

THOMAS KNELT BESIDE the Rubin boys. One held the other's lifeless head in his lap, while silent tears streamed down his freckled cheeks.

Marti. That was the boy's name. Had it really been that difficult to tell them apart?

Thomas put a hand on Sepp's shoulder and said a prayer for Marti. As he stood, he saw Ruedi leading two horses toward him.

"Cap'n, they found Leopold."

"Where?"

"A short distance to the west. I hear the men he is with is giving our boys a hard time."

Leopold. Thomas suddenly wished Seraina were there to help him decide what to do with the 'boy tyrant', as Noll so often called him.

"Lead the way," Thomas said, taking one set of reins from the crossbowman.

When Thomas and Ruedi arrived, twenty Schwyzers

had formed a large circle around the three men. Leopold, his fine clothes and armor splattered with dirt and blood, sat on the ground at Franco Roemer's feet. The captain of the Sturmritter did not look as shiny as the last time Thomas had seen him. Gone was his polished armor and peacock-plumed helmet. He wore simple cotton breeches and a sweat-ringed shirt that may have been white at one time. Now, it looked like it had been pulled from a pig bath. Beside him stood the hulking form of Klaus, his long sword held before him, daring anyone to come within its reach. His armor seemed intact, save for his helmet, which he had either lost in battle or discarded.

"Open a path," Thomas said. He drew his short sword and mace as he walked into the circle. "Throw down your weapons and surrender Leopold." He pointed his sword at Franco.

When Leopold saw Thomas, he screamed. His eyes bulged and he dug his heels into the soft ground to propel himself away backwards, but Franco held him in place with his knee planted firmly in the Duke's back.

"Stay where you are," Klaus growled at Thomas. His voice sounded like he was badly in need of a drink of water. Or, perhaps, he always sounded that way. Thomas was not sure he had ever heard the man speak.

Thomas kept walking, and soon discovered Klaus was not the type of man to warn someone twice. With a loud cry he charged at Thomas. His sword carved a murderous arc straight down at the Hospitaller's head. Thomas swayed his upper body to the side just enough for the sword to miss making any contact. Then he swung his mace hard against the side of the large man's knee. Klaus groaned, his leg buckled, and Thomas stepped in to slid his short sword straight through the man's throat. He pulled it out as quickly as it went in.

A fine spray added to the red of Thomas's tunic, but most of the blood was deflected by the older man's gray beard. It collected there for a moment, hidden from sight, but then it welled up and poured down Klaus's chest. Without even a whimper, he fell over backward, his body stiff when it hit the ground. His unseeing eyes stared at the clouds.

"No!" Leopold screamed and began crawling on his hands and knees toward Klaus, but Franco reeled him in and unceremoniously threw him behind his legs. Leopold fell over on his side, in a fetal position, and with his eyes clenched tighter than fists, began to moan.

Franco raised his sword and pointed it at Thomas.

"You will not find my throat so easily, Hospitaller." He cut the air with his sword. "Come. Let us duel for the Prince's life."

"Ruedi," Thomas called out, keeping his eyes on Franco.

"Cap'n?"

"Shoot this man."

Ruedi bent over, fastened the hook at his waist onto his crossbow string, and with a grunt, cocked the war bow by standing up straight. He pulled a bolt from his belt quiver and set it to the string.

Franco looked from Ruedi to Thomas, and his lips curled in disdain.

"You would have your man shoot me?"

"You have something I want," Thomas said.

"Then fight me for it! I took you for a man of honor when we first met. Will you prove me wrong now, here, in front of your men?"

Thomas felt his blood rising. Why should he care

anything for honor?

"I was told my entire life that only the nobility and knights are capable of true honor. Well, as you may have noticed, I am neither." He waved his arm over the men surrounding them. "There is not a drop of blue blood in any one of us. But what we do have is loyalty. Loyalty to our countrymen, our children, our wives and husbands, our friends. So tell me, with all this, what need do we have of honor?"

Franco was quiet for a long time as he glared at Thomas.

"Your men have been executing prisoners. And do not deny it, for I have seen it several times already."

"I know. I gave the orders. From this day forward, any man who comes into our lands with intent to do us wrong, must expect to die if he is caught. That is our law."

"Peasants, yes, I can understand that. But a noble man's ransom could make you a rich man! It makes no sense to kill him."

"We do not want your kind's gold. We wish to be left alone. So why would we suffer, even for one day, the company of a man who comes to our door looking to take everything we hold dear?"

Thomas could see Franco weighing his words. Leopold tried to crawl away once again, but Franco stepped on his leg to keep him in place. He stared at Duke Leopold trapped under his boot, and then met Thomas's eyes.

"Very well. I will agree to lay down my sword and be executed, but only if you allow Duke Leopold to live."

"You negotiate a poor bargain," Thomas said. "This is my counter-offer. You will take Leopold from our lands and see him delivered safely to Habsburg. When his mind has recovered, you will explain to him that if he ever sets foot within our borders again, his life will be forfeit. As will the lives of anyone he brings with him."

Franco's eyes narrowed. "You would let us both go?"

"Someone must tell what happened here today," Thomas said. He pointed at Leopold cowering behind Franco's legs like a child hiding in his mother's skirts. "Since he is unlikely to remember many details, that someone must be you."

Franco sheathed his sword and pulled Leopold to his feet. He pushed the young Duke ahead of him, while he walked behind. He took a few steps and then turned around.

"This is not over. The princes will not let this stand. Sooner or later, one will work up the courage to march another army through your valleys."

Thomas remained silent. What could he say when he knew Franco was right?

"But when they come," Franco continued, "Do not look for me, Schwyzer. For I will not be counted among their number."

He turned back to Leopold and gave him another shove up the road.

***

Seraina stood beside the sacrificial stone with Oppid at her side. The druids closed around her, chanting, while Orlina stooped and carefully picked up Gildas's white robe. The chanting became softer, and no more intrusive than the sound of a nearby creek.

Orlina held up the robe and slipped it over Seraina's

numb shoulders.

"If we are to survive," Orlina said, "there must be balance." She pulled Seraina's head down gently and kissed her forehead. Without another word, she turned and began walking down the Mythen.

Each druid, in turn, followed Orlina's lead, and after kissing Seraina on the forehead, they too began winding down the rocky path. Soon, only Seraina and Oppid stood upon the Mythen's summit. She pulled the robe around her shoulders and knelt next to the white wolf. She wrapped her arms around his thick neck and stared at Gildas's walking stick until she could no longer feel her legs.

The trees told her where to go, but she took her time. Seraina was in no hurry to see Gildas's body.

She arrived at the great pile of blown over trees, and scanned the area. There was no sign of him. She cringed. The Habsburgs took him, she thought.

But then, from the forest a short distance to the east, the wind carried to her a voice. A *singing* voice.

Seraina saw the white robe through the trees as she approached. The druid's hood was up and he stood over a low mound of rocks. He continued singing until Seraina was at his side.

His voice was soft and gentle, and the song was one Seraina did not know the words to, but somehow, she felt it was perfect. When the man turned to her and took down his hood, she was sorry the song had come to an end.

"Blessed be the Weave," he said. It was the man who had stood beside her in the circle. The one who had held her hand so firmly. He was pushing the far side of middle life, but his eyes shone with the wonder of youth.

Much like Gildas's, she realized. Uncannily so.

He smiled, and looked at the stacked rocks. "He was my elder brother," he said.

"I am sorry," Seraina said. "I never knew he had a brother."

The man shrugged. "Gildas was not one to talk about himself. Being an Eye of the Weave, I suppose he did not allow himself the time."

Seraina nodded, and swallowed the emotions building in her throat. "I never saw him much these last few years. He always seemed to be on his way somewhere, searching for new adepts."

"That is because he was the only one of us who could. We all have our part to play in the pattern, but Gildas was the only one who had the ability to identify talent at an age young enough to nurture it. As he did with you."

"But I have never found an adept before. I do not understand why Orlina thinks I can take over Gildas's duties," Seraina said.

"Because Gildas told her that you could."

"And if I cannot?"

The man chuckled. "Every thread in the Weave has an end. Time is sure to outlast us all, Seraina. But some threads twist and wind their way through the pattern of life in such a complicated and unpredictable manner, that it is virtually impossible to find where it finishes. I like to think our kind are one of those."

Seraina liked the sound of that. She had always felt in her heart that it was not yet time for this world to say goodbye to the Helvetii. She stared at the grave before her. Gildas had taught her so much, not just about the

Weave, but about herself as well. She owed it to him to pass on as much as she could.

"I will leave you so you can say your goodbyes," the druid said.

"Where do you go now? What will you do?" she asked.

He scratched at a tooth with his index finger for a moment. "I think I will compile a manuscript."

"A book? Druids have never kept written records. What kind of book?"

"I think I would like… a white one," he said, laughing. "Yes! We need more white books to give our people hope for the future. There are more than enough dark ones already in the world."

Seraina could not help but smile at this. "Do you think it will work?"

He shrugged and held up his hands. "You should ask yourself that question. Unlike you or Gildas, I do not have the sight to know what the future holds. My role, is simply one of support. If you are the Eye of our order, I am but one of many pieces of skin, trying to hold us all together."

"Will I ever see you again?" Seraina asked, hoping the answer was 'yes'.

He nodded. "Even if you do not want to."

He held up his hand in farewell, pulled up the hood of his white robe, and began to walk into the trees. As she watched the man leave, she noticed how small he looked. Speaking to him up close, he had given off the energy and stature of a much taller person.

Just before the druid disappeared into the forest, a soft breeze rustled his cloak, and as the same wind blew over Seraina, for the briefest of instants, she swore she could hear the tinkling of bells.

***

Seraina waited until well after dark, until a time when she knew the celebration festivities in the Schwyz market square would be well under way. She put out her small fire and poured the cauldron of hot herb water that had been simmering over it into a wooden bucket.

Minutes later, with the bucket of warm water in hand, she eased open the flap to Thomas's tent. Still dressed in his red Hospitaller tunic, he sat on a stool with his weary head in his hands, staring at a single tallow candle on the small table before him.

He looked up, his face still streaked with dried blood and sweat. His mouth fell open, but no words came out. He made to stand, but when Seraina saw pain flicker across his face, she stopped him with a hand on his shoulder. She pressed him back down onto his stool and set the bucket down. Then she produced a clean cloth from the pocket of her white robe, Gildas's robe, dipped it in the water, and rung it out. The sound of the water falling echoed in the silence of the small space.

"Seraina, I—"

She cut him off by putting her finger over his lips, and then began wiping his face with the hot cloth. He closed his eyes, and she was thankful he did not speak. For she knew he would have so many questions. Ones that she could not answer because she simply did not know.

Why am I here?

She knew she should not have come. Thomas was the Catalyst, and his time had just begun. He would do things for her people, *their people*, that she would never dare dream. They were about to enter a new era, filled with much risk to be sure, but it would also be one which promised to set her people on a new path. One with opportunities the like of which they had not seen in a thousand years. So long as, no one came between the Catalyst and his gift to sense the Weave's patterns.

She knew the danger. And yet, she had still come.

She dropped the cloth into the bucket and a red cloud billowed out into the scented water. Slowly, she lifted his tunic over his head. Then she removed his chainmail vest and the padded cloth below. Finally, she unbuttoned his shirt and peeled it away. He winced every time she raised his right arm. His sides were covered in bruises but nothing was broken.

Seraina took out a fresh cloth and, starting at the hollow below his throat, washed down Thomas's entire body. When she was finished, they made love. Neither one of them uttered a single word.

Afterward, in the coldest hours just before dawn, with her head resting on his chest, Seraina began to speak. Her words were heavy with the power of her voice, and she hoped that with Thomas being so exhausted from the day's events, she would be able to make him forget how he felt for her. She would have to deal with her own feelings at another time.

She had spoken no more than a dozen words, when she felt Thomas's finger across her lips.

"I want to remember," he said. "I know you think you are doing me a kindness. But if we cannot be together, I do not wish to lose a single memory of you, Seraina. Painful or not, I should like to have them to look back on."

Seraina closed her eyes, but that did nothing to stop the tears.

A kindness. It was the perfect choice of words, she thought. For what is love, if not a *perfect* kindness?

Chapter 30

"ARE YOU JODOCK Schnidrig?" Thomas asked, his voice rough from weeks alone on the road.

The question felt ridiculous, for even before the man nodded, Thomas knew the answer. Standing there with his arms crossed over his massive chest, his pose and stature rivaled that of the rocky peak of the Matterhorn towering in the background. His once blonde hair and beard were marble white, like the tops of the jagged crags that surrounded them on all sides. But his chiseled cheekbones and bright eyes made Thomas think that, in his youth, he had probably been even more handsome than Pirmin.

Several black-necked goats milled about the rocky yard of a small farmhouse nearby. Built entirely of stone, it looked as solid as the man who stood across from Thomas now. Even the shingles on its roof were fashioned from large flat stones overlapping one another.

It had taken Thomas over a month to make it to Wallis from Schwyz. The paths had been steep and dangerous, and he never would have managed it with his precious cargo intact if Noll had not procured for him a specially built alp cart that merchants used for traversing goods over the mountain passes. It was a narrow, two-wheeled, open wagon that was barely wide enough to hold the solid pine box that housed Pirmin's body.

Thomas cleared the dust from his throat. "I brought your son," he said.

"My boys are in Tasch," the man said. His eyes flicked to the box in the back of the cart. Thomas could see him begin to panic.

"No, not one of them," Thomas said quickly. "Pirmin. I have brought Pirmin home."

"Pirmin?"

The giant's eyes went suddenly wide and one leg buckled. He reached out to grab the side of the wagon. Thomas stepped forward and offered his arm, but the man held up his hand. He stared at the box for a long time before he spoke.

"You knew him?"

"Since we were boys," Thomas said.

He reached into the back of the wagon and dragged out Pirmin's great ax. He stood it on end and leaned it over to the older man. "This was his. I think he would have wanted you to have it."

Pirmin's father pulled his eyes away from the casket and looked at Thomas, the ax, then back at Thomas. He shouted out to someone in the house causing Thomas to jump.

"Mattie! Come out here and meet your brother!"

The door crashed open and a young woman half-walked, half-ran out to meet them. The speed with which she appeared, told Thomas she had probably been watching them the whole time. Her hair was the color of honey-dipped wheat, and where everything Thomas had seen so far of this land had been hard and cold, she was the exact opposite. She talked as she walked, the words bubbling out of her in the strong sing-song Wallis dialect.

"Well, I know you Daddy, and I know Mama too. And if this man is my brother, I swear I will milk the goats myself for a week!"

She stopped in front of Thomas and fixed him with a curious smile. Her eyes were the blue of a dawn sky, and her skin had the healthy glow of someone who liked to be outside. Her face was slightly flushed with excitement, which could have been due to the rare events of the day, but Thomas suspected she always looked like this. She was simply beautiful; like only Pirmin's sister could have been.

"Not *him*," her father said.

Did Thomas detect a hint of disgust at the thought?

"The one in the box."

Keeping one hand on the cart, the old man walked around to its side. He placed his massive hand slowly on top of the pine box and spread his fingers.

"His name was Pirmin. And I sent him away before you were born."

The girl's mouth opened as wide as her eyes. She glanced from Thomas to her father, and bit her lip, waiting for either one to speak. After a time, Pirmin's father looked at Thomas. The old man's eyes were wet.

"What is your name, friend?"

His tone, the way he looked straight at you when he spoke, the slight drawl to his words; Thomas saw so much of Pirmin in front of him a lump formed in his throat.

"You can call me Thomi."

"Can you stay with us a while, Thomi? I would like to hear about my boy."

And Pirmin would like nothing more, Thomas thought.

He nodded, and followed the Schnidrigs inside.

Leopold's Fate

WITHOUT RESOURCES, or any real desire to face the Schwyzers in battle again, Leopold spent the next seven years focusing all his energies on helping his brother regain the crown of the Holy Roman Empire. Just when the war seemed to be going their way, Frederich the Handsome suffered a crushing defeat in 1322. Louis the Bavarian took Frederich, and over a thousand nobles from Austria and Salzburg, captive.

The Habsburgs were beaten. But Leopold continued to resist, and by leveraging his political connections with the other German princes, was a constant threat to the fragile Holy Roman Empire which Louis now ruled. After three years of captivity, to Leopold's surprise, Louis suddenly released Frederich.

The last leaves of fall were on the ground turning black when Leopold met Frederich's escort at the gates to Habsburg castle. The two brothers embraced and then Leopold stepped back to appraise his brother's condition.

For a man held prisoner for over three years, he looked exceptionally well. Better, in fact, than Leopold remembered.

Frederich had put on some weight and his eyes were bright, but that could be the glistening effect of the tears of joy he was fighting back at being reunited with his younger sibling.

"You look good, brother. Louis treated you well enough, I see," Leopold said.

"Of course he did. Our cousin is a fair man, and we were friends long before our disagreement over the crown."

Fair man?

Two foiled assassination attempts in the last year alone had Leopold believing otherwise. But he knew there would be no point in telling his brother just yet. Louis had had three years to shape Frederich's mind to his cause, and Leopold suspected it would take some time to undo the damage.

"No need to talk out here in the cold. Let us get you into the keep in front of a fire, and put some good Habsburg wine into your belly. Then you can tell me all about your time away."

Leopold took his brother's elbow to lead him through the gates, but Frederich pulled his arm away.

"What is it?" Leopold asked.

"I cannot go in just yet. We have something to discuss first."

"Surely that can wait until you have eaten some—"

"No. It cannot."

Leopold was afraid of this. Three years was a long time.

"Very well," Leopold said. "What would you have me know?"

"My release was conditional."

"On what?"

"I gave Louis my word."

Leopold felt his throat constrict. Louis knew Frederich's weakness too well.

"Go on."

"I promised to speak with you, and convince you that Louis is the best suited ruler for the Empire at this time."

"You are the rightful heir," Leopold said. He tried to keep his voice low, soothing. But his throat burned with the taste of bile.

Frederich shrugged. "That no longer matters. We must consider what is best for the entire Holy Roman Empire. The German princes have been divided for too long, and as a result, everyone has suffered. Not just our family."

Leopold put his hand on his brother's shoulder.

"Come inside. We can talk more after you have rested."

Frederich shrugged his touch away. "No. I swore I would not set foot in Habsburg until you recognized Louis as the legitimate ruler. I know this is difficult for you, brother, but it really is best. For the Empire as a whole."

Leopold could take no more. "Listen to yourself! These are not your words. Your mind has been poisoned and turned against itself. Think of what you say."

"It is your own mind that swims in poison. Ever since Morgarten." Frederich shook his head and looked at Leopold with sadness in his eyes. "That battle did something to you, Leo. It turned you into a distrusting soul, jealous and petty. Here is a chance for you to let go of all that. To be a true Prince of the Empire once again."

Leopold felt his fist connect square on with the bridge of Frederich's nose. The cartilage gave way with a grinding pop and Frederich fell to the ground.

"Never!" Leopold's clenched hand trembled at his side.

Some of Frederich's escort drew their swords and held them pointed at Leopold, stopping him from advancing on his brother. Leopold's guards at the gate came pouring through, with weapons drawn, and pulled their lord behind them.

Frederich sat up on the ground. Blood streamed from his broken nose and his eyes were wet with tears of pain and disappointment. He looked at his brother.

"NEVER!" Leopold shouted again from behind his men.

Frederich pushed himself to his feet. He mounted up and turned his horse away from the gates of Habsburg.

***

True to his word, Frederich returned to Louis and confessed he had failed to win over his brother's obstinacy. He demanded to be put in chains. Legend has it that Louis was so impressed with Frederich's sense of honor, that he decreed they both should rule together. Louis the Bavarian remained the Holy Roman Emperor, but he agreed to give Frederich the title of King of the Romans.

Less than two months after Frederich the Handsome was crowned King of the Romans, his brother, Leopold I of Habsburg, died. He was thirty-five years old.

Frederich was so upset by his brother's death, that he immediately resigned his regency as King of the Romans and returned to rule over only Austria. Four years later, Frederich the Handsome, was also dead.

Louis the Bavarian continued to rule the Holy Roman Empire until his death seventeen years later.

Author's notes

Swiss Halberdiers and Pikemen

By the end of the fifteenth century, Swiss mercenaries were the most feared and respected fighting units in Europe. They were ruthless, loyal to their employer, disciplined, and because of their exceptional mobility, revolutionized the use of the halberd and pike on the battlefield. Their ability to change up their formations quickly, turned the pike, which was traditionally used defensively to repel cavalry, into a fearsome offensive weapon effective against infantry as well. They were also known for not retreating from a battle. Of course, their practice of hanging the first man to run from his unit may have something to do with this. For over two hundred years, there was scarcely a battle fought in Europe where one side or the other did not enlist the aid of Swiss mercenaries. Even the Pope employed Swiss guards, and still does to this day.

Unlike other soldiers of fortune at the time, Swiss mercenary units were raised and trained by each canton (state or province). The canton arranged the contracts and received a cut from each assignment. The mercenaries themselves had strict rules they had to follow. These included: *Swiss do not fight Swiss, at harvest time we go back home to work the fields, and "no money, no Swiss".*

White Book of Sarnen

It is in the White Book of Sarnen that we first see any mention of William Tell. So named because of its expensive white parchment, it was compiled more than one hundred and fifty years after the Battle of Morgarten (1315). Most historians now believe William Tell was a fictional character created much later than the tumultuous times in which he was supposed to exist.

Helvetia

The official name for Switzerland is *Confederatio Helvetica* (the Helvetic Confederation), which is why its country code today is CH. Helvetia is the female personification of Switzerland. A peaceful, yet protective figure, she is usually depicted wearing a wreath in her hair and carrying a shield and sword. Her image currently appears on everything from Swiss Franc coins to postage stamps. In other words, the *Helvetii* are still going strong to this day. As for the *Druids of the Helvetii*, only one of their kind could tell you of their fate.

About the author

J. K. Swift lives in a log house well off the beaten path in central B.C., Canada. He has worked as a school teacher, jailhouse guard, Japanese translator, log peeler, accountant, martial arts instructor, massage therapist, technical editor, and has called a few Bingo games. He gets his story ideas while traveling in Europe, feeding his chickens, and cutting wood.

...a message from the author:

Thank you very much for reading my work. Reviews and personal recommendations from readers like you are the most important way for an author to attract more readers, so I truly am grateful to anyone who takes the time to rate my work. If you could take a moment to rate my story and/or leave a review where you purchased it, I would greatly appreciate it. It doesn't need to be long—a sentence or two about why you liked it or disliked it would be great. Feel free to contact me through my website and blog with any questions or comments. Thanks very much!

Sign up for the New Releases Mailing List at:

http://jkswift.com/

If you enjoyed this story, you may also like:

HEALER: Keepers of Kwellevonne Vol. 1
(short story series)

Why would anyone try to kill a healer?

Deenah's quiet life as an apprentice healer in the remote village of Brae's Creek is shattered when a stranger gravely wounds her master and flees into the wild. For all her skills, Deenah is unable to identify the strange forces at work on the injury. To save her master's life, Deenah must join the young Warder Kaern, and an aging veteran tracker, as they set out on a manhunt into hostile lands.

FARRIER (Vol. 2)

Deenah finds herself on the outskirts of Tablat, a frontier town full of thieves, murderers, and halfbreeds. Exhausted and hungry, she has no choice but to enter.

But she is not alone. And that thought terrifies her more than anything.

WARDER (Vol. 3)

Kaern and Speller track Deenah to Tablat, where Kaern is forced to relive the events that made him the youngest Warder ever appointed by the Seneschal.

Made in the USA
Middletown, DE
27 June 2020